Chris Bunch is the author of the Sten Series, the Dragonmaster Series, the Seer King Series and many other acclaimed SF and fantasy novels. A notable journalist and bestselling writer for many years, he died in 2005.

Find out more about Chris Bunch and other Orbit authors by registering for the free monthly newsletter at www.orbitbooks.co.uk

CHRIS BUNCH

STAR RISK

BOOK FOUR: THE DOG FROM HELL

www.orbitbooks.co.uk

ORBIT

First published in the United States in 2005 by Roc,
Penguin Group (USA) Inc.
First published in Great Britain in 2006 by Orbit

A CIP catalogue record for this book
is available from the British Library.

ISBN-13: 978-184149-456-2
ISBN-10: 1-84149-456-9

Typeset in Garamond by M Rules
Printed and bound in Great Britain by
Clays Ltd, St Ives plc

Orbit
An imprint of
Little, Brown Book Group
Brettenham House
Lancaster Place
London WC2E 7EN

A member of the Hachette Livre Group of Companies

www.orbitbooks.co.uk

For Richard Knee

Un Gentilhomme d'Honneur
Et sans Reproche

Cerberus: 1. A mythological dog, with three heads, guarding the entrance to Hell. 2. A formidable and often surly guard.

ONE

The castle loomed above them on the bluff, centuries-old stone, dank, brooding. The surrounding moss-dripping dark oak trees seemed as old and decaying as the sprawling fortress.

The sound of the five Star Risk operatives' boots on the cobbled walk was all that broke the wintry silence.

'A hell of a place to get ambushed,' M'chel Riss said, a bit nervously.

'I've seen worse,' Chas Goodnight said. 'Trouble is, I can't remember just where, or when.'

His laugh echoed, sounding forced in the silence.

The sniper focused sights on the oncoming five.

Not the expected, hoped-for targets, but two very beautiful women, one looming monster, a tall man who was very good-looking, and another man who could have been an elderly professor.

Unexpected – but they'd do.

Range . . . check . . . wind . . . not to worry about any wind . . . finger sliding to the trigger . . .

It had started two weeks before.

M'chel Riss, who was on com watch, greeted the other four members of Star Risk (remarkably all on their base world of Trimalchio IV at the same time) somewhat smugly: 'I have a job for us. A nice safe job. A job with children, even.'

'Ugh. Children,' Chas Goodnight moaned.

'What is the matter,' Amanandrala Grokkonomonslf rumbled, 'with small examples of your progeny?'

Grok was large, 2.4 meters in any given direction. He was covered in surprisingly silky fur that, to many humanoids' envy, never needed combing or care. He claimed to be primarily a philosopher, and his race *was* known for Deep Thoughts. It was also known, as was Grok himself, for being more than somewhat murderous, and an evil deity had well equipped them with sufficiency in the way of fangs and retractable claws.

'Not mine, I hope,' Goodnight said. 'I'm most careful about things like that. And don't think I don't like children. I do. At three hundred and fifty degrees, baked for forty minutes per pound, basted with honey and vinegar every hour.'

'Don't be so misanthropic,' Jasmine King said. 'You were a child once yourself.'

'I was,' Goodnight said. 'And a miserable little bastard, too.'

Goodnight was the team's commando expert. Tall, considered more than good-looking, he'd been one of the Alliance's 'besters,' surgically modified to have an assortment of talents, from accelerated reaction time to seeing in the dark, when a tiny battery at the base of his spine was activated.

He'd been used by the Alliance, mankind's fairly ineffectual governing body, as a supercommando and covert action specialist until he discovered that he vastly preferred being a jewel thief to being a hero.

Star Risk had rescued him from a deathcell, and

THE DOG FROM HELL

made him a partner. Even the other four, hardly ethical sorts, considered him dangerously amoral.

'Children can be many things,' Friedrich von Baldur said sententiously. 'Details, if you would?'

'Pickup on Earth,' Riss said. 'Escort eight eleven-year-olds from their residential school to their extended study center on Lefarge XI.

'Payment by certified check, being transferred as we speak to Alliance Credit . . . uh, assuming that the rest of you approve the job.

'Payment five hundred thousand credits retainer, plus one hundred thousand credits per diem, plus expenses, plus another half a mill performance bonus if everything works out.'

'My,' von Baldur said. 'Was that the offer?'

'Of course not,' Riss said. 'That was after I did a gentle bit of negotiation.'

M'chel Riss was 182 centimeters tall, blond hair, green eyes, built like a runway model. She was also an ex-Alliance Marine Corps major, specializing in weaponry, tactics, and demolitions. She quit the marines when a superior got pushily romantic, and ended up the second member of the deliberately tiny Star Risk. She'd been recruited by its founder, von Baldur, (real name Mital Rafinger, never used), who'd left the military just ahead of an investigation for malfeasance, embezzlement, and misappropriation of government funds.

Von Baldur was known for his expertise in not only white-collar crime, but also several species of martial arts. However, the dapper man looked more like someone's rich uncle, or perhaps a most debonair executive.

'A steep little amount they're willing to come up with for a simple piece of babysitting,' Goodnight said. 'Congrats, M'chel. Or should I ask, what's the risk?'

'Our employer — sorry, potential employer — one Amel Friton, said very little. We're needed because the parents of these little charmers — her words, not mine — are uniformly wealthy, and are worried about their nursery angels,' Riss said.

'You believe her?' Goodnight asked.

'Of course not,' Riss said. 'We're not that broke right now. Do I look like an idiot?'

'Earth,' Jasmine King said dreamily. 'Yum. Paris. Double yum. I don't own anything from rue Montaigne. Rue du Faubourg St. Honore. Triple yum.'

King's French accent, like everything else about her, was perfect. She was, impossibly, even more lovely than Riss, and was gifted with an eidetic memory, charm, and perfect business sense. She was so perfect that a previous employer had tried to weasel out of paying her, on the grounds that she might actually be an android, built by some unknown alien civilization.

There was silence for a moment, then: 'Of course, I vote yes,' King said. 'And I assume you do as well, M'chel?'

Riss nodded.

'Earth,' Grok said. 'Little children. Interesting. I shall participate.'

'And I,' von Baldur said. 'I am fondly considering London's bespoke tailors.'

'Oh, hell,' Goodnight said. 'Make it unanimous.'

'Very, very interesting,' Grok said. 'Since the beginning is on Earth, home for you sentimental fools, I assume we're all going on for the inspection?'

'And for the side bennies,' M'chel said.

The sniper, as trained, gently squeezed the trigger . . .

They were just passing a granite facing handcarved

with the words SAINT SEARLES, TRADE PLEASE USE REAR ENTRANCE when Riss caught a flicker of motion and color – purple – out of the corner of her eye, shouted 'Incoming!' and went flat.

She rolled as she hit the cobbles, hand reflexively unsnapping her purse and pulling out a large Alliance-issue blaster.

M'chel saw a figure running from a hide in the brush, had the sniper in her blaster sights, and was squeezing, just as the purple balloon smashed on the ground.

Red splattered everywhere. Riss had an instant of panic, then realized it wasn't blood – and most importantly wasn't *her* blood – and smelled something acidic.

A memory bubbled up.

Catsup. An Earth seasoning. She'd tasted it in London, and her mind shuddered a little at the memory.

Before her pistol went off, she had time to recognize the sniper: A rather chubby little girl with long dark hair, her fat legs twinkling like a metronome as she ran from them.

'Shit!' she managed, catching herself before the gun went off.

Goodnight touched the right side of his jaw, came out of his accelerated bester state, and lowered his gun, a rather small if long-barreled and ornately engraved projectile weapon. He got to his feet.

All five Star Risk operatives had gone flat, and now picked themselves up.

Grok walked forward to the sniper's hide, examined the abandoned weapon without touching it. It was an improvised catapult. Three other full balloons lay beside it on the grass.

Goodnight looked down at the tear on the knee of

his brand-new, trendy suit, black with subdued pin-striping. 'That little bitch,' he growled. 'I shoulda gunned her down.'

'Chas, that isn't exactly—' King began, then saw the smeared red stain on her fresh-from-Paris Chanel jacket. 'You're right. You should have shot her down. Like a damned dog.'

Grok was burbling – his race's equivalent of laughter.

'Children,' von Baldur said mildly. 'You must learn forgiveness . . . and what expense accounts are for.'

'Yes,' the rather severe-looking and -dressed school headmistress, Amel Friton, said. 'Our charges can sometimes be a bit – shall we say – bumptious. But they are full of life, and that compensates for a great deal.'

Jasmine made a note to double the cost of replacing her outfit on the expense account, and forced a saccharine smile.

'The culprit, I rather imagine, will have been Lithia. She has been evincing . . . an interest in ballistic science of late.

'But regardless of youthful high spirits, this breach of proper manners to visitors cannot be allowed. I shall speak to her harshly, and require her to give up her desserts for a week. She has been rather liberal in the avoirdupois area of late, and the deprivation will do her no lasting harm.'

Goodnight was thinking of asking why chubby little Lithia's melon couldn't be wailed on for an hour or so with a club, but held his tongue. No doubt his recommendation wasn't in league with current educational theories.

Friton eyed the five, as if to see if there was going to

be any argument. Four of them, cowed by the memory of their teachers, said nothing. Grok, out of respect for native customs, did the same.

'Saint Searles has existed for six centuries,' Friton said. 'Always with the aim of helping our country's – and later our world's, and then the Alliance's – leaders, busy with the duty of governing the lesser, raising the next generation of women to be capable of stepping into their parents' shoes.

'We have had great success over the centuries, and I am proud to say the tradition continues unbroken. To continue this tradition, we have always been willing and able to provide whatever services our clients require, always remembering we stand in loco parentis.

'Even when the unusual occurs.

'Such has, in fact, happened recently.

'A group of our girls were recently on a field trip. There they encountered a woman who found them not only charming, but reminiscent of herself at their age.

'Her name is Lady Ardent Rosewater-Jones, and she is the principal shareholder on a planet named Porcellis, which is famed within our Alliance for providing recreational opportunities.

'She offered a chance for the girls she'd encountered to study economics on her world for a year or two, and for those who wished to pursue a career in commerce, the chance to enter her employment. This was, you might imagine, a bit out of the ordinary, but my administrators approached the parents of the girls involved, and without exception they approved.

'All of them wished to ensure there were no problems, given these parlous times, in the girls' arriving on Porcellis, and since, frankly, there have been incidents of kidnapping for ransom of pupils at two of our sister schools in Belize and Zurich, I wanted to ensure proper security. Your firm came highly recommended, although the two recommendees wish to remain anonymous.'

Friton tapped a very old-fashioned bell. 'One of my staffers will accompany the girls, to ensure you have no problems in communication.'

A door opened, and a woman entered.

Goodnight held his eyebrows down.

'This is Miss Alice Sims, one of our newer staff members.'

Alice Sims was dark, sultry, and of medium height, and she made her school uniform look like an outfit designed for pornographers. She eyed the five, her chin tipped down demurely, and her eyes lowered for an instant when she saw Goodnight.

Friton introduced Star Risk.

Sims, in a low voice matching her body's promise, said she was pleased to meet them, and would do all she could to ensure their job went smoothly.

'And these are the girls who will be your charges.'

Sims went to another door, and herded in eight girls in school uniform.

One of them was the dark-haired girl who'd sniped at them, Lithia.

Friton named them: Lithia, Lis, Megan, Kel, Erin, Arbra, Jo, and Von.

All of them looked normal, well-scrubbed, and alert.

They politely responded, and were taken out by Sims, who, at the door, looked back and gave Goodnight a look of infinite promise.

'Exactly how you choose to take the girls to Porcellis is your business. I do not intrude in the practices of experts.'

Jasmine had questions about clothing, diet, and so forth. A secretary gave the others a grand tour of St.

Searles. Everything was very old, and looked as if it had been in the care of several generations of furniture breakers.

Hanging in the halls were portraits of former pupils, in their later lives.

Riss was interested to note how many were dressed in various racy styles of previous generations of the demimonde.

They were brought back to the main office, given final good wishes by Friton, and left.

The dankness outside had turned to a light, bleak rain.

Riss turned back to look at the school.

Along a battlement, she saw a line of what she thought, at first, to be particularly nice-looking gargoyles, then realized they were the eight customers.

'At least,' she said, 'that old battle-ax didn't gut us for not using the servants' entrance.'

Von Baldur, who had surprisingly said very little during the interview and was now studying the eight faces high above them, said, 'This should be interesting.'

Goodnight, thinking of Sims's smile, unconsciously licked his lips.

'Yes,' he said. 'Yes, it should.'

TWO

They'd rented not only an archaically named 'chara-banc,' which was a twenty-passenger lim, but a driver, after discovering the British Community still insisted on very archaic driving regulations.

They piled the girls and their not inconsiderable luggage in, the driver muttering in some indecipherable dialect about getting paid by the pound, whatever that might have been. Then they lifted, taking the winding roadway through the nearby hamlet.

'How quaint,' Goodnight muttered. 'Freddie, where are we gonna be able to park the customers while we get our clothes replaced?'

'You might not want to do that,' Sims said. 'My charges can sometimes get, well, a bit mischievous when not closely minded.'

'We do not,' claimed one dark-haired girl, whose name, Goodnight remembered, was Erin. 'We're as good as gold.'

'Wonderful,' Goodnight said, seeing a sign over a brick building that said SAINT GEORGE'S KNEECAP, and showed someone in a medieval space suit slaughtering some poor alien. 'Just bleedin' wonderful.'

They went through hilly country lanes, then pulled onto a throughway. In the back of her mind

Riss was grateful they were in a lifter — the road looked as if it'd been resurfaced about the time that guy with the space suit and long spear had been wandering about.

'Why do we not just lift and go directly?' Grok asked the driver.

The man started, as if surprised Grok could speak.

'Local regs, guv,' he said. 'Posh district, makes their own laws.'

Von Baldur, feeling that he was among his own — or at least the class to which he aspired — relaxed.

'Don't get too comfortable,' King said. 'We have a tail.'

All five looked back, and saw a rather nondescript lifter about a hundred meters behind them.

'You sure?' von Baldur asked.

'It's made the last three turnings with us,' Jasmine said.

'That's no guarantee,' the driver said. 'This is the main road back to London.'

Riss noted the driver wasn't shocked at the idea they were being followed.

'To make sure,' von Baldur said, 'take the next right, and go around on them.'

The driver glanced at him, shrugged, and obeyed. They entered another tiny village.

The lifter turned with them.

'Interesting,' von Baldur said, his hand sliding into his suit coat, coming out with a blaster.

'Here now,' the driver said. 'That's a gun! We have laws about things like that!'

'We have laws, too,' Goodnight said, the small gun appearing in his hand, 'starting with self-preservation.'

'Perhaps it's just a follower,' Grok said, as the charabanc

turned back onto the main road. 'And we don't care who knows we're headed for the spaceport.'

'Negative,' Riss said, seeing two more vehicles – one a heavy lifter, making the same turn they had – up ahead. 'I count three, which makes it a crash team.

'The truck to stop us thoroughly, the front tailer to do whatever they're thinking of – which I don't think is a simple snatch, since there isn't room enough for us all in either the front or rear vehicles – and the last for a blocker.

'Somebody in this pig has nice friends.'

'What's going on?' one of the girls asked. 'Are those guns real?'

Star Risk ignored her.

'Just like that?' Jasmine asked. 'No negotiation, no cheap threats or anything.'

'Guess not,' Riss said.

'Then I think we should mess with them severely, to quote Mr. Goodnight.'

Sims, looking scared, tried to make soothing noises to the girls.

'How far's the nearest decent-sized burg?' Goodnight asked the driver.

'Five, maybe ten minutes,' the driver managed. 'And I want you to know I didn't bargain for this.'

'We'll drop you off, then,' Riss said. 'Or we can figure it into your bonus.'

'I'll have none of that,' the driver said indignantly. 'I've got my life savings in this here charry, and I'll not have anyone pottering about with it.'

'Then shut up and drive,' Goodnight said. 'We'll need a blocker, M'chel, assuming we're going for a nice, simple, tidy thing, without too many bodies.'

'I figured that,' Riss said. 'And it's my turn. Dig out some cash. We won't have time to mess around with cards.'

'Aw shit,' Goodnight said, obeying. 'You get to have all the fun.'

There was, thankfully, some traffic in the small city they flew through, which gave them a little cover. Goodnight saw a man in a rather strange uniform, wearing what looked like a blue multiple-user chamber pot on his head.

The driver looked hopeful when he saw the cop.

Goodnight leaned forward and jabbed him in the ribs with his gun. The man's face fell and he went on.

'At the edge of town,' Riss ordered, 'we'll do it.'

'No kid,' Goodnight said. 'And there's your spot for the blocker.'

'When I tell you, turn left,' Riss said to the driver. 'Not this street . . . not this one . . . now!'

The driver obeyed, and Riss went out the door, landing crouched, almost falling, then recovering. A passing kindly old lady looked shocked. Riss hid the gun sheepishly as the trio of followers went past, intent on the charabanc.

M'chel went back a block to a sign that read LIFTERS TO LET over a small lot with economy lifts in it.

In a few minutes, she came in a nicely polished economy lifter, smiling at the still-babbling agent and calling, 'We'll check it back in London, with a full fuel cell.'

Muttering at her tendency to pull to the right lane, like all proper drivers should, she found an open space, pulled over to the side, and waited.

In about five minutes, the easily noticed charabanc came back through, then its followers. The driver of the lead lifter was looking slightly vexed, and was on a com, no doubt upset at being led onto a roundabout.

Riss pulled out, following behind the heavy lifter and the blocking vehicle.

The road opened up, but still stayed at two lanes.

They passed a school, then two large houses.

Riss decided it was time.

Quite illegally, ignoring the signs about the town's height limitations, M'chel punched full power, and took the lifter off to a height of three meters.

Someone on foot shouted at her, but she paid no mind. She increased lift, took her lifter over the rear blocking car, then over the heavy lifter. Paying no mind to the shriek of collision alarms, she cut power, nosed down and slammed her lifter into the lead follower.

Her vehicle bounced off the follower's hood and skewed sideways as it crashed — which she hadn't intended, but at least she was definitely blocking the road.

Her lifter almost rolled, then settled back on its landing struts, engine screaming.

Riss rolled out her door as the charabanc ahead grounded, and the Star Risk operators jumped out.

The driver of the following car lolled against the steering wheel, unconscious, blood dripping from his mouth.

His partner was digging for a gun, saw Riss's leveled blaster, and froze.

That lead vehicle wasn't going anywhere soon, but to make sure, M'chel put a bolt into its engine compartment.

She spun, crouched, and put two more rounds into the front end of the heavy lifter behind the two wrecks.

She dimly heard shouts and a scream, but Riss was running back to the charabanc.

She jumped in, and the others followed.

'Drive it, buster,' she ordered.

The driver fish-gaped, then obeyed, lifting with a speed that suggested he must have something on his conscience.

'I would suggest you take off as soon as you can,' von Baldur said mildly. 'There may be some people coming around wearing uniforms who will have questions.'

The driver obeyed.

Riss turned around in her seat.

All eight children, and their minder, had eyes like saucers.

'Now,' Riss said, calming her overactive lungs, 'that is Lesson One on one way to deal with drivers who follow too closely.'

THREE

They paid off the charabanc outside London and took three cabs to the airport itself.

M'chel was feeling a bit sorry for the driver, who'd have to contend with the law sooner or later, since his unwieldy vehicle wasn't the least bit anonymous looking. But he was suspiciously cheerful, especially after von Baldur gave him a tip that equaled his fee, which made her suspect he was more used to irregular customers than he let on, or else he had some impressive friends with badges.

She immediately forgot him, and began pondering who was after them and why.

Riss kept coming up with nothings, and so she asked Jasmine, the usual repository of wisdom.

She, too, was drawing a blank.

All Goodnight could offer was that one of the children had clearly irked someone with a criminal mind and a certain organization, which gave them nothing.

While they thought about who the villains could be, they had more than enough to do with their charges.

It started as Jasmine, being the normal paymaster, was shepherding luggage and tipping handlers.

Grok saw something odd, and inquired of the little

girl bending over the drinking fountain just what she was doing. The girl was named Lis.

'Making punch,' she said blandly.

'Which means?'

'Which means I'm wedging this bit of chemicals down beside the spout,' she explained.

'Which makes?' Grok inquired.

'Which makes whoever takes a drink have a little taste of my chemicals,' she said.

'Which makes?'

'Them pee bright purple for a while,' Lis said gleefully.

Grok took the chemical block away.

At least, he thought, Lis was honest.

Goodnight was the next up.

Goodnight happened to see Megan holding her right hand very oddly as she strolled close to a prosperous young man wearing a vastly oversized collarless jacket – the current style for men in Britain.

He recognized what she was doing, came in fast, took the girl by the arm, and moved her into a corner, a forced smile on his lips.

Kel was following closely.

'Bad stance,' Chas hissed in thieves' cant. 'That kind of dip is too easy to go shy, and bump the sucker wise.'

Megan, who'd begun putting on an angry face, lost it.

'What *should* I be doing?' she asked.

'Not trying to teach yourself pickpocketing,' Goodnight said.

'But I couldn't find any schools to teach me. Not in England,' she protested.

'Tough. So you can stay straight, before somebody breaks off your ickle pretty fingers,' he said.

'Who would do something like that to a sweet little girl like Megan?' Kel asked.

'Me.' Goodnight said.

The two girls considered the expression on his face, and believed.

Arbra and Jo, looking terminally innocent, were strolling toward a duty-free jewelry shop. Grok intercepted them, and put on what he considered a friendly smile.

The two froze, seeing a face promising incipient anthropophaging and paled.

Grok had no idea what they'd been intending, but they went rapidly back to the main group. Grok himself decided to work on his smile.

Alice Sims was giving Von a severe, if very quiet, talking to, and Von was wailing loudly and contritely. Riss thought the wailing was maybe a little too contrite, theatrical, and eye-attracting. Suspicious, she looked around and saw Erin, in sad-faced conversation with a benevolent-looking elderly couple. She edged closer.

'You see, Reverend,' Erin was saying, 'when my beloved parents were dying, they gave me all of their Madagaskee money, which was to pay for my education here in England as a Bible translator. But no bank I've found will convert to English money. They tell me that what I need is someone who'll stand good for the amount until it clears, and I saw your faces, and knew that—'

That was enough for M'chel.

'Erin,' she said, 'it's time for prayers.'

Erin glared in a most unholy way at Riss.

'In just a minute,' she said sweetly.

'No,' Riss said firmly, taking the girl's hand. 'Now.' She dragged Erin away.

'I almost had them going!' she protested.

'Maybe,' M'chel said. 'And by the way, where were you going to get these Magawhatsit bills?'

'Oh, I'd figure something out,' Erin said. 'The important thing was for me to get my hands on their poke.'

'Right.'

Goodnight was watching Jo and Lithia slide down a corridor, past a sign reading BAGGAGE HANDLING.

He went after them, taking his time.

He arrived in a back room. A knot of kneeling men looked up as Jo bent, picked up a pair of dice, and said, 'All right, I can deal with any bets up to twenty pounds.'

Bills and coins hit a blanket spread on the floor.

'You covered,' a very light-skinned man said. 'But I don't like takin' money from a babe.'

As Jo started to cast the dice, Goodnight stepped in, took her hand, and slid the dice out of her grasp.

'Sorry, gents,' he said genially. 'Gambling's against the law, especially for minors.'

'And who the hell are you,' a large, scarred man growled, 'nudging in like this?'

Goodnight bounced the dice in his hand.

'I'm a fool protector,' he said. 'Watch. A four and a two are faceup. I tap them once, then I let idiots like you put their money down, and then I throw.'

He did so.

The dice bounced a couple of times, and six showed.

'They'll put out fours and twos all day long,' he said. 'Until somebody taps them for another set of numbers. Come, girls. Your warm milk and cookies are getting cold.'

As he herded them back into the central waiting room, ignoring the snarls coming from the gamblers, a speaker came on:

'Passengers with last names beginning with E, T, A, O, I, N are instructed to report to their loading areas, and be prepared to have your tickets checked for auth . . . authenticity.' The voice sounded very young.

Friedrich von Baldur was on his feet, slightly purple-faced, even though he had no idea what crime that announcement was intended to conceal or promote.

'Enough and more than enough!' he almost shouted, and stamped toward a woman in an official-looking uniform.

Money changed hands, and the girls were shepherded into a VIP lounge, where they were the only occupants.

'And, by the Lord who made us all,' von Baldur growled, 'no one – but *no one* – will leave this room until they call our ship.'

Jasmine King immediately got on a com, trying to reach contacts to find out who'd been trying to crash them on the way into London.

M'chel Riss looked around the room, saw a sideboard with bottles on it, poured herself a drink, knocked it back, forced a smile, and said, through her teeth, 'Well, well. What a *brisk* start for a day!

'I wonder what exciting excitement comes next?'

FOUR

The liner was, of course, palatially huge.

It had been designed to look most secure, so the two engine pods were strut-mounted slightly below and behind the main capsule, which resembled an obese, rounded cylinder. In fact, the struts were subject to great stresses in hyperspace, and constantly required inspection and not infrequent replacement.

The design should have dictated that the ship would be used in deep and hyperspaces only. But no one actually thought those who could afford a cabin would stomach – literally – having to use shuttles, the potential of zero g's and transshipment. Instead, the liner required an inordinate number of ground-mounted antigravity generators to land on a world with the slightest amount of gravity.

There were stories, cheerfully propagated by Interstellar Cunard, that the liner – *Imperial Victory* – had passengers living aboard who'd given up any landside holdings to cruise forever and ever around the Alliance worlds.

It had ten decks just for passengers, not including crew, engine, and service spaces. The *Victory* stretched for almost two kilometers, had wholly redundant power and life-support systems, featured every possible luxury

and recreation from gambling halls to swimming pools
to theaters to boutiques to exercise salons, could carry
nine thousand passengers cosseted by at least five
staffers each, crewed by . . . and the mind was numbed
by statistics, regularly reeled off by attendants.

It also cost a baby mint for a ticket.

But that was of little concern to Star Risk, nor to St.
Searles, nor to Lady Rosewater-Jones, who would be
footing the bill.

Assuming the claims were true of St. Searles's pupils'
parentage, the girls' families would have been unutter-
ably shocked – shocked – if the fruit of various loins
had been treated in any lesser fashion.

'Not least,' Goodnight told von Baldur, 'because this
Rosewater-Bilgewater is willing to take all of these
little sociopaths off their hands.'

'Do not be so cynical,' von Baldur answered.
'Especially when in hearing range of the cash customers.'

More money had changed hands, and Star Risk now
controlled an entire passageway on one deck, with the
operatives' and Alice Sims's suites at either end, to keep
rein on their charges.

'Not,' Riss said to Jasmine, 'that I think that'll slow
the girls down more than a nanobeat.'

It didn't.

Since the wealthy have perfected the art of ennui, it
was possible to be bored on the *Victory*. One way to
relieve it was to get involved in one of the many pools
the ship's staff ran, betting on the number of meals provided, fuel consumption, ships 'seen' in a day's passage,
and so forth.

Grok and Jasmine were initially interested, until
they calculated that Cunard was taking a very sizable
chunk out of the money wagered – enough to reduce
the odds enough so as not to be worth considering.

One of the most popular pools, since it lasted for days, was guessing the exact time of arrival at the *Victory*'s next port.

The first clue to the girls' involvement was when Sims tracked Jo, the gambler, and Arbra, her general companion, to the crew's quarters, which were off-limits to passengers, especially little girls.

Sims went to Goodnight and asked him what he thought was going on. No one bothered to think or say the word 'might.' They all knew better by now. 'Your little chickadees are too young to be slamming some handsome steward . . .' he said, 'I hope. So further investigation is warranted.'

A bit of lurking, and then some raw physical intimidation, revealed the scheme:

Jo would bet on a certain time of arrival. This time would have been decided as within possibilities by her contact, a woman in the radar section. A second crewman was also bribed, who just happened to be assigned to astrogation.

That made it easy to minutely jiggle time out of hyperspace, time orbiting destination, and so forth.

Or, rather, it would have been easy.

Goodnight took his information to von Baldur, who put on his best suit and air of indignation and went to the captain.

'Although,' he sighed after the 'ring' had been broken up, 'it is a bit of a pity that it would have been so imprudent for us to have involved ourselves in the conspiracy.

'There is good, solid money to be made in a scheme such as this. I predict a great future for young Jo.'

'If,' Riss said darkly, 'someone doesn't murder her before she makes it to adolescence.'

*

No one ever found out what the girls' next project was – but it must have been eminently profitable, since all eight of them were suddenly very flush, spending money on everything from cosmetics to candy, with never a credit transfer from any parent having been made.

Alice Sims was disconsolate, feeling that she was nothing but a failure.

Jasmine King, feeling sorry for the woman, arranged to put a bug in Erin's suite.

The playback depressed every adult even further:

ERIN: Everybody comf?
    Chorus of various yesses.
ERIN: Has anybody thought about what we're going to do on Porcellis?
MEGAN: Get rich, of course. Richer than our parentos.
LITHIA: Of course, dummer. But how?
KEL: Take the old hide for everything.
ERIN: Stupido! That's a good way of killing the goose!
    Chorus of agreement.
JO: No. We won't take advantage of Rosewater-Jones. At least until we figure out how things shake. Porcellis is a pleasure world. So they'll have gambling.
ERIN(*Impatient*): Of course. But that's not big enough to make all of us rich rich. And we're too young now to get away with much.
VON: Boys. They'll pay.
LITHIA: For what? Having us take our clothes off, like my cousin always wants me to do?
ARBRA: Eeeech! He's the one with all the pimples, right? He wanted me to show him the stables, right before last hols. Offered me five credits if I did. I told him to get kicked by a mule.

LITHIA: But you thought about it, didn't you?

ARBRA: (*Giggles*): Of course. Wouldn't you . . . if he weren't so heinie-ugly?

LITHIA: Maybe. If it'd been fifty credits.

MEGAN: Eeech! Sex! And how much you want to bet that any boy on Porcellis that would pay to do dirty things to you would have pimples? (*Primly*) I'll bet any boy who's good-looking doesn't have to pay for it. Or else he'll want you to do all kinds of weird things that'll hurt and everything. And I don't want to think about some dirty, hairy, drooling old man.

ERIN: Megan's right. That idea doesn't go anywhere. Doing what boys want is liable to get you all kinds of ugly rots. My aunt told me.

LIS: I read that the only people who make any real money out of things like that are the ones who have girls working for them. And we're not old enough to get anybody to do that yet.

LITHIA: And I don't want to work for anybody, ever. *More agreement.*

MEGAN: Stealing. That's it. Jewels and things like that. And you know a richie like old lady Rosewater'll have rich friends with all kinds of goodies.

ERIN: But you have to have a fence after you steal them, so that's out until we know more about Porcellis.

KEL: Drugs. The holos say there's lots of credits in that.

LITHIA: And guns. And bodies. And lots and lots of jail time if you get caught. No.

LIS: What about doing what these Star Risk people do? They don't seem to work very hard. And they get to carry all kinds of sharpy things like guns, and get to fly real fast without worrying about cops. And they're not bad. For old farts.

ERIN: But you got to have training to do what they do. Like experience in some kind of army, and I for one don't want to join anybody's army and get ordered around and eat shitty food and get told what to do by people who need to wear a patch to remind them of what their names are. That's ugly ugly. What we need to do is come up with some kind of new sin.

Mutters of agreement . . . various voices saying they don't have any ideas, then silence.

ERIN: Well, we've all got something to think about, anyway.

Jasmine turned off the recorder.

'Then they all started talking about who their favorite singer is, which I didn't figure any of you cared about.'

Sims and the Star Risk operatives stared at each other.

Finally, M'chel said, 'Old farts, hmm?'

There didn't seem to be anything else to say.

That 'evening,' the girls tried something new. After their seating for the third meal, they grouped in Erin's cabin, changed into their best, and set out, en masse and with speed, out of their passage into the recreation areas. Erin had called this a 'bomb burst' tactic, figuring that Star Risk couldn't corral all of them, and at least a few would find something profitable to do.

She still wasn't aware of the bug in her suite.

The girls roared down the corridor and encountered Star Risk, Alice Sims, and a dozen stewards.

Shortly thereafter – in spite of struggles, storms, and

wails – they were returned to their suites, and the doors locked – which should, Jasmine said, have been done on takeoff and left barred until they reached Porcellis.

Alice Sims was miserable.

Chas Goodnight offered her a drink and some comforting.

'I'll never make a good teacher,' she groaned, knocking back her glass of guaranteed-from-France-on-Earth champagne.

'Probably not,' Goodnight agreed, refilling her glass. 'But you might do fine as a prison guard.'

Sims drained that glass as well.

One thing led to another, and she found herself kissing him.

An hour later, she surveyed the bedroom of his suite, littered with their clothes.

'I have an excuse,' she said. 'It's been a long time for me.'

'I don't bother to look for one,' Goodnight said smugly, reaching for her.

It was morning, ship's time, when, looking rumpled but happy, Sims let herself out of Goodnight's suite and crept down the corridor toward her own cabin.

She heard a girlish giggle from behind her and whirled, not in time to see which door closed.

'This,' she murmured, 'isn't going to make my job much easier.'

But, somehow, she didn't give much of a damn.

Two days after Goodnight and Sims's tryst, alarm bells shrilled.

'All passengers, all passengers, report to your cabins at once, and prepare for emergency procedures and moving to your lifeboat stations. All crewmen, to your emergency stations.

'Stand by for further orders'

'All deck officers go immediately to assigned secondary command posts.

'This is not a drill.'

FIVE

M'chel Riss was never that happy in any situation without an escape hatch, and that exactly fit the *Imperial Victory*. She never believed that any civilian ship as big as the *Victory* could conceivably have enough lifecraft, nor would they be within her reach in the event of a catastrophe.

So she always tried to make friends with the crew, in the vague thought that if disaster struck, she'd at least have somebody to talk to before the smashup.

Riss buttonholed one of the ship's officers and asked her what the hell was going on.

The woman leaned close, and said that they'd had a com — she didn't know from where or from whom — that there was a bomb aboard.

Since the woman looked rattled, M'chel put on a calm face, and said, 'Probably just a hoax from some sick fool.'

The officer looked slightly calmer as she bustled away.

M'chel wondered how many times she'd given some placid reassurance in her career shortly before the doors blew off. She set that thought aside and made for the other Star Risk operatives to give them the word.

Then she planned on a long, satisfying meal on her fingernails.

But no bangs banged, and the *Victory* popped out of hyperspace and made for the Alliance world of Cygnes IV.

Babbling comfort, it set down at a remote spaceport. Military and police swarmed aboard, and the passengers were shuttled to IV's capital. Every hotel and pension was filled to the brim while the *Victory* was tooth-combed for explosives and such.

Von Baldur contacted St. Searles and told them why they were delayed, gave Rosewater-Jones's representative on Porcellis the same message, and found an exclusive girls' school to put his charges in for the estimated week that the *Victory* would be dry-docked for the search.

On the third day after their arrival, a pair of patrol craft – or so the media reported – made a quote *daring raid* end quote on the drydock, and scattered incendiaries along the length of the ship's hull.

The *Victory* burned merrily, and every emergency team on the planet swarmed the shipyard, worried that the ship's power plant would go up.

Von Baldur had other worries.

'The question I have,' he told the other Star Risk people, 'is whether or not I should allow myself to be paranoid and think this whole mess has anything to do with us.

'First a bomb scare – that is what I am calling it, since the last report said that no explosives had been found aboard the *Victory*, and no further communiqués had been received from the bombers. Then a successful firebombing while the ship lies helpless.

'So the first question to worry about is this: What do our charming innocents have control of or access to that can justify the total destruction of a multibillion-credit ship?'

'That's one good worry,' Riss agreed. 'A second, incidental, one might be what the girls are now up to.'

'Uh-oh,' von Baldur said.

M'chel gestured for Grok to explain.

'I was making a routine check of the rooms our clients are occupying, just to ensure there was no mischief at hand,' the alien said, 'and I found a nice, compact little laboratory in Lis's closet.'

'Making what?' Jasmine asked.

'That took a bit of analysis,' Grok said. 'It turned out to be a substance from Earth's dark ages. Something called lysergic acid diethylmide, a derivative from the fungoid known as ergot.

'It basically instills in the taker a psychotic state, resembling what humans knew as schizophrenia.

'It was very popular at one time, taken recreationally before listening to rather primitively structured music.'

'People got messed up on it for *fun*?' Jasmine asked.

'They did,' Grok said. 'Which is why Lis was making it – for sale to the older students. It was becoming the newest fad when I intervened.'

'Oh, brother,' Goodnight said. 'So next we'll be accused of turning a bunch of children into drug addicts.'

'Possibly,' Grok agreed. 'But if so, that eventuality has already occurred, and is not worth concerning ourselves with.

'I confiscated the chemical gear and destroyed the portion Lis had already formulated.'

Grok was silent for a moment.

'Except, I shall confess, for a single dose that I calculated to be correct for my body mass.'

'You took this swill?' M'chel asked, incredulous.

'I did,' Grok said. 'And found it a quite pleasant experience. It provided great insights into various metaphysical matters that I have been pondering. Besides Earth's grappa, it was one of the most enjoyable substances I've ever ingested.'

'*Wonderful*,' Riss said sarcastically. 'Not only do we have a murderous alien as a partner, but one that's now an addict as well.'

'This has nothing to do with my theory that all this may be aimed at us,' von Baldur said, a trifle impatiently.

'Not enough hard data to operate from,' Jasmine said. 'At present, no more than an interesting conjecture at best.'

'I did not think it worthy of more than mention,' Friedrich said. 'So I suppose we just sit here until Cunard sends a replacement for the *Victory*.'

'Hopefully,' Riss said, 'we'll be allowed to do just that.'

They weren't.

It was quite a professional kidnap attempt.

They came in just before dawn, evidently planning to take off with their prey and bury themselves in morning commuter traffic on the nearby throughway.

There were four lifters. Two were medium capacity, two were heavy-duty. One heavy-duty antigravity lifter orbited the school, the other three made straight-in approaches and slammed in on the school's flat roof.

Fourteen men and women armed with gas guns and blasters, wearing dark body armor, dashed out. Eight of them carried what could only be called kidnap kits — restraints, gags, blindfolds, sedatives.

The roof appeared free of any security precautions.

There'd been none when Star Risk arrived.

All there'd been time enough for was for Grok to jerry-rig a proximity braking unit from one of their own rental lifters to use as a warning radar, which yammered out a warning instead of hitting the braking unit.

The raiders blew the door to the roof open, and then were stopped. The stairwell had been thoroughly blocked with old desks and furniture.

They milled about indecisively for a moment, giving Star Risk time to yank on clothes and combat harnesses.

Jasmine thought, later, that it was as if their plan had gone only so far, and now they were improvising.

The attackers grabbed furniture and threw it out of the stairwell, clearing the way.

By that time, Grok had smashed a window in his room two floors below, and was eeling up the side of the building, using the ever so ornate and sturdy red ivy as a climbing rope, Riss and Goodnight after him.

The stairwell came clear, and the first pair of raiders started down it.

Jasmine King and Friedrich von Baldur were waiting, and blasters thundered, the bolts ricocheting up the passageway into soft targets.

The raiders flinched back, straight into fire from the three who'd reached the roof.

They might have been well prepared up to a point, but they weren't ready for a combat assault.

Rounds from their blasters were going high, wide, and handsome.

Riss and Goodnight pulled themselves onto the rooftop, and were in prone firing positions. Grok held on to the ivy with one enormous paw and started shooting promiscuously into the raiders' midst.

Someone shouted, 'Extract!' and three or four of the raiders ran for the largest, rearmost lifter.

The engines had been left running on the lifters, and the pilots were gunning their engines, eager to pull out.

The rear lifter, not full, came off the ground just as two more raiders grabbed for the still-open ports.

The pilot of that lifter pushed at them, trying to get them to let go while he tried to clear the lifter in front of him.

Distracted, he didn't use enough power, and the bigger lifter tore into the top of the small one in front.

The pilot lost control, and the heavy lifter cartwheeled and spun.

Grok carefully put half a magazine of bolts into the control compartment of that lifter, and it twisted down, crashing and exploding in the school grounds.

The lifter it had smashed into also tried to get away, and Riss sprayed a burst into the engine compartment.

Its engine died, and it crashed back down on the rooftop, rolling onto its side.

Riss killed the pilot as he tried to jump out, then ran to the lead lifter and chattered the rest of her magazine around its interior.

She crouched against it for cover as the few remaining raiders ran from Goodnight's deadly blaster fire toward her.

One of them might have been lifting his arms to surrender, but was a little too slow and died with his fellows.

The rooftop was smoke hung, and Riss heard, over the ringing in her ears, the screams of the students in the floors below.

Goodnight put a bolt into one raider who was still moving and trotted to Riss.

The fourth watchdog lifter recognized the predicament he was in, broke out of his orbit, and put on full power away from the school.

Riss braced, took careful aim, and realized her blaster was dry.

She changed magazines and retook her stance as the sole surviving lifter went low, just above the trees, and was gone.

'You all right?' Goodnight said.

She nodded.

Chas looked around and saw that Grok was uninjured, as Jasmine and Friedrich burst onto the rooftop.

He considered the bodies and the girls now cautiously peering up from windows, the wisping smoke, the blaster holes everywhere.

'Well, *enough* of this shit,' he snarled.

SIX

Chas Goodnight went ship hunting as soon as the schoolgirls had been relocated to a luxurious but defensible hotel, and a dozen armed security types had been laid on.

With him went Friedrich von Baldur. This was one of Freddie's favorite side benefits of being a mercenary — being able to shop for exotic toys with someone else's money.

He still recalled most fondly a brief interval when he'd had his own battleship, until one of Star Risk's accountants took a look at the wallowing warship's operating costs and rather sternly told him that he could either dump the barge or rapidly find a client with a good-sized fleet willing to let him play admiral.

Von Baldur couldn't, and so the battleship vanished into the mists of history.

At the third shipyard they got lucky, finding a recently built research vessel, intended, von Baldur thought, for small expeditions that'd cover its real use as a yacht that was quite operable by a crew of three.

It wouldn't be economical to operate, but it was sleek and very, very fast, its engine spaces fully automated. And besides, von Baldur told Goodnight

reasonably, the fuel costs would be the clients' problem.
'And no doubt dear, sweet Mrs. Rosewater-Jones can
field the ticket, especially since she owns a gambling
world.'

'True,' Goodnight said. 'All she has to do is kick
the vig up a point, and she'll never ever notice the
pain.'

One of the biggest virtues of the ship was having
crew quarters very separate from those of the 'research
fellows.'

'We can stuff the kids in the suites,' Goodnight said,
'and not have to worry about what they're plotting.'

Friedrich pouted a bit about not being able to
occupy the owner's suite, but subsided when Chas
glowered at him.

Better yet, from Star Risk's perspective, the partner-
ship that owned the good ship *Monkey Business* was
more than willing to turn it loose on a short-term lease
rather than sell it outright, particularly when
Goodnight had no objections to an all-inclusive insurance policy.

'I'm betting they can't dump a fuel hog like the
Business with a gun at somebody's head, and are hoping
like hell that we're going to do something nice and
high-risk with it,' Goodnight guessed. 'Which, of
course, we are, since I'm assuming the bastards would
like to have another try at us.'

Von Baldur wasn't paying any attention. He was
trying to figure how he would convince the others that
the captain's quarters should rightfully be his.

M'chel Riss, on the other hand, had been brooding.

After a while, her dark thoughts were so productive
she roped in Jasmine King, who, in turn, involved
Grok in the project.

When Chas and Freddie came back to the hotel, full of technobabble about the performance of the *Monkey Business*, they were summoned to Riss's suite.

'And what,' Goodnight asked jovially, full of testosterone and adrenaline from his test flight, 'would Her Supreme Marineness like?'

Then he noticed the pile of odd artifacts on the bed and, in a chair, looking as if she were about to either panic or burst into tears, sat Alice Sims.

He also noticed she was restrained with cable ties around her wrists to the arms of that chair.

'Uh-oh,' he said, brilliantly.

'Yes,' Riss said. 'It is time for us all to have a word with our liaison officer here.'

She indicated the objects on the bed.

'I started thinking about Lis suddenly coming up with her chemistry set, then I thought of all the other interesting things our lovely ladies might have squirreled away that might prove to be a discomfort.

'So I decided to shake them.

'Then another thought came – or, rather, a series of thoughts. Such as, how the hell did these baddies find out that we'd taken refuge in that school?

'I guessed that they knew who and how many they were after. So why eight neat little snatch packages? Were they planning on leaving Sims? That was the most logical explanation.

'But then I gave in to my paranoia, and wondered if Sims was expected to leave with them – of her own free will. If Sims was in with them, that would answer my first question.

'At this point, I brought in Jasmine, to tell me I was just thinking weirdly.

'Instead, she came in with a question of her own. If our kidnap team was so well prepared, why did they suddenly go to square zero when they actually hit the grounds?

'Had they been expecting more data?

'Too many questions . . . so Jasmine and I decided to shake not only the girls, but tender young Alice, as well.

'This is what we got.'

She indicated the collection on the bed.

'A couple of nasty little push daggers, some paralyzing gas, rigged dice, three fixed game capsules, two marked decks, those very pretty knuckle-dusters and so on – all just about what we could have expected from the juvenile set.

'Then these two items.'

She picked up one.

'A high-powered multiband radio receiver.

'Property, Miss Alice Sims.'

Sims squirmed.

'I got it used,' she said. 'I like to listen to the radio late, and didn't know what was in it.'

'What it is,' M'chel said, 'is also a medium-powered transmitter. Of *course* she didn't know that.

'The second item here is Sims's private com. A bit strange that she would take along equipment that wouldn't necessarily broadcast on whatever public frequencies are used on Porcellis.

'We asked Grok to disassemble it, and found that not only would it work on Earth, but also on an unassigned frequency.

'An outgoing signal on that frequency would also set off a small homing device in Sims's com.'

'And, by the way,' Jasmine put in, 'I checked with the local library, and found out what com frequencies are used on Porcellis. None that the chips of this com are set for.'

'At that point, we thought it was time to bring in our principal. So far, we've gotten nothing but a few sobs and bleats of innocence.'

'So you decided it was time to call in the wrecking crew,' Goodnight said. He went to Sims's chair and stroked her hair gently. She flinched.

'Now, Alice,' Goodnight said. 'I don't suppose you've studied torture at all. It's pretty much a cheap trick, and is only worth considering if you're under the pressure of the moment and need easy information that you know the other party's got.

'Or else if you've got weeks and months and want to know everything about the person who you're slowly skinning.

'But desperate people do desperate things.

'I'd like you to think about how desperate we are — and remember that none of us particularly liked getting shot at the night before last, so we may be feeling a trifle barbaric around the edges.'

She looked at him, eyes wide in fear.

Goodnight smiled, sweetly, innocently, and his eyes were dead pools.

'I didn't know . . . I didn't mean . . .' she blurted, and the story came out.

There'd been this man back at the school who'd met her in a bar one night, and it was very lonely with all of the 'friddly farts' at St. Searles, and these 'slithery little bitches,' and he was very good-looking, and she didn't have any money, and all he said he wanted was to know what was going on, because he had some friends who were interested in investing in Porcellis, and they'd pay well, and—

'And who paid you?'

'Henri did. In cash.' By this time, Sims was in tears.

'Did he tell you who he worked for?'

'No. Honestly, he never said a word. Just . . . friends.'

'So she tipped them, which got us our tail and the first attempt on the way down to London,' Riss said, her face as hard as Goodnight's.

Another 'friend' of Sims's had contacted her aboard the *Victory* and told her what she should do next.

'All it was was to turn on my com when we reached our next port, no matter where or what it was. I did.'

'That let them trail us to the school here on Cygnes,' Riss interrupted.

'And then?' Goodnight asked.

'I guess I must have turned it off, or something,' Sims said.

'Which is why they didn't zip right inside and grab the girls,' Riss added. 'They expected to have a roadmap, which was turned off. I don't think old Handsome Hank is very pleased with you right now, Alice.'

Goodnight considered.

'If we had six months, and a nice clean psych lab . . . or three days and a soundproof room and a good collection of knives,' Goodnight said, 'we could maybe find out if she's lying or not—'

'I'm not! I swear to you!'

'I happen to believe she is speaking the truth,' von Baldur said. 'Grok, if you'd take her in the next room, and Chas, if you would keep her from getting into any mischief . . .'

The two obeyed. Grok came back.

'It is not unlikely,' von Baldur said, 'that whoever the boyfriend is was working a false flag, or that he in fact told her nothing.

'Those apparati are a bit unusual, however. Grok, can you tell anything about them?'

Grok took an amazing number of tools from a belt

pouch and set to work on the com. After a few minutes, he grunted, set it aside, and began autopsying the radio.

'Interesting,' he said. 'Neither device has any maker's marks on it, nor can I find anything on the components themselves. Interesting to find something . . . somethings . . . that sterile.'

'Maybe,' King said coldly, 'but not that unusual. Grok, you and I know a company that works like that.'

Grok whuffed air in surprise.

'We do. We do. And I should have Goodnight torture *me* a little for general stupidity.'

'Cerberus Systems,' Jasmine said, unaware that she was hissing like a cobra.

Cerberus was one of the largest security firms in the known galaxy, known and feared for their complete amorality and ruthlessness. Cerberus was King's exemployer who'd tried to get out of paying her by accusing her of being a robot. Grok, too, had worked for Cerberus, leaving their employ both out of boredom and because he disapproved of their unwillingness to back their personnel if anything even vaguely catastrophic happened.

The alien had no particular feelings toward Cerberus now, but King hated them with a bleak passion.

'So what does Cerberus want with these girls?' Riss said. 'Or maybe, more likely, with Porcellis, Miss Rosewater-Jones, *and* these girls.'

'We do not know, and I would like to very much,' von Baldur said.

'The second question becomes,' Riss continued, 'whether Cerberus wants the girls as a threat to someone, conceivably Rosewater-Jones, or for blackmail purposes; and whether, worst case, they're willing to physically harm them.'

'I find that hard to accept,' von Baldur said. 'They

certainly kill adults . . . look at the numbers of times
they've tried to kill *me* . . . but children?'

'I think they're capable of anything,' King said. 'But
I freely admit to prejudice.'

'I suspect,' Grok said, 'that we have to operate on the
assumption that they'll do anything – and guard ourselves accordingly.'

'Confusion and more confusion,' Goodnight muttered.

'And it is very damned unlikely we'll get anything
from Sims,' Jasmine said. 'It sounds like they ran a nice,
clean operation.'

'The question now becomes,' M'chel said, 'how
quickly you can get your spitkit ready to lift, Freddie.'

Von Baldur nodded, went to a com, began dialing.

'And,' she added, 'what we're going to do with
Sims.'

The *Monkey Business* was fueled and supplied within the
day, and the girls were rushed aboard.

Von Baldur had the lifters take circuitous courses
from the hotel to the yacht.

As they loaded aboard, Erin asked where Miss Sims
was.

'She got a com from Earth,' Goodnight answered. 'A
family emergency, and she was very sorry she didn't
have a chance to say good-bye to you.'

'Oh,' Erin said, looking puzzled. 'I thought she once
told me she didn't have any family.'

Goodnight made no answer.

M'chel waited until the girls were on the ship, then
leaned close to Goodnight.

'So what happened to the idiot? Did you leave her
facedown in some back alley?'

'I wouldn't dream of such a thing. In fact, I consulted

a map, and found a primitive area not an hour's flight from where we were. I left her in the middle of that, making sure she wasn't tied too tightly and would be able to work herself free and walk back to civilization in a day or so.'

Riss looked at him skeptically.

'You're generally not that soft-hearted . . . or happy with loose ends, Chas. Are you telling me the truth?'

'M'chel, I'm hurt! Would I ever lie to you?' Goodnight said.

He smiled innocently. Riss snorted.

SEVEN

'This is Cygnes Control . . . clear for lift, over.'

Riss, at the controls of the yacht, glanced back.

'First thing, we get offworld, is to check for bugs.'

'No kid,' Goodnight said. 'But first jump us nice and random, twice.'

'A deal,' she said, and the *Monkey Business* lifted from its staging position on antigrav, cleared atmosphere, and went into hyperspace.

Riss touched sensors.

'Jumping again,' she said into the intercom, heard a groan from the passenger section's link, then a voice:

'Kel's puking.'

'Shit,' King murmured. She waited until the *Business* emerged from the strange whorls of hyperspace into normality, then unstrapped and went back to play medic.

The others helped Grok as he hastily modified receivers on three space suits. He found a standard field scanner in the ship's tiny electronics space, and fitted himself into his custom-ordered suit.

Leaving Riss at the controls, they went out, and floated around the *Business*, looking for any transmissions.

M'chel kept the ship's scanners on Rove.

Grok's suit radio crackled:

'I find nothing. And this suit I paid too many credits for was not properly fumigated. Reboarding.'

The others followed him, also reporting that they found no sign that any tracer had been installed.

'Of course, you realize this proves nothing,' Goodnight said. 'It's too easy to put in a telltale that doesn't work on any of the usual freqs – or one that, say, would kick in when we jumped or during the time we're in hyperspace.'

'Thanks, O cheery one,' Riss said, touching controls.

'Jumping,' she announced.

They blipped out into normal space – and less than a dozen seconds later, they had company.

'Oh, joy,' Riss said.

'I have it ID'd as a standard customs ship,' Grok said. 'More or less. And it will be armed, I would anticipate.'

'Hang on, people,' Riss said, as a screen flared. 'I have a launch!'

The missile hurtled at them, and Riss's fingers danced across the control board.

The missile blew about a hundred meters distant, and several screens flared, then went dark.

'Jumping!'

Again, the *Business* went into hyperspace, and, again, within a minute, came back out.

'Well,' Goodnight said, 'this time the bastards weren't interested in just grabbing the negotiables and negotiating.'

The other ship appeared a moment later, and another missile spat out of its tubes.

This one almost hit, and its detonation flash took other sensors down, then they flashed back up on secondary or emergency power.

'Jumping! That was too goddamned close!' Riss announced.

She started to key in a random setting.

'No!' Goodnight said. 'Go back to where we were before.'

'Huh?' Riss asked. But she obeyed.

'Maybe the bastard'll think that he hit us, and put the drive on frammis, so we're stuck,' Goodnight explained.

'Gotcha.' Again, the *Business* went into hyperspace.

This time there were several wails from the girls' section, and they heard King swearing.

'I wish,' Grok said calmly, 'that we had invested in a good, serious, well-armed destroyer.'

'Or a battleship,' von Baldur tried, as Riss sent the *Monkey Business* to its previous location.

'Good, good, very good,' Chas approved. 'Now let's hope they think we're stuck in a groove, and they'll jump back to where we were before, and be waiting to dry-gulch us good.

'M'chel, let's go somewhere new.'

Riss, concentrating on her piloting, nodded, and again the *Business* jumped.

This time, they were not far off an unknown world ringed in deep purple and green.

With no follower.

'Good,' Riss said. 'It worked. Now let's go where we're going before they catch up to us.'

Two jumps later, they were off Porcellis, and gratefully turned themselves over to Landing Central.

Riss insisted that she had to stay at the controls, but it was very all right for the rest of them to go back and help Jasmine clean up the passengers' quarters.

'I'd love to help you,' she said piously. 'But duty calls.'

Lady Ardent Rosewater-Jones was tiny, and wore a floral hat, a print dress to match, and white gloves.

Her mansion — really a series of barely connected houses — stretched for kilometers, and seemed to be decorated in every style of kitsch the galaxy had known.

She cooed over the girls, said that they would have so much fun together and learn so many new things, and it would be just a delight having them around.

Then she shooed them off to a late-afternoon meal composed mainly of desserts, and turned to the Star Risk operatives.

'I understand you had a bit of trouble getting here.'

'A bit, yes ma'am,' said von Baldur, who was uncomfortably aware of how much Lady Rosewater-Jones reminded him of his own great-aunt. 'But nothing we couldn't handle.'

'Do you have any idea who the culprits might be?'

'We do,' Grok said.

Lady Rosewater-Jones looked a bit surprised, as if astonished that something that primitive-looking could talk.

'An organization called Cerberus Systems,' he went on.

'Oh, them,' and she laughed in a little, tinkly manner. 'They *are* rascals, aren't they?'

'That's one way to describe them,' Riss said. 'There are others.'

'They never seem to give up,' Rosewater-Jones said. 'And don't really understand the meaning of the word "no."'

'You're, uh, familiar with them?' Goodnight asked, trying to keep incredulity out of his voice.

'Oh, yes. Very,' the old woman said. 'At one time I made the error of retaining them to manage the security here. There are, would you believe, men and women who seem to think that anything intended to give pleasure to the people should be vulnerable to various schemes, and it takes constant watch to dissuade them.

'At any rate, they made me an offer to keep Porcellis secure, which I accepted on a trial basis. I was most disappointed in their performance. They seemed to think I was a bit of a simpleton, and used false bookkeeping and other forms of what I can refer to only as chicanery to wildly inflate their bill.

'I retained other, more reliable, investigators, and they were of the opinion that not only was Cerberus Systems crooked, but they had actually been behind some of the very schemes that had caused me to hire them.

'They thought me, in short, a fool.

'I may be, but I purely despise being thought such. I might add that the culprits might also have been remote members of my family, who've been most distressed at my not cutting them in on my operation.'

She laughed again and waved her hand, dismissing Cerberus.

'But all that is a thing of the past, and you have fulfilled your commitment admirably. I've examined your bill, and approve of it. Your charges are steep, but you deliver, and I've added a significant bonus to your fee. Thank you very much for helping an old woman in her hour of need.

'Now that the girls are safely here, I look forward to what I've been thinking of as my second girlhood, teaching these young women things I've learned the hard way over the years, so they'll have, I hope, none of the grief I've experienced in growing up. I do hope that I'll be able to guide them into professions they'll be happy and successful in.'

Jasmine thought Rosewater-Jones deserved a warning.

'Ma'am, one thing you should be aware of, is that the girls are a little, well, high-spirited.'

'Prone to high jinks,' Goodnight added.

'Aren't we all?' Rosewater-Jones beamed. 'I think that I, too, was a high-spirited lass in my day. And I'm sure that none of the girls will step over the bounds of good, safe fun. Or I shall be unhappy with them.

'*Most* unhappy.'

Her smile swept the five Star Risk operatives.

Riss noticed, with a chill, that the smile didn't go above her lips, and her eyes were cold as ice.

She decided there was a reason that a wide-open world like Porcellis was controlled by one person, and that person was someone who could dismiss the thugs of Cerberus as rascals.

And then she thought they'd tried to alert the wrong person.

They should have warned the girls.

EIGHT

Eight men, all prosperous-looking, sat around a long table. Four, including the chairman, were there in person, and the others were holo images, projected from various parts of the galaxy.

All of them were experienced in long-range communications, so the various delays from their distant fellows was allowed for reflexively.

They were the division heads of the enormous Cerberus Systems, plus the chairman and chairman emeritus.

Cerberus was headquartered on Alegria IV, one of Alegria 87's multiple worlds. Earth might have been the Alliance's ceremonial home, But Alegria was one of the half dozen planets where the working bureaucracy was located.

Alegria headquartered the Alliance military, plus Intelligence, which was why Cerberus had been sited there.

Cerberus's CEO was fairly young, in his forties. Since his hostile takeover, he had sent the sprawling security company into newer, more 'activist' directions. Never known for its high ethics, Cerberus was now famed – or rather, notorious – for being willing to accept any assignment, provided the fee was high enough and any

broken laws could either be ignored, taken care of sub
rosa, or blamed on erring employees.

Ral Tomkins prided himself on being self-made; a
boast that was occasionally responded to, well out of
Tomkins's hearing, as 'damned correct, since no one
else'll take credit for the little bugger.'

His inheritance, close to a billion credits made in
military scrap, was never alluded to.

'Success,' Tomkins was fond of saying, 'makes anything right.'

Mostly, his fellow board members agreed with him.
The company had a long tradition of skullduggery to
support that belief.

The chairman emeritus had taken over the firm more
than fifty years earlier, when he'd used his retirement
funds and contacts within Alliance Intelligence to build
a small private investigation company into an industrial
giant.

He deliberately sat at the far end of the table from
Tomkins. Eldad Yarb'ro's face held the residue of a
thousand covert operations, and as many sins.

All of them, he was privately arrogant enough to
boast, had been carefully concealed, as were those
crimes he'd committed building Cerberus.

There were those who, well out of Yarb'ro's hearing,
repeated the old quip that the company motto should
be 'Never been indicted,' although that wasn't quite
true. 'Never been convicted of anything that couldn't be
settled, appealed, or buried' might have been closer.

'I think,' one of the men said, 'we can regard the
Nahroo matter as closed. Miss Angress has accepted our
offer, and will plead guilty, and the presiding trial officer has agreed the investigation will not be pursued to
any higher level.

'Our client is most pleased.'

He picked up another fiche, touched its surface, read, and then frowned.

'Another matter that, unfortunately, should be closed is the Porcellis affair. All of our efforts – either on behalf of the estranged members of the Rosewater-Jones family or in our own interests, which of course were never revealed to the family – have failed, and the candidates we had planned to further our interests are now in the hands of the originally intended party. I recommend that we distance ourselves from any further dealings with anyone and everyone in this regrettable case.

'I so move it.'

Tomkins said, 'Seconded,' looked around the table, got nods. Cerberus sometimes gave the air of being democratically run. It was not, of course. All dissension was resolved before any meeting.

'Carried,' he said. 'Although I'm most displeased by the loss of valuable resources and personnel in the matter. Move on.'

'No,' Yarb'ro said. 'I don't think the matter should be dismissed at all, although I certainly agree that we should have no dealings with either the family or the world.'

'What, then, are you saying?' Tomkins said, voice chill. There was little fondness between the two men.

'I'm referring to this minuscule organization that calls itself Star Risk that was our opponent in this matter. No more than five principals, yet again they've managed to cleverly bollix up the works,' Yarb'ro said. 'We have allowed them to do this time and again. This is absurd. Our reputation as a firm to be dealt with most carefully is potentially at stake.

'We've always prided ourselves in dealing swiftly and finally with any competition, yet these beings have been allowed to continue in their financially and otherwise embarrassing ways. There is a complete fiche available on their activities on the agenda, and any of you are welcome to review it, although I think the summary at the top of the file is adequate.

'I wish never to see their names again.'

'And you propose?' came from one of Tomkins's lackeys. 'What? An End Certificate on them?'

That was Cerberus's code phrase for assassination.

'I do not,' Yarb'ro said. 'We have been, as I've said before, too quick to extend our responses to the limit, which is not only unnecessary, but expensive and potentially lays Cerberus open to legal action.

'That is not necessary. I think that we should put full pressure on this firm, in all areas, to remove them from the field. I have an executive ready to coordinate this attempt, one of our more capable operatives named Nowotny. He has already been placed on standby.'

Several of the men, or their images, nodded familiarity with the name.

Tomkins touched sensors on his desk, scanned the screen that appeared. He looked up.

'You are certainly right about this Star Risk, and we don't need to waste time discussing how they should be dealt with. They may be no more than a gadfly, but even mites can be annoying, especially considering a future contract that promises quite incredible profits.

'It is time, and past time, to deal with them conclusively.

'I so order, and see no reason to waste our time with a vote.'

NINE

It started small.

M'chel Riss had recently gotten fascinated with the ancient Earth martial art of salat. She thought she was doing well — as well as she ever allowed herself to think she was doing — and was surprised when her instructor, one Stiff Perr, told her he didn't think she had a chance of advancing to a higher degree, and was dropping her from the class.

She was hurt, then angry, then thought about whipping up on the man.

From behind, knowing his skills.

But she remembered he was a notoriously eccentric sort, shrugged, and forgot about it.

The next hitch was an inquiry from Trimalchio IV's Immigration Bureau, asking if Grok's papers were in order.

Jasmine sent an immediate response back saying of course they were, and why were they bothering him?

No reply was received, and Star Risk considered it had merely been some officious bureaucrat they'd silenced, and so gave Grok a proper ration for being illegal, which he failed to find amusing.

Nor did Jasmine, Grok's closest friend, especially when she discovered Trimalchio's Immigration was used for nothing other than polite extortion when a notorious and successful white-collar criminal sought asylum on the world.

The next trouble was not amusing for anyone. Alliance Credit, their longtime banker, told Jasmine that there had been unspecified complaints about Star Risk playing fast and loose with their credit, and 'requested' that Star Risk take their banking elsewhere.

No further explanations were offered.

Jasmine, muttering under her breath, found a new banker.

She also caught the next bomb. Their insurance company canceled all coverage, including the team's personal medical plan, with only the bland explanation that 'in these troubled times, we're forced to consider all clients very carefully.'

M'chel took King out for a drink or six. Jasmine complained plaintively, 'I feel like I've been shot at and missed and shit at and hit.' M'chel couldn't offer much beyond sympathy and another round.

The firm picked up a quick and easy contract, helping a system find advisors to train their military.

All that would be necessary was for Star Risk to hire reliable people – and, even in the flaky field of mercenarying, there *were* such – coordinate on a syllabus with the client world, and inspect the work done once or twice an E-year.

Jobs like that, never bragged about in resumes or bars, paid the rent.

Goodnight contacted Hal Maffer, a fairly reliable contractor, told him what they needed, and moved on to another project.

Within the day, Maffer, sounding worried, was back on the com, saying that three of the four teams he contacted didn't want to accept a contract with Star Risk, having heard the company wasn't that reputable, and was getting a very nasty reputation for not paying its people when it should.

Goodnight hit the roof, knowing well how many deadbeats worked in his field, and how desperate circumstances could become if Star Risk got the reputation of being a deadbeat.

Maffer said he'd stand by.

Goodnight started checking the rumor mill, and found that, indeed, someone was spreading the word that Star Risk *had* had a good rep, but they'd gone sadly downhill.

Nobody knew where the slander had come from, nor who'd started it, but 'everyone' had heard it.

Goodnight managed to piece together a team for the contract, but it became necessary to post a bond. Since Star Risk's banking was awry, that required some financial jiggling, almost enough to make the job not worth handling.

Goodnight retired to a bar — any bar — fuming gently.

Freddie was the next target.

A rather nubile journoh showed up, claiming to be a freelancer interested in doing a major piece on Star Risk as an example of a reliable, moral mercenary outfit.

M'chel tried telling von Baldur to get away from her — that journohs, any journohs, are always the pilot fish of disaster for soldiers.

Von Baldur pooh-poohed her, saying that he was good with people, and could tell there was no malice in this woman. He gave her everything — including, Riss suspected, some exceedingly after-hours attention, and they parted as smiling friends.

Two weeks later, it appeared the smile had been

on the face of the tiger, as one of the biggest-selling
tabs in the Alliance appeared with a screaming head-
line:

DEADLY MERCENARY RING ACCUSED OF
WAR CRIMES.

And the drop:

STAR RISK, LTD. NAMED IN CIVILIAN ATROCITIES.

There was nothing to the story, except some wild
rumors that had been floating around for years about
never-to-be-named soldiers of fortune who were utterly
guilty of some ugly crimes.

Suddenly Star Risk was named as the guilty party,
even though the firm hadn't been in existence when at
least five of those atrocities had been committed.

'*Wonderful*,' Freddie muttered.

'Indeed,' Riss said, trying not to gloat.

'Come on,' she said. 'I know the bar where Chas is
hanging his hat these days.'

She did hope the episode would slightly reduce
Friedrich's proud boasts about being an unerring Isaiah.

'Cheer up,' she told the pair, after uniting them over
alcohol. 'It can only get better.'

It didn't. It got very much worse.

Next was a tax audit. This, however. was no particularly big deal. Among the original settlers of
Trimalchio IV had been several tax evaders, so the
Revenue Division of the planet's tiny government was
small and ineffectual.

But this, coupled with a 'safety inspection' of Star
Risk's offices, was enough to drive Jasmine King to the
bar.

Grok came along, amiably, since he'd found a definite fondness for Earth cognac.

The four were joined by Chas Goodnight, who
announced that he'd picked up a tail, and, worse yet,

that there were other lurkers outside the bar, clearly waiting for their assigned targets to leave.

'It's not that I'm doing anything nefarious, and if I can still pronounce that word I'm definitely not drinking enough gin,' Goodnight said. 'But just the presence of a shadow is enough to inhibit my style.'

He drank, then looked at his partners.

'You know who's behind all of this crap.'

Before anyone else could answer, Grok said, most positively, 'Cerberus Systems, of course.'

There was not a shadow of disagreement or of other candidacy.

'Just frigging wonderful,' Riss said. 'They've got how many operatives – five thousand?'

'Double that,' said King, who kept track of such things.

'I don't want to think about how many people subverted, how many ships, how many millions of credits,' Riss went on. 'So what are we gonna do about it?'

Silence, then Goodnight tried, 'Hope they get tired of teaching us moral lessons?'

Jasmine snorted disbelief.

'All we can do,' she said, 'is hang on until they run out of ideas and find someone else to screw.'

'This is not a cheerful conversation,' von Baldur said. He signaled for another round.

The next morning, his mood hadn't improved, even seen through the lens of a hangover.

He took M'chel into his office.

'I think,' he said, 'since you and I are original partners, that we had best be preparing for a doomsday plan, before someone gets killed.'

'Like what?' Riss asked, knowing the answer full well.

Von Baldur just looked at her.

She nodded, went back to her office, began figuring.

That night, while von Baldur and Riss were separately glooming over how far Star Risk might be forced to cut and run — and coming up with worst-case scenarios — an industrial accident occurred.

In spite of statistical improbability, the antigravity generators that made the Star Risk building so architecturally stylish and improbable-looking failed momentarily. Worse, the backup and emergency generators cut out just on the forty-third floor for a few seconds.

The building didn't topple, but the forty-fourth floor dropped one story before the backups came on and lifted things to where they should have remained.

Holos were already screaming about the catastrophe that had been predicted, which was why the tower had relatively few tenants. Star Risk considered the damage from a lifter hovering just off the building.

'The offices are pretty well squashed,' Goodnight said. 'Naturally, nobody's talking sabotage yet.'

'And probably they won't,' King said. 'Cerberus's Industrial Section is a lot better than most arson/accident teams.'

'What about our insurance?' Goodnight asked.

'What insurance?' Jasmine King said. 'We were canceled, remember? And I haven't gotten an approval from the companies I've been getting quotes from.'

'Wonderfuller and wonderfuller,' Riss said. 'So what have we lost?'

'Totally? Not all that much, really,' King said. 'We're backed up, twice, in offsite locations. We'll come back up all right, but it'll be the devil's own time putting things in operating order.'

'During which time, we won't be getting any jobs,' Goodnight said. 'I just hope the building management's coverage is nice and covered.'

King nodded, didn't answer.

'Talking will not solve our problem,' Grok said, trying to sound cheery and undisturbed. 'So let's set to work.'

Von Baldur looked at Riss. He didn't need to say anything. What would happen if the next 'accident' happened during working hours?

Five versus ten thousand?

They set to work.

What came next should have been a joke, but no one considered it funny.

Star Risk had been working almost around the clock, on rented furniture with rented computers.

They were very proud of themselves that they'd almost put Humpty Dumpty together again, and figured they'd reopen for business in a week, no longer.

Trimalchio IV's Animal Cruelty Society showed up with a list of questions. Was this strange creature they called Grok really sentient? If not, was he there of his own free will? Did he need liberation? If so, what zoological gardens might accept him? Was he to be considered nonhostile to humans? If not, were there proper security precautions to prevent him from harming people? Had his custodians posted a proper bond to provide for any accidents or runnings-amok?

Star Risk ignored them.

But even ignoring further frayed tempers.

'We're being nibbled to death by ducks,' Goodnight growled.

The grand finale came next.

It was a very slick deal, everyone at Star Risk agreed.

Three aircraft, most likely small strike ships, attacked just after midnight on a weekend, when Trimalchio IV's business section was almost empty.

Two held, orbiting five hundred meters over Star Risk's tower, and the third came in hot.

It launched what was probably a five hundred kiloton conventional homing bomb, which hit the Star Risk suite through Chas Goodnight's office window.

The blast utterly destroyed the suite, and the shock sent the tower rocking on its foundations.

The second ship came in, firing a dozen small incendiaries.

If there had been anything left of Star Risk's assets, they were destroyed in the fire. Firemen from a dozen companies responded, and the fire was out by an hour after dawn.

The five Star Risk operatives looked up at the smoke curling from the building's midsection.

M'chel Riss, her voice as empty as her prospects, said, 'It's over.'

There was no need or energy for argument or discussion.

TEN

'Does anybody see a way to break it off in Cerberus?'
Chas Goodnight demanded harshly.

M'chel Riss shook her head.

'One — or rather five — against a gazillion . . . that
only works in the holos.'

After that, there wasn't much to say — or, rather,
there was a great deal to say, but the Star Risk operatives, being soldiers, weren't good with words or
emotions.

Even Grok had learned human habits in that regard.

Jasmine gave each of them a thick envelope full of
high-denomination bills, from her secret emergency
fund.

They all made insincere promises to stay in touch.

Jasmine gave M'chel the alloy nameplate for her
office, and Riss almost started crying.

Instead, she managed, 'So, what now?'

Goodnight had seen the glisten in her eye, and
added, hastily, a cheerful 'We'll just keep on keeping
on.'

Then he spoiled it by adding a very tentative 'I
guess.'

With that, Star Risk, Ltd., was done.

ELEVEN

Of them all, Jasmine King and Grok had the least clear idea of what they wanted to do next.

King was, in spite of laudatory retraining efforts by M'chel Riss, still too much the bureaucrat, so she immediately rented a small suite of offices in a nondescript part of Trimalchio IV's capital.

She privately thought that Freddie had made Cerberus's job much easier with Star Risk's high visibility – the flashy suite in the high-rise and the even flashier name.

Her new offices had a very small sign on the door, saying RESEARCH ASSOCIATES.

She invited Grok to share them with her.

'And what are we going to do?' he wanted to know.

'Make money,' she said.

'How, might I ask?'

Jasmine hesitated for a little, then said, 'What's the matter with what we were doing? Except with a *much* lower profile?'

Grok considered, then nodded his shaggy head.

'That is as good a way as any to pass the time, since I am not yet bored with this odd trade of mercenary-ing.'

Jasmine smiled, a little wanly.

'It won't be as much fun as Star Risk was.'

'Perhaps not,' Grok said. 'But the profit-sharing plan with just two of us is a great deal more favorable.'

And so they put the word out, thinking there was no reason the lead Star Risk had pioneered – to have no more than the absolute essentials eating up the normal payroll, and contract hiring as needs and jobs presented themselves – wouldn't still work.

In about a week, Grok came in, beaming.

'I never thought I would have the human satisfaction of a mere job, working for someone else. But my horizons are continually expanding, and I think we have an excellent prospect here.'

He was right.

Two systems, longtime enemies for some absurd reason, had recently had changes of government. Both were authoritarian, which meant they needed to have a nice little war going so the citizens wouldn't notice they were being robbed blind.

And so Quast and Folv declared war on each other, each claiming, naturally, to be the injured party.

'And both sides,' Grok continued, 'are putting together their armies, which reduces the unemployment, and therefore the visible taxes, leaving the next generation to pay for all this nonsense.

'God, but I love people!'

The problem on both sides was that neither had much of a star fleet.

'So,' Grok concluded, 'it should be a simple matter for us to start getting on the com to various people, and then to provide our clients, whichever they shall be, with ships and their crews.'

'Simple enough,' Jasmine mused. 'But I have a bit of an idea.

'First of all, I've got to guess that every merc on their

side of the galaxy is sending Quast and Folv the old resume, full of blood and thunder.'

'Probably,' Grok said. 'But we can resort to telling the truth, can't we?'

'Seems a little pedestrian,' Jasmine said. 'Let me muse a trifle.'

She did, and within a day, had her inspiration.

'We're going to become merchants of death,' she said.

'That doesn't sound like much of an improvement,' Grok said. 'Even if we ignore the basic suppliers like Thompson or Kerley, our old friends Cerberus can provide battleships by the kilometer.'

'But I,' Jasmine said, 'can beat them all. For we have a secret weapon.'

'We do?' Grok asked. 'Lying around this office? It's so secret you haven't told me about it.'

'That's because I just thought of it,' King said. 'We can have both sides as clients – and we, and any of our employees, won't stand the slightest chance of getting killed.

'Now, I'll give you the spiel, and then we'll each get on the com to Quast and Folv. I'll be Research Associates, and you can be, umm, Defense Contracting.'

'I am bewildered,' Grok said.

'You won't be for long,' King said.

Half a century before, there'd been a sudden fad for a new kind of warship. It was called an Assault Command & Control craft – ACC.

The older C&C ships, both in-atmosphere and space, had been around forever. Their intent was to provide maximum communications and battle analysis for commanders, who could sit a bit away from the fray, coolly figure out what was going on in a battle, and come back with the appropriate response.

Of course, if the general or admiral was a clutter-brain, being able to see fourteen different projections of a battle did little good. But every military leader worth his gold braid had to have one or several of them.

The only problem a C&C ship had was if the foe was able to sneak or force its way within range. C&C craft were notoriously soft-skinned, underpowered, and lightly armed, since their entire hulls were full of electronics.

Few admirals really like being in the line of fire, let alone getting hit, so some genius came up with the ACC. It had a cruiser's armament and defenses, and so there were many, many takers.

Unfortunately, there is no such thing as a free lunch when it comes to warships, and the ACCs weren't quite 'smart' enough to 'outthink' the oppos in that their mere size couldn't provide the electronics suite that a moonlet or even a converted liner could, plus they were dangerously vulnerable to anything bigger than a heavy destroyer.

In a very short time, the ACCs whose construction had made weapons' designers and shipyards very wealthy sat in mothballs or hung uselessly in bone-yards.

Jasmine, as part of her omnivorous reading, had noted a piece on the debacle of the ACCs, and routinely filed it.

But King never forgot *anything*, and when Quast and Folv started putting fleets together without much in the way of combat experience, her memory came alive.

Grok understood immediately, and growled his pleasure.

And so they set to work.

The initial spiel was King pretending to be a reporter for *Janes* – still quaintly called *All the Galaxy's*

Ships – contacting first Quast's and then Folv's military public relations departments.

That gave her the names of various admirals, especially those in or close to the purchasing department. She also found out the names of government members who'd served in what passed for the two worlds' navies.

The pair next flipped a coin, and Grok made his choice. He contacted Folv's J-4, Logistics, and using a voice synthesizer, pretended to be an electronics company, asking what classes of ACCs they had that might be in need of upgrade.

Told Folv had none, he pretended shock, and said he would have a colleague – also Grok, without his synthesizer – talk to them.

'After all,' he finished, 'Quast has three of them. Not the most current, though, I'm afraid.'

When Grok II got through to the purchasers, they must have checked with their flag-bridged superiors, and were very interested in Assault Command & Control ships.

Grok just happened to have a couple, freshly refitted, available: the *Giap* and the *Rentzel*.

Interest grew, and Grok contacted the scrapyard where he'd found the pair of ships, and bought them on a per-kiloton price.

They were hastily towed to shipyards, painted, and given heavier-duty fuses and slightly more recent electronics.

Then it was Jasmine's turn to deal with Quast, which, of course, had no ACCs – at least, not before King began her machinations. When she was done, they had three: the *Marshall*, *Li Po*, and *Von Moltke*, all three marginally more modern than the two Folv had bought.

When Grok's turn came, Folv inquired worriedly as

to how many ACC spacecraft it was 'ideal' to have. Grok advised at least four.

That added the *Hoffman*, the *Suleiman* and the *Mahmud* to the Folv fleet, after their parliament decided they didn't want to do things by halves.

The *Arslan* and *Giuscard* were next bought by Quast.

A rather stricken Grok came to King.

'A disaster!' he proclaimed.

'What?'

'I can't find any more of those damned ships for sale!'

Jasmine worked her end of the galaxy, and also couldn't find any.

'Oh well,' she consoled Grok. 'All good things have an end. We made several kilos of credits. And, if it matters, nobody got killed.'

'True,' Grok said, then sadly shook his head.

'But as you have said, it wasn't nearly as much fun as with Star Risk.'

TWELVE

M'chel Riss lay naked on the sands of her island, dreaming of money.

If she restrained her lower impulses to occasionally run amok in a high-fashion district, to attend theoretical physics conventions on distant worlds, and to take profligate lovers, her finances were more than sufficient to carry her for two full lifetimes.

Since she didn't have much of a tendency toward gigolos, she was probably fairly safe with the other two.

But still . . .

Riss hadn't been raised to be a flake, no matter how hard she tried to convince herself otherwise.

But she did feel a little hurt, like any good marine, at being driven from the field with her banner in tatters.

God *damn* Cerberus!

Lying in the sun, she thought dreamily of somehow, someway, making a one-woman assault on wherever their headquarters were, grenade between her teeth and a dagger in each hand.

And getting away with it.

That was, indeed, a rub or two.

She didn't want to think about Star Risk and what had happened. Riss believed in enjoying the moment when it was good, and moving out at high port when it changed, and never looking back.

Star Risk had been a hell of a dream.

But it was over, she reminded herself.

She thought of getting up, going into her villa, and making herself a very tall, very cool drink.

But Riss didn't drink much before midday, especially alone.

So she shut off her mind and concentrated on UV rays and skin cancer until the com blatted.

She grunted, grabbed the unit, made sure the visual was turned off, and answered it.

The grating voice was ex-Warrant Officer Naysmith. Not many former military sorts retired to Trimalchio, since the planet's government-by-somnolence didn't match the careerists' requirements and budgets. But Naysmith, a master ex-armorer, had prospered; he was not only selling various weapons to the citizenry, but maintaining several police departments' arsenals.

Plus, he also was the conduit for offworld 'safaris,' and most anything else that had anything to do with guns or gunnery, while keeping his dealings strictly legal.

He'd customized several blasters of various types for Riss over the years, and they'd become as friendly as any hard-bitten warrant could become with an officer — even ex-.

'You know anything about music?'

'A little,' Riss said cautiously. In fact, she knew quite a lot. Her family had all been amateur musicians, and so she'd grown up surrounded by every kind of instrument from banjo to sitar to theremin.

She herself played guitar.

Badly, she freely admitted. But on a long deployment, any marine who managed to drag along anything capable of making sounds would be prized, if she didn't make a pain out of herself by twanging away while others wanted to sleep or expecting special favors.

M'chel Riss's big problem was that she prized vocal music for the lyrics, which always brought up the old joke about why a bunch of people were moving jerkily to music, with the explanation that they all liked music for the words.

'You ever hear,' the warrant went on, 'of Lollypop and the Berserkers?'

'Gesundheit. Problem with your sinuses, chief?'

'Lollypop and the Berserkers, I said. They're a pop music group. Lollypop is looking for a good bodyguard.'

M'chel knew she shouldn't, but she thought an interview might at least be interesting, so she called the com number Naysmith gave her and was in touch with the group's new managerial firm.

The meeting was set two days distant, which made Riss think that this Lollypop might be in earnest about wanting a bodyguard, and decided to up her price tag.

It was held in the management company's — Music Associates, a nice nondescript name — offices, which were outside Trimalchio's capital, set in a rolling estate carefully styled to look like an Old Earth plantation.

Riss was met by one Arn — no last name offered — one of the two heads of Music Associates, was told that hiring a bodyguard was only one item scheduled for today's band meeting and that the group and its support people were 'one big democracy,' and led into a large conference room packed with various people.

She was introduced to a pair of lawyers, the head of the sound crew, the head of the holo crew, the head gaffer, the publicity man, the group historian — she boggled slightly at that — the still photographer, who wanted to take her picture and had to be forcibly told no, the head of the fan club, the chief songwriter, the lead costumer, and the head of security, whose name was Folger.

She wondered what the group itself had to do except show up, hit a few notes off a lead sheet, and look spectacular.

The only other name that stuck belonged to the band's one present member, a tall, handsome young man with long brown hair and haunted eyes, who played the distinctly archaic bass guitar. His name was Maln.

Again, no last name was offered. Riss couldn't figure if she was supposed to know it, or if everyone in the room leaned slightly to the fugitive side.

Everyone looked at M'chel as if expecting her to start the meeting. She knew better, from countless staff meetings at which she'd been the junior party, than to begin things.

Besides, the real client hadn't shown.

After a few minutes, which M'chel thought was deliberately calculated to build suspense, Lollypop entered.

She was young, but Riss noted that she had very old eyes that seemed to have seen everything and didn't want to see much more. Lollypop was about M'chel's height, had blond hair that couldn't have possibly been made lighter, a thin build that, except for huge breasts, approached the skeletal.

'I'm Lollypop,' she said, curling a lip to illustrate her obvious superiority. 'And you're the woman who wants to be my bodyguard.'

'I don't know about wants,' M'chel said easily. 'I might possibly be interested in the job – *you're* the one who's supposedly looking for a bodyguard.'

Lollypop frowned, clearly not used to disagreement.

There was a snort – of amusement? – from Maln, and a wordless but displeased murmur from Arn.

'Why?' Riss persisted.

'Why else?' Lollypop said. 'Someone wants to kill me.'

'Do you have any idea who?' M'chel asked.

Lollypop gave a dirty look at Folger as if it were his fault the culprit hadn't been found.

'None at all,' she said. 'If I did, I'd be screaming to the frigging police.'

She stared skeptically at M'chel.

'I'm not sure you're my idea of a bodyguard.'

Riss didn't ask what a bodyguard was supposed to look like, reached into the portfolio she was carrying, took out a one-page resume, and handed it to the singer.

Lollypop frowned at it, passing it to Arn, as if not happy or used to reading. The manager scanned it, and his eyes widened twice in surprise.

'Yes,' he said. 'Your credentials are . . . more than adequate.'

Lollypop nodded, as if she agreed with the vetting.

'The first time,' she said, 'someone pushed a speaker off the rack – we have our own sound, set up on a tower – and almost got me.'

'Could it have been an accident?' Riss asked.

'I thought like that at first,' Lollypop said. 'But we have Mag-Clips to hold things down. And they were pried loose.'

'And there were scrapes on the tower deck,' Maln put in. 'Somebody had to push it pretty hard to move it.'

Lollypop gave him a look that suggested his contribution was unwelcome.

'Then . . . back here on Trim . . . someone tried to run me down with a lifter when I was leaving a club.'

'Lollypop got its registry number,' Arn said. 'We traced it, and the lifter was stolen.'

Riss nodded.

'That could mark a professional,' she said.

'That's when I got scared,' Lollypop said. 'The third time was just last week. Someone rigged a gas bomb – at least, there were fumes after a bang – at my front door.'

Riss glanced at Folger, who nodded slightly.

'Did you report this to the police?'

'I did,' Arn said. 'They seemed to think it was some kind of publicity stunt.'

'Our latest log,' Maln put in, 'we called *Street Warrant*. Maybe that gave somebody the idea.'

'Or maybe not,' Lollypop said.

'It does sound,' M'chel said, 'as if you have a problem.'

Lollypop looked at Riss scornfully, as if she shouldn't have bothered to bring up the obvious.

'If I take the assignment,' Riss said, 'which I'll know after I do some research, there'll be three others, minimum, plus myself My rates—'

'I don't care about that,' Lollypop said. 'Arn talks business for me – for us.'

'Just so you're aware of the way things work,' Riss said. 'That means somebody will be with you all day, every day, and every night. Plus we'll use backup if we decide it's necessary.'

'That's going to put some kind of crimp in my sex life,' Lollypop said. 'Try to have some cute guys with your team.'

There was a short laugh from Maln, and a very hateful look from Lollypop.

'No offense,' Riss said, meaning offense, 'but my team will be there to keep you alive. We won't want to even be your friend, let alone anything more.'

'That'll put you with the majority,' somebody across the table said. Lollypop's sweeping glower didn't ID the voice.

'We'll put our best efforts behind finding whoever's after you, as well,' Riss said.

'Just keep me alive,' Lollypop chirped, and a bit of fear came into her voice.

'That's our job,' M'chel said. 'After all, dead clients don't pay.'

Riss mentally doubled her price as Arn rose and beckoned her out of the room. He wanted to haggle. M'chel, who was already wondering why she wasn't just passing on the job, didn't let him.

The eventual rate was 200,000 credits per month, plus all expenses.

'Steep, very steep,' Arn said.

M'chel shrugged.

'What's your client's life worth?'

Arn couldn't come up with any answer but a nod of concession.

'I'll have my team in place within a week,' she said. 'I need to study the situation. One of the women in the meeting was IDed as the group historian. I'll need her full cooperation. And Folger's as well.'

'Your timing is perfect,' Arn said. 'The group will be going on the road in two weeks.'

'On the road?'

'Sorry. That's an archaic term for touring.'

Once the contract was signed and a retainer check cleared her new bank, M'chel started doing her homework.

She rapidly discovered that the anonymous voice was right. Lollypop had all the best friends money could buy, and not one more.

There was good reason — not that M'chel got much

help learning the negatives from the group's PR man, a fat sycophant named Sonlev, to whom everything was wonderful (and if it wasn't, he paid no attention). The true history of Lollypop came from Yalt, the band's historian, a mousy little man with dozens of downloads on Lollypop, and Dimet, president of the group's fan club, a heavyset woman with a tendency toward a mustache who insisted on using what M'chel thought might be youth slang. Lollypop was, to her, 'the ginchiest,' which Riss assumed indicated some sort of approval.

Lollypop was actually named Miki Gubitosi, and started life as a minor star named Little Miki, all ringlets and flounces.

M'chel had enough morbid curiosity to dig out one of her recorded songs, a sentimental wallow called 'My Heart and Family,' that made Riss's teeth ache.

When Little Miki had the temerity to reach adolescence and developed breasts and an attitude, her career was history. She, in turn, dropped her family, who'd vampired her into stardom, and vanished into the jungle of her home planet's runaways.

Those had their own music, which, as far as Riss could tell, was judged solely on how badly it disgusted adults.

Miki ended up as part of the Berserkers, which was successful enough to get a booking agent, a manager, and a recording contract.

Success of a sort came, but then the Berserkers peaked. Railing on about how everything sucks has, after all, a limited audience.

A normal group would have broken up at this point, but Little Miki, now calling herself Mik the Murderer, was unbelievably ambitious, having tasted a bit of fame, and wanting it back.

Either she was contacted by Music Associates, or she went to them. No one knew.

But suddenly the Berserkers were released from all contracts and were free agents.

Riss, very cautiously, asked how that had happened, feeling that toes must have been stepped on.

Even she knew that the music industry's contracts were, for the talent, as ironbound as slavery.

Maln gave her the explanation: They knew some 'hard boys,' from their days on the street, who didn't mind 'reasoning' with people.

Credits for these goons changed hands – 'Not ours, 'course,' Maln said. 'Folger was one of the thugs who went out and worked on people's kneecaps. I'd guess that Arn and his partner put up the geetus for the goon show.'

And then the Berserkers were signed by Music Associates.

The contract also wasn't for the usual fifteen to twenty percent managers charged. Their flat fee was forty percent, plus additional points for the choreographers, costumers, songwriters, and such.

Riss couldn't find out how much the Berserkers themselves got, but estimated around twenty percent.

'But it don't matter,' Maln said. 'They do everything for us, from taking care of our houses to . . . to making sure we're happy.'

Their material changed radically. Now all was mooning about lost lovers and new infatuations, prime interests to the subteen set.

The songs, Riss thought, truly sucked, being simplistic in both their lyrics and chord changes.

The group now made millions, both with recorded logs and in their tours. That figured, Riss thought cynically. Pop music never did go for the intellect.

THE DOG FROM HELL

Riss wondered to herself if the Berserkers, when the smoke cleared, had more credits in their pockets now than before, but didn't say anything.

She also hoped they were saving what they made, pretty sure the Berserkers' fame had about the half-life of a laboratory-formulated element on the very far side of the periodic table.

Part of the change to the group had been Miki's deciding she needed a new name. Arn supposedly came up with 'Lollypop.'

It made the band sound absurd, but M'chel thought she was maybe being too much of an adult.

Their new audience of prepubescent little girls loved the name, and buried Music Associates's secretaries with requests for Lollypop's picture and advice.

The Berserkers thought their audience was quite too dumb to reach adulthood, but their manicured press never gave a clue that the band didn't think every person in their audience wasn't a budding saint.

Lollypop herself became known as a harridan on roller skates, insisting on her way all the time, which included contracts for concerts that had specific clauses about what food was to be backstage, which depended on Lollypop's latest fad diet; the color of the lims they were to be transported in; the number of temporary aides they were provided with, the precise number of backstage passes, and so forth, down, Riss suspected, to a description of their touring bed partners.

Lollypop was also infamous for discussing, the next morning, in public, just how incompetent her night's lover, of whatever sex, had been. Of course, she'd already gone through her bandmates, and now only used them as pimps when the group was on the road.

Riss decided she definitely had no desire or talent for

a career in music, and certainly not this method of being a wandering troubadour.

At least she'd had no trouble finding three solid backups. Two were women, which Riss thought was preferable, since they would be seen as less of an obvious threat. All of them had not only active military service, but field duty, and all of them had been seconded to various dirty deeds divisions.

Best of all, two of them had held civilian risk management jobs, but not long enough to have bad habits thoroughly ingrained. M'chel thought she could train them the way she wanted in a short time, hopefully before the nameless assassin(s) tried again.

And she'd learned a good, solid reason why she shouldn't tell Lollipop and Company to pack their asses with salt and piddle up a rope, as Chas Goodnight had been wont to say:

Music Associates had hired additional security after the first attempt on Lollypop — Cerberus Systems, who'd utterly failed to find the culprits, but had still charged an enormous fee.

The idea of being able to break it off in them, no matter how slight, even though Cerberus was unlikely to hear of her success, was like a shot of mother's milk.

With ancient brandy.

Riss put that aside, and started trying to play detective, which she thought she was completely incompetent at.

She began with the assumption that the unknown enemy was either within the organization or without.

She found that appallingly brilliant, and her feebling around hadn't produced anything by the time the tour began.

Lollypop and the Berserkers were flush enough to be able to charter a small liner.

Cabins were assigned by rank, M'chel learned.

Lollypop and Arn, being at the top of the pyramid, got the largest staterooms, the band the second largest; the 'executives' of the various branches the third; the crew the fourth; and hangers-on – unless they were screwing or otherwise kowtowing to someone significant – what was left over.

M'chel was beginning to get the idea that in this 'one big democracy' some people had more clout than others.

She herself and her three operators were given small rooms aboard ship, what Riss thought would be considered third tier. But that didn't matter – she didn't consider that part of real status, nor did she plan for anyone to have enough leisure time for anything other than eating and sleeping.

She also secured a largish storeroom for her group's 'tools.'

These ranged from tiny, easily concealable and non-ferrous blasters to gas projectors to sniper weapons to antipersonnel radar and night vision to various scanning devices for unobtrusive searches.

An operator was outside Lollypop's stateroom door or with the singer at all times.

One of her women reported that Lollypop had made a fairly serious pass at her. She'd been either drunk or in some sort of altered state at the time.

'What did you tell her?'

'Not what I wanted to,' the woman said. 'Which was that I wouldn't screw her with her own dildo.'

'Your reticence was fairly wise,' Riss said dryly.

'I told her I'd taken a vow of celibacy until the Shire was granted its rightful place in the comity of nations.'

M'chel laughed.

'Good on you.'

'Naturally,' the woman went on, 'she had no idea where the Shire was.'

Riss laughed even harder.

The third performance was on Defelter VI, in the planet's largest amphitheater.

Two local groups, the most popular among the teenies of Defelter, opened the gig.

Riss had the word 'gig' defined to her, and looked up its origin out of curiosity.

She finally found something in a dictionary of archaisms that left her even more puzzled. Why a musical performance used the same word as an ancient term for a military criticism was quite beyond her.

The group carried its own sound system with it, which she'd been told simplified life no end. It was mounted on a double alloy tower that was bolted together by the crew.

This was something that had impressed M'chel. The grips took only a few hours to set up the huge structure, its myriad cables – more reliable and less bother than wireless transmission and speakers and monitors and mix boards here, there, and everywhere. There were also cameras and lights scattered all over the tower.

Riss was a bit awed with how much all this gear had cost. Lollypop and the Berserkers, regardless of whatever else they were, believed in giving a hell of a show.

Maln set her straight: The tower and all equipment belonged to Music Associates. 'That way, when we fall off the charts, they have things ready to go for whoever's standing in line to replace us.'

M'chel now had an idea where Maln's haunted look came from.

The band, short Lollypop, deigned to make a sound

check, then retired to their luxury hotel, which of course had been paid for by the promoter.

For the performance, two of Riss's team and M'chel danced attendance in the stadium. It was vital that they learn who belonged where and when, so anyone out of place intending harm could be quickly tagged and neutralized.

One operator stayed with Lollypop.

M'chel decided her command post would be atop one side of the tower.

That far up, it was very hot, very sweaty, and very loud.

But certainly nowhere as bad as combat, she reminded herself. And a lot safer — at least for anyone except Lollypop.

The two opening groups played hard, but not that hard. M'chel had heard that anyone outdoing the Berserkers would find it hard to get paid until much, much later in the tour.

The fact that they had to provide their own sound gear and were forbidden to use the group's didn't help them shine.

Riss put sound filters in her ears and scanned the huge stadium, concentrating on first the audience.

All she saw was the core listeners and a few bored or appalled parents. Neither group seemed motivated enough to be assassins.

Riss forgot about them, swept the stage.

Standard procedure, she'd learned, was for the Berserkers to play two numbers, and then, to the audience's carefully choreographed screaming, Lollypop would bound onstage.

The group was halfway through its intro number when M'chel saw something. It was on the catwalk atop the other side of the tower, and if it was anything dangerous, as it appeared, she didn't have time to go back down to the stage, push her way across and clamber back up.

Riss swore and swung out on the narrow lighter connecting the two parts of the tower, restraining an impulse to gibber, claw at an armpit, and look for a piece of fruit.

If anyone below saw her, they must have assumed it was part of the act.

M'chel reached the other side as the first number finished and the Berserkers, not waiting for the applause to die, launched into the second one.

The device was pretty impressive.

It was a cut-down blaster, mounted on a folding tripod.

The blaster was topped with a small radar set and camera, focused on the front part of the stage below. A radio contact was wired to the trigger.

It took only a moment to figure out.

The radar would track anyone forward of the group and the camera would remote the image.

Of an innocent dancer.

Or Lollypop.

The radio would be used to fire the blaster from a distance when it had the proper target in its sights.

Lollypop, of course.

M'chel wrenched a servomechanism linked to the radio free of the trigger, snapped the blaster's magazine out of its slot, and defanged the chamber.

She sat staring at the weapon, ignoring the roars of girlish glee for the star below as she smashed into her set.

Lollypop was definitely not imagining things. Someone was surely trying to murder her.

THIRTEEN

Friedrich von Baldur suppressed a yawn, smiled as brightly as he could manage at the two other people at the table, and said, 'If you'll excuse me for a moment . . .'

Without waiting for a response, he stood, bowed to his opponents, then to the handful of spectators, and, accompanied by a security man, left the hall.

There weren't any rules against taking a fresher break, even in middeal.

He'd checked before entering the tournament.

Von Baldur didn't object to the security man going into the toilet with him, nor lift an eyebrow when the man checked the booth to see if anyone had stashed a card for him.

Baldur used the facility with relief, pun only half-considered, his mind intent on the cards and the table behind him.

It hadn't been that much of a pretext – this was the thirty-fourth straight hour of competition.

But he'd really gone out not only to rattle the two men still in the game a little – or so he hoped – but to freshen up.

He washed his face in hot, soapy water, dried carefully, straightened his fashionably off-white shirt and tucked it in, combed his thinning hair, and went back out, sat down, and picked up his cards.

He was in fairly good shape on the table, even though the other two still had about a third more money in front of them, and the rules were table stakes.

Von Baldur had taken three of the last four pots, all three without a bluff. The cards were running in his favor.

The tournament had some grandiose name, and the game was the archaic seven-card stud poker.

Baldur's open cards were two tens and one jack. In the hole, he had a pair of jacks, and felt fairly comfortable with his full house.

One of the other players was, Friedrich was pretty sure, bluffing, with two low pair showing, who'd bet heavily on the last card, trying to convince the other two that he'd either made his own full house or had four of a kind.

God forbid.

The other player had played a very consistent hand, and had three kings showing.

The fourth king hadn't materialized on the table so far.

All in all, though, it looked fairly good for him.

The first player gave von Baldur a hard look, and picked up the deck.

He dealt three cards, faceup.

As far as Friedrich could tell, no one had improved his hand.

Unfortunately, that included von Baldur.

He looked bland and checked.

The first player, ostentatiously not counting his stack of chips, shoved a pile into the pot, trying very hard to convince the other two he now had the winning hand. Friedrich didn't think so, but couldn't be sure. He didn't think the first man was a very good player, but he was very lucky, and had a large stake behind him.

He watched closely the second man, whose face stayed blank, and the man simply called.

That was potentially not good. He might be sand-bagging.

Von Baldur raised, was raised back by the first player. The second player just called. Again, an unknown.

Friedrich tried to avoid looking at his increasingly slender stake. If this went on, they could buy him out of competition.

He called, as, to his great relief, did the others.

The last card was dealt, down and dirty.

Von Baldur casually lifted its corner, and, he hoped still calmly, set it back down.

It was the fourth jack.

The first player checked, as did Friedrich. The second bet heavily. It took almost all of von Baldur's pile to stay in the game. The first player, suddenly seeming unsure, merely called.

Friedrich did the same.

He felt sweat trickle down his sides.

The first player forced a smile, shrugged, and turned over his three hole cards.

Junk.

The second man looked smug, and showed what von Baldur thought he might have held — a full house, kings and sevens.

Friedrich flipped over his four jacks, and raked in the pot.

That gave him his strength, and, a dozen hands later, the first player was out, and a few hands later, so was the second.

There was applause, and Freddie bowed.

Friedrich von Baldur had a very large pot in front of him.

A chip girl, smiling her availability, asked if she could cash him in.

Von Baldur waited until three holo photographers got their pictures, then told her to go ahead.

He'd be in the bar.

By the time his drink, a very expensive vintage Earth cognac with a water back had materialized, so had the rather large check, and a scattering of cash.

The chip girl smiled invitingly.

Von Baldur smiled back, and tipped her a one hundred credit note.

She looked disappointed, moved away.

There would have been a time when von Baldur would have followed up on the invite, but he was feeling a bit of his years, and all of the thirty-five hours.

Von Baldur hated to make promises he might not be able to keep.

Friedrich drained about half of his drink – this was the first alcohol he'd allowed himself beyond the single drink every eight hours when he was playing – and relaxed.

He wanted to finish the brandy and order another, but didn't want to suddenly pass out in the middle of his triumph. He would wait for a minute.

This was one step, the third successful one he'd made.

If he could keep up the winning, his goal – setting up another Star Risk, this one keeping well away from anything resembling Cerberus Systems – was getting closer.

He wondered, if he was successful, if he could track down his former partners and see if they were interested in trying again.

Probably not, he thought, a bit sadly.

Things never went that smoothly.

A waitress, unbidden, set another snifter down in front of him.

He was about to ask, when a man his age settled down in the next chair.

'It is good, Mital,' the man said, startling von Baldur by use of his real name, 'to see you being a success.'

It took a moment to recognize the man. He, like Freddie, had aged.

His real name was Laurence Chambers, von Baldur remembered, and he hadn't seen him for ten, no fifteen years. The last time had been in the middle of a disastrous retreat, all screaming, blood, and crashing starships.

Chambers had been in charge of an elite reconnaissance team, detailed, quite out of its specialty but typical for the military, to help von Baldur evacuate the supply depot he'd been in charge of.

It had been a very long and defeated week.

'I thought you were dead, or at least disassembled a bit,' Friedrich said.

'It was all smoke and flame,' Chambers said. 'They got me out and patched me up.

'I remember you and I'd been talking about—' Chambers looked around to see if there was anyone in earshot. 'Decent and civilized ways to make money, and you'd convinced me that being in the middle of shooting, shitting, and shouting was a mug's game.

'When I got out of the hospital and was waiting for my retirement papers to go through, I started looking for you.

'Without luck.'

'I got off that hellworld . . . I don't even remember its name,' von Baldur said, 'as quickly as I could, and found a nice, safe job, way behind the lines. And then I found it . . . expedient to leave the military.'

'So I discovered,' Chambers said. 'I did, as well. Running security for a gaming world.

'As sort of a hobby, I kept trying to find you.'

'At the time,' von Baldur said, 'I was distinctly interested in not being found. More so, later.'

'I learned that, too,' Chambers said.

Neither man mentioned the reason − that Mital Rafinger, now Friedrich von Baldur, had resigned from the Alliance shortly before an investigating commission arrived at the quartermaster regiment of which he was in charge.

'Finally, I tracked you down. Running that Star Risk, which sounded like fun until the shit came down.' Again, Chambers looked around, but there were still no eavesdroppers. 'I heard about the raw deal Cerberus gave you people. I'd heard from other sources what shitheels they were, and didn't have any trouble believing you'd run afoul of them.'

'But you kept on looking,' von Baldur said, trying to keep suspicion from his voice.

'I did,' Chambers said. 'Not just out of curiosity anymore. Especially after I heard what you were doing now. I came here, and saw that you were lucky − if a little underfunded.'

'This is true,' von Baldur admitted.

'I'm now running my little world after a certain high-stakes game,' Chambers went on. 'But I've got a problem. Goddamned bust-out artists have been moving in on me. I don't know if it's a conspiracy, but I've got 'em thicker than flies.'

'That is not good.'

'What I decided I needed was a Q-ship. And, maybe, somebody who's good enough to find out who's running the operation, since you've done some interesting things since the Alliance let you go.'

'Ah?'

'Someone,' Chambers went on, 'who can show up in a game, looking fairly innocent, and go after the sharpies.'

'What makes you think I'm a supershark?'

'I don't,' Chambers said. 'But I want somebody on the floor who clearly isn't part of my team. Let's say I can generally make the cards run in your direction.'

'How *very* interesting.'

'I thought you might like it,' Chambers said, with a tight smile.

'I'll pay a salary, bankroll you, and let you play in any tournaments you want. That'll attract some folks who might want to go head to head against you, which is good for my operation.'

'Mr. Chambers,' von Baldur said carefully, 'this is worth discussing, although I feel that I've run across a shark much bigger than I am.'

'That,' Chambers said, 'is one thing that'll keep you honest — which, of course, means *on my side*.'

FOURTEEN

The woman was simply amazing.

From her carefully coifed hair to her coyly painted toes, she could only be called spectacular.

Still more impressive, she appeared rich without being a snob, exquisitely dressed and jeweled without being a clotheshorse, seductive without being whorish.

Chas Goodnight might've wanted to take her to bed, were he not a man who never confused work and pleasure.

She was costing him two hundred credits an hour, plus expenses, and Chas thought – from the adoring looks she was getting from the two clerks and the manager of the jewelry store – she was worth every bit of it.

Her name was Marnie, and her voice was like pure water over stones in a purling brook.

She turned to Chas, who was impeccably dressed as a rich man of leisure, fully suitable for Marnie's companion, and asked if he was *sure* this store carried really fine rubies.

He didn't have to answer.

The two clerks scurried, and the manager told her they had the finest rubies on the planet – nay, the system, no, the cluster itself – fit for a princess or a queen such as she was, and showed her to the appropriate counter.

Marnie justified their faith in her, and asked to look at the second most expensive necklace in the case.

She tried it on, posed in front of a mirror, frowned slightly, and asked to see another item, this one the *most* expensive ruby necklace in the case.

It was reverently put before her, resting on a black velvet cloth.

She picked it up, let out a small squeal of delight, and then, somehow, accidentally, the string of the necklace broke.

Gems scattered across the carpet.

Marnie squealed again, this time in pure dismay, knelt, and, apologizing, started scooping up rubies.

The two clerks and manager were around the side of the counter, on their knees, helping.

The tiny knife with which Marnie had cut the string vanished, unseen.

No one seemed to notice Goodnight's move to the rear of the counter, or his sliding the back of the counter open, a small silk bag coming out of his jacket, and gems being shoveled in.

Then the rubies were recovered, and Marnie, blushing and in tears, couldn't be more shamefaced, telling Goodnight she had to go back to the hotel, her amour propre was shattered, and maybe they could come back later, but she certainly couldn't pick anything out at the moment after this embarrassment.

Making the appropriate noises, Goodnight escorted her to the door.

It was then things went awry.

The guard, slightly older than God, came out of his alcove burbling something about stop thief, they wouldn't be allowed to get away with this, and by Heaven he'd see the law put both of them away forever, and so on and so forth.

More to the point, his hand was bringing out an elderly nickel-plated but still deadly gun.

Goodnight had allowed for the possibility of the retiree's rather pointless bravery when he planned the holdup, hoped he wouldn't have to take extreme measures.

His hand flashed across his cheek, and he went bester.

He was inside the old man's guard before the man could take the safety catch off his pistol, and rigid fingers seemed to merely touch a nerve ganglion in the man's neck.

The man gargled and his eyes rolled back. He started to fall backward.

Goodnight came out of bester.

Gun and guard went to the floor.

The manager was just beginning to shout something when Marnie took a small, svelte gas grenade from her sleeve, and, thumbing the timer, flipped it toward the three employees.

It went off, and they went down like stalled oxen.

Goodnight, not trusting the filters in either his or Marnie's noses, had her by the arm and spun her out the door into the street.

A dozen steps away, a lifter sat, its engine ready.

Goodnight unlocked the door, got the woman inside, and was behind the controls in an instant.

Without ceremony, he lifted the car, putting a large dent in the luxury vehicle parked in front of him.

Three blocks away, another anonymous lifter waited.

They changed vehicles, and were off again.

'Well?' Marnie asked.

'Goddamn that impotent old fart playing hero,' he said, not sounding that disturbed. 'He's going to get himself killed and some poor goddamned thief up on a murder rap if he's not careful one of these days.

'Just because old bastards like him don't care if they get themselves killed doesn't mean they're entitled to cause so much frigging trouble, damnit!'

'Did we get what we came after?'

Goodnight grinned.

'We did. So you'll get your bonus at the spaceport. Your flight's boarding in an hour. I want you gone and away within the hour, since you're a little on the high-profile side.'

Marnie made a face.

'I was afraid of that,' she said. 'I would have liked to stay around and play with you.'

'Another time, princess,' he said.

She pouted, and rolled between her fingers two of the rubies she'd palmed.

'Why is it the people you want to stay around never can?' she asked. 'What are you going to do?'

Goodnight, for a change, told part of the truth.

'I've an idea for another job on another world, darling, that I thought of while we were hauling ass. Something that'll be well worth risking my handsome young person for, not like this small-time action.'

'Can I help?' Marnie asked. 'You're fun to work for.'

'Afraid not,' Chas said. 'This one'll call for just plain ordinary thugs and smash-and-grab goons, no one of your talents.'

FIFTEEN

By the seventh concert, M'chel Riss knew that the assassin-wannabe was one of them and not an outsider.

There'd been another attempt – this one with a conventional bomb in one of Lollypop's semiportable costume trunks – and Riss refused to believe the handful of gape-jawed fans who followed the tour had brains enough to plan a murder, let alone the desire.

She also was developing a healthy respect for any touring musician. She and her trio of bodyguards had already fallen into the eons-old 'If this is Tuesday, this must be Belgium' thinking – whatever a Belgium was.

And the tour had barely begun.

All that existed for them now was the tour, and the people on it. Everyone else was either a help, a hindrance, a citizen in the audience, or a blur, and each world consisted of the road to the chosen hotel, perhaps a glimpse from a lim window of a local landmark pointed out by a promoter, the stadium, and a larger blur that was the planet.

Space was a doldrum of stupid games, hearing jokes and stories that'd been told a thousand times before, and practice, at least for everyone but Lollypop.

It might have been tough on the musicians – they set up, played, and then wanted to collapse when the fans wanted to throw a party afterward, but it was harder on the crew. They had to set up, make all the equipment checks and deal with the venue problems and vagaries, keep the show running, and then, when the musicians could collapse in sweaty relief, tear the set down, load it in the liner, and get ready for the next jump, with seldom an overly concupiscent fan for a hasty intermission.

There was, Riss realized, a quantum difference between the classic idea of a musician — one woman with a guitar and synthesizer, making her own way from job to job, frequently playing the same place for a week or a month — and these dinosaur monolithic one-night stands.

At least, Riss thought, she and her people weren't constantly facing attempts at various seductions from their assigned job of keeping Lollypop carnate.

Not that the singer became any more civilized or easy to handle. Now she was noted for snarling, at regular intervals, how anyone and everyone within range could and would be replaced by someone more efficient, 'like, say, a rock.'

But none of the four trying to keep her alive had, as yet, reset her clock for her.

But while Lollypop was still alive, Riss hadn't gotten anywhere finding the would-be murderer.

She wished that she had either King or Grok with her. They weren't formally trained detectives either, but at least they had analytical minds, which Riss couldn't seem to find in her bag of issued gear.

She couldn't go out and hire a *real* cop in midtour, and anyway she didn't know the difference between a doorknob rattler and a holmes; a padded porker and a detective.

She thought of bouncing her ideas off the group's

own security man, Folger, but didn't want to involve anyone within Music Associates.

She felt she was falling down on the job, although Arn seemed pleased with her efficiency.

M'chel Riss knew better.

She thought maybe it would be helpful if she sat and made a list of everything she knew about people on the tour, particularly their relationship with Lollypop.

She already knew everyone's resume inside out.

She was surprised, and pleased, to find she knew quite a bit more than she thought she did.

Unfortunately, none of it seemed to lead to a homicidal sort.

She was glooming in a ship corridor one day and heard Lollypop savaging someone. It was Dimet, the fat, somewhat mustached head of the fan club.

'No, you dumb bitch!' Lollypop shrilled. 'You never, ever let those dumb little shitsuckers know when I'm going to be anywhere or what I'm doing. You think I want to be buried in their pimply little dreams and get shrilled to death?'

'But Lollypop, it was just to present you with a plaque,' Dimet whined. 'I thought—'

'Thought! Thought! Goddamnit, lardass, don't go doing things you don't know how to! I told you once, you're prunes when this tour is over! Just prunes!'

Bootheels slammed away.

M'chel waited a sufficiency, then went around the corner.

Dimet was still snuffling, leaning against the bulkhead, and Riss was amazed at the somewhat less than adulatory look she was throwing in the direction Little Miki had taken.

She paid no heed to Riss, who hurried past, embarrassed.

Lordy, lordy, M'chel thought. If looks could kill . . .

That stopped her cold.

No. Not only no, but goodness gracious no.

Dimet couldn't be the plotter. She would cheerfully have died to save Lollypop's ingrown toenail.

Which, of course, was why she was treated the way she was.

Lollypop, like any self-respecting sadist, loved a target that volunteered.

Poor Dimet.

To have her lips torn off by that bitch, and, like most fan-club types, to not have a friend in the world. Or, at least, on the tour. Except maybe for Folger, who treated her with amused politeness.

Dimet wasn't even vaguely on the suspect list. For openers, she didn't have the skills to be able to pull off the kind of killer devices the murderer had progressed to.

Hell, the only ones who did, unless somebody was a close student at the Build a Bomb and Other Nasty Gimmickry Mail Order Institute, were Riss and her three assistants – innocent, of course, because the killer predated them.

So there was no one—

Riss's mind, obedient, if not especially prompt, fed her the recording of Maln, some weeks back, talking about the thugs who'd help break the Berserkers' original contract: 'Folger was one of the thugs who went out and worked on people's kneecaps.'

Folger.

Goons frequently had training in other areas of mayhem.

Folger.

Dimet's only friend.

Son of a bitch.

*

Once they knew where to look, and for what, it was easy.

Riss and two of the others buzzed Folger to his compartment, and the third bodyguard brought Dimet down.

There were sketches, cryptic notes that were now easy to interpret, receipts for odd items used to make even odder devices, some traces of interesting chemicals that had been swept up at the bottoms of lockers.

Dimet took a look at the assembled garbage, and Folger's carefully innocent expression, and burst into tears.

She then started volunteering a confession.

Riss had to immobilize Folger with a knife-hand strike, and then gag him.

Halfway through the blurt of how Lollypop meant everything, and if Dimet couldn't be around her idol, her dreamie, she didn't want to live at all, and therefore didn't want Lollypop to live, and Folger had a built-up hate going back for years, the singer burst into the compartment, which was now getting crowded.

She had a gun in her hand.

M'chel guessed that she shouldn't have told Arn who the guilty party was until everyone was safely locked away.

To alarmed expressions from the others, Lollypop burst out with a profane accusation and betrayal of trust that sounded like it'd been lifted from a fairly bad daytime holo serial, dragged out a medium-sized blaster, and aimed it at Dimet.

'You don't really think,' M'chel said tiredly, 'that with some kind of maniac running around we were going to let anybody but us have live guns, now, did you?'

Lollypop pulled the trigger, and the blaster made a disgusting noise, courtesy of a small sound box that Riss had substituted for its normal powerpack.

Lollypop gaped, and started to throw the weapon at Dimet.

Riss clipped her, quite hard, on the side of the neck.

Lollypop scrawked like a poleaxed chicken and went down.

That was, M'chel reflected later, about the only part of the day that she'd really enjoyed.

At least she was off the frigging tour.

And wouldn't listen to live music for at least a century.

SIXTEEN

'I hope,' Jasmine King sighed, 'that you've had a day more productive than mine.'

'What was the matter?' Grok inquired, as he poured them each an after-work cocktail. Grok had become partial to Earth cognac, and King drank some awful combination of liqueurs called a Veronica's Revenge that did a great deal to encourage the belief that she was an android – no normal stomach could have handled the drink.

'I was lazy, and spent the day being a sentimental slob,' she said.

'Ah?'

'Chasing down our former compatriots and hoping they were all well and happy.'

'I confess,' Grok said, 'to a slobbish, almost human tendency these days to mawkishness . . . and curiosity, as well.'

'M'chel is currently the favorite of the fast set on Trimalchio,' Jasmine said. 'Everyone famous wants her to play bodyguard for them. Freddie is being a little high profile, on some gambling world, with his own gaming tournament.'

'I assume it's rigged,' Grok said.

'I hope so,' King said. 'But nobody said.'

'What about our pet delinquent?'

'I couldn't find a trace of Charles, although there was a jewelry store robbery on one of the Fringe Worlds that sounded like his work.

'I dropped a line with a couple of recruiters that said they heard from him now and again. I left a note with the other two that we're glad they're going well, and if they're in the area, to please visit.'

King shrugged.

'I guess I can't seem to let the past go. Tell me about your day, and that we made some money.'

'We did — and I, too, encountered a bit of the past.'

King lifted an eyebrow, and Grok explained:

'I shall probably be long-winded about this.

'A contact of ours told me, a couple of weeks ago, about a system — eight planets, plus asteroids just outside the system.

'The name of the system is Alsaoud, which had been inhabited by humans for about three hundred fifty years, originally colonized, grudgingly, by two systems who'd fought over who had the rights.

'For some reason the Alliance, usually so reluctant to get involved in anything that might involve danger, had brokered a peace, which required that both systems settle Alsaoud.

'Both wanting to make very sure Alsaoud wouldn't do anything absurd, such as develop delusions of independence, crippled the system with a government that required a premier from one system, and a prime minister from the other, and a parliament to boot.

'Then both systems had promptly lost interest, leaving Alsaoud with the muddle.

'Time passed, and Alsaoud's second and fourth world became heavily settled, and the third, riven by volcanoes, more sparsely.

'Life was further complicated when a third group, running from a sun going nova, decided to move in. The only major, somewhat habitable real estate that wasn't now occupied was the fifth and sixth worlds, and these refugees, who called themselves only the People, occupied them.

'They've recently started settling on the capital world itself,' Grok went on. 'Since their birth rate is about double that of their fellows, that's making the original settlers a bit nervous.

'But their main settlement is in the asteroids, which has a cornucopia of easily exploited minerals, and so they built bubble settlements and such.'

'This sounds,' Jasmine King said, touching a tongue to her lips, 'like a situation made for a nice, profitable war.'

'Actually, *several* internecine sagas of butchery over the years,' Grok said. 'Not to mention things like smuggling, piracy, and general mopery – enough of a problem so the Alliance has actually sent in finger-waggling expeditions from time to time.'

'A problem, indeed.'

'Now, my contact told me, they seem to be getting ready for another round, with special bloodlust for going after the People – and the People reciprocating.

'I approached the Alsaoud government, and found they were in the market for deep-space mines, which I just happen to have access to. They were mightily thrilled at my help, and allowed as how they were in the market for almost any sort of weaponry that might work against what they rather colorfully called "space bandits."'

'You *did* have a good day,' Jasmine said. 'I just might buy you dinner tonight.'

'I haven't reached my point of interest yet,' Grok

said. 'One of the people I was speaking to happened to say there are several mercenary outfits and freelancers swarming around the system.

'One of which is Cerberus Systems, which currently seems to have the inner track with the newly elected government.'

Jasmine licked her lips thoughtfully.

'How nice for them,' she said. 'Is there any way we can somehow ruin a good percentage of their day? As I said, I'm a sentimentalist, and I definitely bear a grudge.'

'I don't know,' Grok said. 'Further of interest, however, since this isn't the richest system known, is that I haven't been able to see how they can pay for Cerberus, given their usual fees.'

'So something stinky is going on, eh?'

'It might be.'

'I wonder if there's anything there for us?'

'I don't know,' Grok said. 'But, remember, we've agreed to, as Goodnight said, "take our lumps" and go our way, and let them go theirs.

'They are a great deal bigger, as we've discovered.'

'Bigger,' King agreed. 'But not necessarily nastier. Oh well. It might be nice to have another shot at them. One that we win, this time.

'But bygones are bygones, and big bullies are big bullies, who generally seem to get away with their bullying.

'Damnit.'

SEVENTEEN

The world of Zion had been settled for a baby forever — and it showed.

Its central city might have come right out of medieval Earth, turning its back on the coast it fronted on toward the close mountains, cut through with narrow lanes and close-set buildings.

Many of its people also looked archaic, dressing all in formal black, with beards and long side curls.

Many of them practiced a religious faith/lifestyle that was just as ancient, dictating everything from dress to manner of worship to diet.

Zion's main commerce was equally antique: diamonds.

Here was one of the four great diamond markets of Man's worlds, the other three being Tel Aviv and Amsterdam on Old Earth, and Sternopoli.

The trade was founded on mutual trust and knowledge.

There was little crime here but the petty variety.

All that, Chas Goodnight willing, was about to change.

Two ships broke into the world's atmosphere at speed, both homing on the city.

One was an archaic Alliance destroyer, stripped of almost all of its weaponry, save two missiles. If all went well, there would be no need for violence after the first assault.

Both ships were running less than five minutes behind a sleek transport, escorted by a pair of corvettes, all three provided by Cerberus Systems.

Weaponry wasn't the most important part of the Cerberus operation's security – secrecy was.

No one was supposed to know the transport's schedule.

Almost no one did.

The transport was intended to pick up cut and polished diamonds, some in their final settings, which would be shipped toward retail markets on a thousand thousand worlds.

The old destroyer carried two pilots, Chas Goodnight, and twenty heavily armed, suited men.

Only one of them was a double agent.

No one had ever dared Zion's security.

Chas Goodnight was daring it.

He'd considered the fact that Cerberus was providing security, and his sensible vow to never cross tracks with them if he could avoid it. But he wasn't stepping on their corns, since he was planning to jack the diamonds before they became Cerberus's responsibility.

Besides, this was an incredibly juicy target . . .

The transport landed at the central city's spaceport, its two escorts seconds behind.

Lifters were waiting to load the vastly precious cargo aboard.

The old destroyer, its pilots ignoring the yammering from Ground Control, dove on the transport, and launched its pair of missiles.

Both, fired at point-blank range, slashed into the Cerberus escort ships and blew their sterns and their drive mechanisms apart, immobilizing them.

The destroyer came in for a hard landing between the escorts and the transport, never giving either corvette a chance to fire on it.

A pair of locks slammed open, and the robbers ran out toward the lifters. Each of them carried on his back a modified antigravity lifter.

As they did, Goodnight's emergency backup ship, an ultra-modern medium speedster, crashed down into a park less than five hundred meters from the port.

The speedster destroyed a statue of a dignified man, fronted by a plaque heralding his life as a statesman and philanthropist.

The plaque didn't say that he'd started his career as a diamond smuggler.

The destroyer pilots slid out a forward hatch, and scurried away from the spaceport toward the speedster. They moved quickly, because they'd triggered a gas bomb in the destroyer, intended to cover the robbers' exit.

The plan was for the robbers to break into the lifters, grab one lifter's worth of diamonds, and then head for the speedster.

Goodnight already had fences and transport in place on a dozen worlds.

This caper would give him – even after the heavy expenses of the two ships and hiring the twenty very expensive pros – enough to retire on.

Or, at least, to relax while he figured out another job, he thought realistically.

Each of the robbers had a timer above his suit's viewscreen, and orders to take no more than five minutes before they went for the speedster and escape.

Less than a minute after the landing, Cerberus sprang the trap that the man who'd betrayed Goodnight's scheme to them had helped set up.

There were no diamonds in any of the waiting lifters.

Instead, doors and panels fell open, and crew-served weapons opened fire.

The gunners had been given orders that there was no particular need to take prisoners.

There was little cover on the spaceport's open tarmac, and about half of the robbers went down in the first blasts.

The double agent had been given instructions by Cerberus to go flat, and pop a purple smoke grenade. He'd been promised that would keep him safe to collect the huge reward.

Cerberus was not known for keeping its promises, but this time it may have meant them.

But two gunners, in a frenzy of excitement, saw the purple smoke, didn't remember what it was supposed to mean, and chattered bursts through the agent.

Goodnight had only seconds to realize how thoroughly he'd been mousetrapped.

He rubbed his cheek against the inside of his helmet, and triggered bester.

Goodnight became a blur, zigging, ducking, and running as hard as he could.

He ducked behind a lifter, flipped a grenade in its rear as he went past, and went hard for the park, as the last of his robbers was shot down.

His suit mike gave him the sound of sirens starting to scream, then, to his accelerated ears, going down the scale to bass.

He knocked a gaping pair of guards down and was

past them in a moment, through the doors and in a terminal building.

Goodnight knocked a door on the far side off its hinges, saw a pair of ranking men in uniform grabbing for holstered blasters, then was instantly past them and around a transport.

In less than a minute, he was at the park, ahead of the running pilots.

Back at the field, the bomb aboard the destroyer went off, gas billowing into the air.

Goodnight hadn't bothered telling anyone else about the bomb, so it was a surprise to Cerberus, putting them on momentary tilt.

Goodnight was aboard the speedster, cursing himself for being a sentimental slob as he turned and took the time to yank the two pilots aboard.

He squirrel-chattered an order, realized he was not completely in control, triggered himself back out of bester, and shouted, 'Lift it, goddamnit!'

One of the speedster's pilots gawped, then obeyed, hitting controls.

The airlock slid shut, and the drive boiled.

The speedster came off the ground, went vertical, and drove upward.

That caused the day's only civilian casualty — incinerating an old man who came to the park every day to leer at the young girls playing handball on nearby courts.

Goodnight ignored both the babble of questions from the four fliers and his own extreme hunger pangs from the body energy his extended bester state had burned.

He wheezed in air, slumped down into an acceleration couch, and hoped he still had enough in his savings to at least pay off these fliers.

'I think,' he finally managed, 'I could have done with another rehearsal when I planned this operation.'

Then he wondered what the hell he was going to do next.

EIGHTEEN

Friedrich von Baldur swore under his breath.

They had him cold.

And it was his own damned fault.

There were four of them, and they were all pros.

Now, if he hadn't had the hubris to suggest to Laurence Chambers that he had a big enough name to draw people to Chambers's planetoid who'd be interested in bringing von Baldur down, and would bring the credits to play with . . .

But he had.

He also should have allowed Cerberus Systems the blatant unprofessionalism of still wanting von Baldur's ass on toast . . .

But he hadn't.

The tournament was called, simply, The First Annual Von Baldur Stud Poker Tourney, and the players did, indeed, materialize.

Among them were these four particular professionals, quite illegally and unethically teamed.

They'd laid low through the preliminary rounds, then begun their play.

The four were the main card man, a scholarly looking, meek-sounding sort; his secret partner, an exceedingly handsome woman; the lookout; and a cover, who unobtrusively wandered around, pretending slight drunkenness and casing the other players and their hands when he could. It was a winning combination.

Von Baldur should know – he'd used similar tactics himself.

Of course they had signals.

When Friedrich had his suspicions, he put holo crews, shooting from the Eye In The Sky – the ceiling watch chamber that every casino has had since time immemorial – and screened, centimeter by centimeter, the footage.

But the team was good – Friedrich wasn't able to translate nor even identify their sign language, so he couldn't put pit bosses on the alert to pitch them out of the tournament.

The team was also well-covered – the main player was sponsored by another gambling world, so they couldn't just bar him from the tournament without any better cause than that he was winning.

Von Baldur had their rooms searched.

They almost looked innocent. But looking back at the entries on their passport fiches showed too-remarkable sets of coincidence, and all four of them had recently 'happened' to 'pass through' Alegria IV, which Freddie remembered as Cerberus's headquarters.

He added one and a hypothesis and got two – plus a bad case of the sweats.

The team did increasingly well as the tournament progressed, and von Baldur did not. He was paying too much attention to the Cerberus operatives, even though they weren't playing against him yet, and not enough to the immediate competition.

Finally he forced himself to concentrate on the business at hand.

That put him in the finals along with, unfortunately, the two Cerberus players, plus two other sharpies.

One of the sharpies was just lucky, the other was plain good. Friedrich, had he been able, might have admitted that the woman was as good as he was.

But he couldn't, of course.

He told Chambers what was going on, and Laurence glowered at him.

'For Chrissakes, Mital – I mean Freddie. We have ways of dealing with things like that.'

Von Baldur nodded reluctantly. He would rather have cleaned Cerberus's clock honestly.

But he reminded himself it wasn't how you played the game, but whether you won or lost.

Single deck 'shoes' were used to deal the cards in the tournament.

They were rigged by Chambers's people.

But the rigging somehow went wrong, and the team did even better than before.

Chambers couldn't figure out what the matter was.

Von Baldur could.

Cerberus had more money than Chambers, so the makers of the shoes would have provided the security company with rigging methods Chambers, and von Baldur, knew nothing about.

Von Baldur had watchers, with binocs, in the Eye, and a tiny buzzer in his groin to signal what cards were held.

But the Cerberus team covered their hands most carefully.

The final round was reached deep in the night, and went for almost twelve hours.

The game was table stakes, so the players had almost all their money on the table.

It made a considerable pot – von Baldur thought it

would be well over a million credits, about a third of which was his, winnings that had been sucked away in the course of play.

When the last card was drawn, von Baldur had a straight to the ten.

The lucky player had folded on the third card.

The Scholar had a pair of fours and queens showing, and had been betting like he wanted everyone to believe he had a third queen in the hole. Von Baldur thought he was bluffing.

His secret partner, who von Baldur thought of as the Beauty Queen, had four hearts. Probably a bluff, since there were three other hearts in other hands around the table.

The other woman had a pair of threes and a nothing card showing, and von Baldur couldn't figure what in the hole.

There were raises and counterraises, and finally von Baldur called.

The woman with the threes folded. She'd been bluffing, and was beat on the table.

The Scholar matched the call, as did the Beauty Queen.

Von Baldur, not sure, turned over his cards.

The Scholar sighed, smiled falsely, and turned his cards facedown. He also had been bluffing.

For an instant, von Baldur thought he'd won.

Then the Beauty Queen turned over the fifth heart, and her flush ended the tournament.

Von Baldur was wiped out.

Chambers wouldn't stake him from scratch. At least, not the size of the stake he'd need for a fresh start.

He managed a courteous smile, and stood back from the table.

Cerberus, once again, had gotten him – and, he realized, they would continue to pursue him to the grave.

Which, the way things were going, might not be that distant.

Friedrich managed politeness while his guts churned.

What in the seventh circle of hell was he going to do now?

NINETEEN

M'chel Riss sat on a float in one of her island's lagoons, glooming gently, and trying to keep from jeering at herself.

It was not so long ago that she'd been carefully husbanding tenth-credit coins, wondering where dinner would be coming from, and desperate for any job.

Now . . .

She looked at the path leading from the lagoon to her main house. Whoever'd developed the island had done so with skill, taste, and subtlety.

Human signs of development barely showed.

But, even though she couldn't see or hear anything, she imagined her com buzzing, buzzing, buzzing. She'd had to hire an answering service back in the capital to handle the calls.

Lollypop may have been an obnoxious client whom M'chel cordially loathed, but she and Music Associates had evidently been singing Riss's virtues to the heavens.

Now, every half-witted celebrity on Trimalchio IV not only had to have a bodyguard, but it had to be M'chel Riss, whether they were threatened or not.

Three holo shows had wanted to do features on her, and had only been dissuaded by threats of violence.

But the calls persisted.

She didn't want to take any of them, having had her fingers burned to the elbows with her one contract. But on the other hand, it was work. High-paying work. Safe, high-paying work.

She considered the com from Jasmine.

Part of her really wanted to hare off on this Grand Quest to Shaft Cerberus, although King hadn't yet defined what they'd do or how they'd do it. All she had was her and Grok's feelings that Cerberus was somehow in over its head.

Not enough.

Not to mention that it would involve real danger.

Her adrenaline count was nice and low these days, thank you.

On the other hand, maybe she should just take off, hunt down Redon Spada, her sometimes lover, and see what trouble the mad pilot was getting into these days.

That would not only be dangerous, but who knew if there was any money there?

More sensible to go play with Jasmine, Grok, and maybe the other two former members of Star Risk.

She snorted, brought her thinking back from romantic realms.

She – and the others – had gotten their asses on toast the last time around, and that wasn't even going directly against the huge security firm.

A woman could get killed messing with them again.

She heard a whisper, looked up.

High overhead a couple of ships were sporting about. Idly she decided that both of them were identical attack craft, probably Alliance.

She wondered what the interstellar government was doing on Trimalchio, yawned, and considered her already perfect tan.

The whisper from above got louder.

The two ships were flying in a tight pair, in a near-vertical dive.

M'chel frowned. She wasn't fond of the sounds of war when she was at rest.

Especially from a couple of flyboys showing off.

The ships were getting closer — she guessed only a couple of thousand meters above her.

Sometimes M'chel wished that Trimalchio had a few more laws, about things like noise pollution or hazardous flying over a populated area.

But—

Her thoughts broke off as she realized the ships were still closing.

Riss swore, vowing she'd notify whoever was the local Alliance muckety about his goddamned cowboys, if they didn't pull out in the next few—

Riss saw bomb bay doors open on the ships, and reflexively rolled off the float and underwater.

She surfaced, head close to the float, and saw bombs fall out of their bays, toward the island — goddamnit, *her* island.

The ships pulled out, and Riss saw, with a chill, that neither of them had any hull numbers or any other marking, and the ships themselves were anodized a shiny, searchlight-reflecting, probably radar-absorbing black.

Then the bombs slammed in, and trees and bits of what had been her house pinwheeled up.

The ships banked back.

Riss didn't know whether to get out of the water, knowing how water carried shock effect, or stay where she was, hoping the next set of bombs would also strike land.

They did, and Riss saw more of her real estate get shredded.

The ships came back a third time, very low, and autocannon roared.

Then the ships climbed, at full drive, for space.

Riss found herself standing on the float, shouting up at the attackers as they vanished.

Smoke and flame rose from the shore.

M'chel found tears runnelling down.

She knew, goddamnit, oh, she knew the attack wasn't a mistake, and who was behind it.

Cerberus, of course.

The bastards wouldn't leave her alone until . . .

She didn't allow the thought to complete itself.

A bit of doggerel ran through her head, written by an ancient Earth outlaw:

> *I've labored long and hard for bread,*
> *For honor and for riches,*
> *But on my corns too long you've tread*
> *You fine-haired sons of bitches . . .*

'Just frigging so,' she said aloud.

If they wouldn't leave her alone, then their asses were up for grabs.

She dove off the float and swam toward shore, wondering if her little lifter had survived or if there was an intact com to get transportation to the mainland and a spaceport.

Jasmine King might be a little surprised at the com she was going to get.

A bit of her mind was still trying to recall what had happened to that Old Earth robber.

Had he been hanged, or drawn and quartered, or electrified, or . . .

Something unpleasant, she was sure.

TWENTY

Surprisingly, it was Goodnight who first started to bring some sort of order to a very joyous, if a little paranoiac, reunion.

The five had filtered back onto Trimalchio IV, and been shuttled by one of M'chel's friends to an out-of-the-way conference center on one of its moons.

'Awright, awright, settle down,' he growled. 'We're all glad to see each other and all of that. Pour drinks, siddown, and let's figure out what we're going to do next.'

'If anything,' Riss added.

The other four obeyed.

Grok presented the situation on Alsaoud, and his and King's belief that there had to be a profit hiding in the confused system for the giant security company to get involved.

When he finished, he looked at Riss.

'It is for you, M'chel, to take us the next step.'

'I think.'

Riss half smiled.

'First,' she said, 'it's agreed that all of us would like to break it off in Cerberus, right?'

'That's maybe not the way to put it,' Goodnight said.

'The question seems to have become do any of us have any sort of *choice* against taking on Cerberus?'

'Sorry, Chas,' M'chel said. 'I was starting too deep into things. Let's take up Goodnight's question.

'Do any of us have any sort of choice?

'*I* don't,' she went on. 'I'd taken my lumps and was quietly going about my living and the bastards shot up my home.

'I got the idea they aren't gonna let me alone. Not unless I go dirt farming and marry some clodheel or something. But for sure get out of any kind of adventuring.'

'That's one,' Jasmine tabulated. 'If I may speak for us, Grok?'

'You may.'

'I could say that we could continue on our merry way, but we haven't come up against Cerberus, one way or another, and don't know if they've got us on their, uh—'

'—shit list,' Goodnight said.

'Yes,' King agreed.

'Perhaps we aren't,' Grok said. 'But given these two, maybe three, outstanding examples, who can take the chance of skulking around looking over your shoulder?

'Assuming you have that capability, which my race does not.'

'Hold your vote,' von Baldur requested. 'I can cast a very certain ballot, so it is two yesses.

'Cerberus came after me quite directly.'

'You're sure that team was from Cerberus?' King asked.

'I backtrailed them a little,' Friedrich said. 'And until I ran out of money, I found they'd been around the fringes of several Cerberus operations. Close enough for my decision, at any rate. So it remains, from my perspective, a definite yes.'

'As for me,' Goodnight said, 'the best I can provide is a definite maybe. I can't tell if they tried to trap me just because they were providing general security for Zion's diamond merchants, or if I'd specifically set off some alarms.'

'We have two definite yesses, one maybe,' Grok said. 'Jasmine?'

'I'll vote us for a probable yes, but I'm voting my emotions. I want those bastards on toast,' she said fiercely.

'That kind of loads it on the probable side,' Goodnight said. 'So, I guess we should—'

'—I don't think we can make a decision yet,' Riss said. 'There's another question.

'None of us are rolling in green. We've got some capital, but not enough for a full-scale war.

'And bashing Cerberus won't be cheap.

'If we go against Cerberus, we'll have to figure a way to make a credit out of it. Or through it.'

There was silence, then grunts and nods.

'Any ideas how?'

Again, silence.

'There's *got* to be money in Alsaoud,' Goodnight said. 'Cerberus wouldn't be there if there weren't. All we have to do is figure out what and where it is, and snatch it out of their greedy little fingers.'

'And perhaps leave them with at least a few of said fingers badly bloodied, or, ideally, missing,' von Baldur said.

'Well, this operation, if we mount it, is one we'll have to be pretty sneaky about,' Riss said. 'At least the moving-in part. So I don't think it'd be wise to put the word out that Star Risk is back in business and looking for trouble.'

'No,' Goodnight agreed. 'That'd be sure to get a bomb in our shorts.'

'But there is nothing that says four friends and one alien — who, perhaps, must remain out of sight — could not visit the Alsaoud System, is there?' Grok asked.

'The holos suggest it is very beautiful this time of year.'

'When the credit trees are in blossom,' King said. 'Yes. Most romantic. Let us go a-touristing.'

TWENTY-ONE

They decided to visit the Alsaoud System in two groups. Friedrich, M'chel, and Goodnight went via one of the few scheduled liners into the system – and even then, it was a way-stop, even though Alsaoud was one of the standard nav posts for travel in that sector of the galaxy.

This they found interesting.

It looked as if not many wanted to go to Alsaoud, and even fewer wanted to take them.

The other contingent was Grok and Jasmine, who slipped into the system via a chartered 'space yacht,' acquired and piloted by Redon Spada. It was actually an armed fast scout that someone had done a fast shuffle on when registering.

This was done not only to keep all of Star Risk's hatchlings out of one basket, but to keep the somewhat noticeable Grok from being noticed. It also gave them a possible back door, if Bad Things started happening.

M'chel found it interesting that Jasmine insisted on traveling with Grok, even though the Alliance liner *Normandie* was far more luxurious. Interesting indeed, although she didn't make any comment.

The approach to Alsaoud was also interesting. The ship had only about half a full manifest of passengers, and so they were cosseted. Especially those in first class.

Friedrich had insisted, even though they were supposedly conserving credits, that this remained the only
way to travel.

M'chel tried chatting with crew members about fascinating topics such as why no one seemed to
particularly want to go to Alsaoud, even though the
guide fiches made it sound 'fascinating.'

No one talked, not even by indirection.

As the ship blinked out of hyperspace, the passengers
were encouraged either to go to one of the lounges to
use the huge screens or remain in their cabins and use
those sets, so they could, to quote the intercom's com-
mentary, 'admire the spectacular Maron Region.'

Riss was more interested to note that the *Normandie*'s
two missile stations were manned as the ship hung
beyond the Maron Region as the crew set up for the
jump deeper into the Alsaoud system. There was also an
escort ship that waited on them.

M'chel remembered what Grok had told her about
piracy in the system.

But then she concentrated on spectating.

The Maron Region, consisting of the asteroids outside the system and possibly formed by a planetary
collision eons earlier, was spectacular. The tumbling
rocks, anywhere from decent planetoids to fist-sized
boulders, looked – especially from a distance – like rows
of loose planetary rings, minus a planet, held in their
loose orbits by the system's own light gravity.

Riss guessed if the rings came from a collision, there
must have been seriously huge planets involved.

The intercom guidebook-type chatter told her that
the interesting thing about the Marons was they were
inhabited, by a hardy race that called themselves the
People. 'Hardy race' sounded like it'd been read in
quotes.

Again, there was no mention of piracy or anything else that might upset the eager traveler.

The second world was Khazia, close to E-standard, the capital of the system. Its capital city was Helleu.

Its medium-sized continents were primarily in the temperate zones, studded with small lakes and seas.

Riss had read that it was primarily agricultural, with some light manufacturing.

It was interesting that the *Normandie* didn't port in Helleu, but sent the handful of passengers down via lighter.

The port appeared easily approachable.

Riss also wondered why the crew of the lighter was not only armed with Alliance heavy blasters, but kept giving their passengers odd looks, as if they thought them demented for wanting to go near Alsaoud.

Riss admitted to herself that most of them didn't appear to be just gawkers, but the sort of people who get very interested in other people's problems and in finding a way to exploit them.

On the approach, Helleu appeared a most welcoming city. It nestled in the crook of a large bay, against a range of spectacular mountains. The respectable-sized city, if not a metropolis, looked well laid out, and included several of the offshore islands.

The buildings gleamed white and lovely under the sun.

But the closer the former Star Risk team came to the landing field, the more they saw things that were missing.

Such as the upper half of a skyscraper, jaggedly smashed off by a heavy missile impact;

Such as unscarred lifters – most of the ones they saw darting above roads were heavily armed and armored;

Such as any sign of traffic direction;

Such as shopping districts that didn't have sand-bagged bunkers, here and there, and whose shop fronts weren't heavily reinforced;

Such as strolling pedestrians – those they saw scurried about quickly, and M'chel thought most of them were armed;

Such as a normal-looking landing field. Half of the ships had been badly shot up, and others were warships, either by design or modification.

'Wonderful,' Riss said.

'Be it ever so humble,' Goodnight added, 'there's no place like this.'

They landed, and were hurried with their baggage into a customs shed. The lighter didn't wait for more than a few moments before taking off again.

The customs shed was sandbagged, with the sandbags holed by small arms fire, and the customs officers all wore body armor.

'It would appear,' Friedrich murmured, 'as if the political situation might have worsened since anyone last surveyed the situation.'

The customs official didn't give their passports more than a perfunctory check, and ignored their baggage.

Riss thought she could have had a small howitzer in her suitcase for all the officials cared.

Looking at the holed buildings beyond the terminal, she thought more than a few passengers might've had just that sort of weapon stashed away – or higher calibers.

'I can barely wait to see what our hotel looks like,' Goodnight said.

Their cab had steel plates welded around the passenger compartment, and the driver's cockpit was also armored.

The cabby, a slender, wiry-haired man, was quite friendly, and helped them load their gear.

The last bag was in the trunk when an unholy screeching tore the air.

Riss involuntarily shouted 'incoming,' and the three Star Risk operatives flattened, beaten to the ground by the cabby.

A few hundred meters away, a small building lifted off the ground and disassembled itself into dust as the rocket barrage exploded.

The cabby picked himself up, checked a watch finger.

'A little early today,' was his comment.

'Does this go on all the time?' was Goodnight's rather incredulous question.

'Oh, no,' the cabby said. 'It's a good deal more exciting these days. Elections were two weeks ago, and they're still deciding who *really* won.'

'Interesting,' von Baldur said. 'The Excelsior Hotel, please.'

'Ah,' the cabby said. 'You are going to be some of our movers and shakers.'

'What makes you say that?' Friedrich said. 'We picked the Excelsior from a guide fiche.'

'Of course, of course,' the cabby said, clearly not believing a word. 'For your information, sir, the Excelsior is where those who, shall we say, wish to have a voice in the future of our system stay.'

Riss made a face, leaned over to Goodnight.

'Maybe it's not a good idea to hang our hats there.'

'Or maybe it is,' Chas said. 'We can't expect to do business without meeting businessmen.'

Riss grinned.

They reached a checkpoint, set up in the middle of an otherwise ordinary street. It was a sandbagged position in the center of the street, with a crew-served autocannon, an alert gunner, and two sentries outside.

M'chel also saw a recoilless rifle hidden in a storefront. Half were men, half women. All were in clean, tailored, dark green uniforms, without rank or unit badges.

One sentry checked a metal plate the cabby held out with a small bill wrapped around it. The other squinted at the passengers suspiciously, a blaster in his hand, then waved them on.

'Our new president's men,' the cabby said. 'Sharp-looking, aren't they?'

Friedrich grunted noncommittally.

There was another checkpoint a few blocks on. These guards weren't as flashily dressed, their uniform was a little shabbier, and their weaponry wasn't as new.

But they were just as alert.

'And who do *they* belong to?' M'chel asked.

'Our prime minister,' the cabby said carelessly. 'He's on the outs. This week.'

He pointed down a road. 'Now, there's an avenue you want to stay off of. There's a new post about half a klick down there, set up by the People, and *they* don't like *anybody*.

'Bastards. Not only are they swarming the Marons, but they breed like rats, and are gonna crowd us off our own worlds if we – or somebody – doesn't stop them.'

He turned into a lane that led to a high-rise just off the beach.

Another set of security guards checked the cab, waved to the door.

Obsequious men wearing the same uniform as the security team unloaded them, and took their baggage inside.

Friedrich took out a decent-sized bill, rolled it, and handed it to the cabby.

'Oh, thank you, sir! Will there be anything else? I hope.'

'We might need a driver on an irregular basis,' Friedrich said.

'Always available, sir. Safest, fastest transport in Helleu. I know everybody, everybody knows me, and I know who not to know. My name's Jorkens, sir. Tell the concierge to call Breakside 438 for me. Anytime, anywhere.'

They checked in to the hotel.

'You'll be on the tenth floor,' the congenial clerk said. 'High enough so any, umm, loud noises, explosions, like that, will be softened, but not high enough to be a target for the crazies to aim at.'

They were escorted to their, as always, suite, then standard procedure cut in:

Goodnight used a couple of innocuous-looking devices in their luggage to check for bugs, found three. Two were audio, one was visual. He carefully starred the lens of the visual pickup as if something accidental had happened to crack it, so it would show nothing important.

Of the two bugs, one he judged ancient, and not worth worrying about. On the other he put a small distorter that would mar whatever was transmitted enough to be indecipherable, but still kept 'casting.

Friedrich checked the suite's alternate exits, where they would lead, and the location of fire exits and other emergency back doors.

Riss, with a collection of smallish bills, hunted down the floor's maids, and made very good friends with them, with the promise of more, larger payments if they told her anything interesting or if anyone became curious about them.

It wasn't that they were expecting any trouble.

But it wasn't that they *weren't* expecting any trouble, either.

There'd been no message from Spada, so he evidently hadn't arrived yet.

Riss dug another innocent-looking little box out that supposedly played background music, keyed a code message into it on the frequency Spada's ship would be monitoring when it arrived.

There being nothing else to do before dinner, M'chel went wandering along a nearby arcade.

Being near the Excelsior, it was, naturally, a collection of expensive shops, with everything up to and including Earth imports.

Life, Riss decided, went on. Even in a war zone, rich bitches and bastards still had to flaunt it.

After a fashion.

A couple of the shops had been rocketed out of business, and were boarded up. But the others kept on with business as usual.

Riss admired a store selling designer holsters, plus grenade and ammo cases to fit most of the currently popular smaller blasters, in an interesting assortment of colors.

She weakened and bought a small thigh holster with what looked like black lace that wouldn't get in the way of a rapid draw.

After a quiet consultation with the sales clerk, she paid an only slightly out of line amount for a matching, quite lethal, hideout gun to go with it.

She went on along the promenade. She saw several obvious mercenaries — a little too loud, a little too swaggering, their eyes a little too hungry — and their chosen partners, clearly looking for work.

She spotted one that she'd hired a couple or three assignments ago. She didn't think the woman would recognize her, but she ducked into a store specializing in seductive undergarments and body armor that was promised to be 'comfortable for any occasion,' until the mercenary passed.

As she came out, she heard the howl of a lifter under power and backed into the storefront as the lifter with men hanging out shooting back at a second lifter, also with gunnies at full tilt, roared past.

It turned out this was the payoff-in-progress of that month's particular pastime: kidnapping – for either immediate profit or for political advancement. Generally, no one got hurt, and there was an amicable exchange. Frequently this week's kidnapper became next week's kidnappee. Only when things went distinctly sour did the guns come out.

After a fashion . . .

Another evening, Goodnight – feeling either bullet-proof, cat-dead curious, or inordinately full of bravado – paid a very reluctant Jorkens to take the crew down 'that street' to see what the People were made of.

'If we go and get grabbed, sir,' he said, 'I'm depending on you to ransom me out. M' old woman surely won't pay a damned disme.'

Goodnight agreed.

The People's quarter was a blaze of color and noise. The stores were mostly open-air bazaars packed with tiny booths.

No one seemed to discuss anything below a shout or a shrill. But the food was good, if spiced into the pain level, the costumery was equally breathtaking, the people were striking, and the artistry singular.

The People seemed to laugh a lot, but Riss noted that most of the men, and a near majority of the women, carried knives. Some of them were quite elaborately worked, but all were worn in very functional sheathes. M'chel inquired about the custom, and was told that a woman or man was given a knife when she or he was considered a full citizen, and they only gave them up when they decided to bear children or to otherwise practice nonviolence. Duels, either 'to the blood' or 'to the death,' were fairly common.

Children swarmed everywhere.

M'chel and Chas ended up in a small amphitheater, with a band that seemed made up of 'run what you brung' musicians.

'It looks almost civilized here,' Chas told M'chel, his impression confirmed by his first taste of what the hostile, but terribly efficient, waiter called a Slammer.

He offered a taste to Riss, who had barely that, and had trouble speaking for the next few minutes.

Chas didn't notice – he was watching a dance that had begun on the floor that seemed to be little more than people coming onto the floor, spinning around from person to person, then ricocheting back into the audience.

The waiter, somewhat superciliously, explained that this was one of the People's Great Dances, symbolizing how they had been ejected by invaders in their own homes, which were beautiful beyond words or even music. They were driven out, but sooner or later – and this was signified by all of the dancers suddenly rushing back onto the floor – they would return and claim their heritage.

'A sad story,' he told Riss.

'If it's true,' she said cynically.

'Why should it not be?'

'I've never heard of any refugee, anywhere, who didn't claim he was unjustly driven from his wonderful home . . . or else he fled a tyranny.'

'You should have more faith and trust in people,' Chas said, trying to sound pacifistic as he signaled for another Slammer.

'Why?'

Chas had no answer to that.

One night they went down to dinner, stopping at one of the hotel bars for a cocktail. It was appropriately dark, with nooks and crannies and snugs galore.

Two rather goonish sorts who had obviously been drinking for a while got into an argument about who was going to pay, each insisting it was his turn.

Knives came out, and flashed silver for an instant in the light from the light-bowls on the tables.

The bar's conversation slackened and mild curiosity turned to the floor show.

Both the mercenaries went down, clutching themselves, and writhed about.

Waiters dragged the casualties out, and the murmur of conversation picked up again.

The three of them went in to dinner, and when they got back to their suite, a message waited.

Redon Spada, Grok, and Jasmine were on the ground.

They could start looking for trouble.

And work.

TWENTY-TWO

The coordination with Redon Spada, Grok, and Jasmine took only a little while. Grok was pretty well trapped in Spada's ship, at least until Star Risk was able to come into the open. Jasmine slept in the ship one night and in the hotel the next, and again Riss wondered about her arrangement with Grok, but said nothing.

Spada was a little more complicated for M'chel. He made calves' eyes at Riss, clearly wanting to resume their former romantic relationship, but M'chel held back, at least for the moment. She wasn't, she told herself, in this for romance.

First was to find out who Cerberus's client was, and, hopefully, what they were hoping to gain from this backing.

That was a bit easier than they'd figured it would be in the beginning, even though things got a little complicated thereafter.

A beginning assumption was made that Cerberus was backing the new president, considering his militia's flashy new gear and all, not to mention the Dog from Hell's love of always backing someone on top.

So, an unobtrusive electronic net was put around the presidential palace and set to transmit on a frequency Grok decided no one else on the planet was using.

Star Risk had rapidly expanded beyond one suite at the Excelsior. One room of one suite was set up as a purported laboratory, and the maids had been banned from it. In the room were all of Star Risk's necessary electronics. In another larger and equally well-sealed room, was stored the part of their weaponry not aboard the yacht.

'All that we have to do now,' Goodnight told Riss, 'is watch the monitors and see who crops up that looks Cerberus-y.'

'Which means?' M'chel asked.

'A certain air of complacency, crookedness, amorality, and such.'

'Be careful,' Riss warned, 'you're not looking in a mirror, Chas.'

But it was actually quite simple.

Jasmine was skimming fiches of the bug planted on the main entrance, and suddenly she started gurgling.

At first, Grok thought she was choking, and was trying to remember the first aid techniques he'd been taught for use on humans, then realized King was combining growls of rage and spatters of obscenity.

She finally pointed to the monitor.

'That is he,' Jasmine said quite calmly.

'Not quite, at least as I understand the language, my dear,' Grok corrected. 'That is – holy shit! as you beings say, it *is* him!'

M'chel, who'd been at another console, looked utterly perplexed.

'That,' Grok managed, 'and please forgive my overly human excitement, is one Frabord Held, of Cerberus Systems.'

'Ah-hah,' Riss gloated. 'The liaison!'

'Probably a great deal more than that,' Grok said. 'He is a *very* high level operative.'

Jasmine recovered. 'He is also the person who decided it would be a feather in his cap if I were declared a robot, not human, and one of Cerberus's possessions.'

'Oh, dear,' Riss said.

'Oh, no,' Jasmine said. 'Not oh, dear. Maybe oh, pity the fool. He is now in my — sorry, *our* — frigging web.'

'Your language,' Riss said. 'You're talking like Goodnight, now.'

King caught herself.

'I am, aren't I? But Held's the one who . . . who ruined me!'

'No,' Grok corrected. 'Having read some rather amusing early Earth Vickytorian works of the imagination, as I believe the period was called, being ruined is what would have happened, as I understand it, if he had plans to cozen or bludgeon you into his bedchamber, and work his lack of will on you.

'As for any other sense of the word, the best thing that ever happened to you was being cast out of Cerberus.'

Jasmine caught herself, grinned a bit sheepishly.

'I'm sorry. I *was* making a production out of it, wasn't I?'

'A production out of what?' Friedrich said, wandering into the room.

'Jasmine's found our scumbucket,' M'chel said.

Grok explained further, and ran the playback. Von Baldur studied the image carefully.

'He looks somewhat self-satisfied as well as self-assured, does he not?'

'He's that,' King said fiercely. 'The bastard is all of that.'

Riss shook her head.

'You're still taking this too seriously, kid. Come on.

I'll buy you a drink. I found a new bar that nobody but artists drink in. Guaranteed nothing but trouble, but not the kind we give much of a damn about.

'And we can plot the demise of Mister Held and the ruination of Cerberus.'

The bar, Minnie's Home, was a prize — if you liked things a little on the rowdy side.

M'chel figured that Minnie must have been raised in either a carnival or a gladiatorial arena.

Minnie might have been the rather modish, very soft-spoken woman whom Riss had seen walk up to a trio of obnoxious drunks, sucker punch one, offer the second a drink, kick him well below the belt when he smiled acceptance, and then club the third with a candelabra, but M'chel would never be able to ask, since she was instinctively terrified of her.

Minnie's was in a bad part of town, between two warring militia check points, with wandering bands of thugs practicing nefariousnesses between them.

The bar was signposted, if that was the right word, by a quadrant of lasers positioned around the closest crossroads, all of whose beams centered on a mirror outside the bar that, in turn, directed the beams in through a transom window.

If Minnie's ever closed, no one seemed to know about it.

There were bands playing incessantly and loudly, but no one listened.

In the front room were the heavy drinkers.

In the back room were the heavy drug users.

No one bothered anyone.

Or so the sign promised.

Everyone bothered everyone.

That was the reality.

But it didn't get physical. At least, not more than once an hour.

Riss had fallen in love with the joint because all of the incessant arguments were heated, and none of them were about anything important, at least as far as she was concerned.

Riss had seen, in her short time at Minnie's, life-long enmities and some interesting brawls happen over such vital points as whether Mars was settled before Earth; whether Michelangelo learned what little he knew about sculpture from the Vegans; whether war is the only thing that keeps humanity evolving; and other important matters.

No one seemed to give a damn about Alsaoud's politics or personalities, which, after a hard day of scheming on how to make money and eternal damnation to Cerberus out of the system, was just what Riss needed.

When Jasmine and M'chel walked in, a rather large sort was wrapping his nostrils around an inhaler. He saw King, his eyes bugged out even more than the drug was already making them, and he stepped in front of her.

'Hody, sister, awrap for some cuddlin'?'

Minnie, if it was Minnie, was suddenly between them.

'First, "hody" is no way to greet someone, second, this woman isn't your sister, third she would rather cuddle a slug than someone with your breath, and fourth you're out of here.'

The hulk looked at Minnie, and his lower lip pouted out.

'Awww . . .'

'Barred, barred, barred,' Minnie snarled. 'For at least three days.'

Obediently, he lurched toward the exit.

'See?' Riss said, and led Jasmine to a tiny bare table somewhat drenched in beer.

A few hours later, a bit awash in beer and the brandies of Alsaoud they'd sampled as chasers, plus Jasmine's occasional Veronica's Revenge, they started back for the hotel.

'I think we should call Jorkens and ride back,' King said.

'It's a wonderful night for a walk,' Riss insisted.

King shrugged and followed her out.

They'd not even gotten to the first laser when two lifters rode over the sidewalk before and after them and skidded to halts.

M'chel didn't even have a moment to reach for one of her two hideout guns.

They were covered, front and rear, by two crew-served blasters, whose gunners kept them covered while two other types shook them efficiently down.

'Now,' one of the men said, 'if you two ladies wouldn't mind getting into the first vehicle, you may consider yourselves kidnapped.'

At least, M'chel thought a bit forlornly, feeling like an idiot for not taking Jasmine up on her suggestion of calling Jorkens, the thugs were courteous.

TWENTY-THREE

The kidnappers were not only polite, but efficient, as well.

Neither Jasmine nor M'chel was blindfolded. It wasn't necessary.

The windows of the lifter were opaqued.

The two lifters sped along, taking several turns that M'chel was pretty sure were intended to keep them from being able to ID their destination.

Then the lifter canted down, and, from that and the echoing sound of the drive mechanism, she figured they were going underground.

The lifter braked to a stop, and the doors came open. They were in an underground garage.

Again, two men stood ready with blasters, and the pair was hustled to an elevator. Two gunnies went in first, two after the women.

Jasmine couldn't see what floor sensor was touched.

The old-fashioned elevator lurched upward, King thought, through many floors.

She glanced at Riss to get a lead on how to play things, and was shocked and worried to see her face twisting as if fighting back tears.

The elevator stopped, and their captors pushed them out, down an expensively carpeted hall.

They stopped at a door, the entrance to an apartment that the number had been removed from, and hurried inside.

All of the windows except one had drawn blinds. That one looked out on a balcony and the city of Helleu.

Sitting at ease on a sofa were two men.

There was an upholstered bench across from them, with a table between.

One was amazingly ugly, but very expensively dressed.

The other could have been considered good-looking, if no one noticed his dead eyes. He wore what might have been a uniform, with all patches and rank badges removed.

The ugly man stood up.

'Welcome,' he said, in an educated, calm voice. 'You may call me . . . Rabert is good enough. My colleague here can be called Aren.'

'Please sit down,' Rabert said. 'Could I get you some water? Or we have tea.'

The two women obeyed.

'Tea, if you could,' Jasmine managed.

M'chel let out a wail.

'Please,' Rabert said. 'Try to keep yourself under control. We're not murderers.'

'Not unless we have to be,' Aren said softly.

'I . . . I can't,' Riss said plaintively. 'I'm afraid of what . . . what you're going to do to us.'

One of the gunmen brought a cup of tea and set it down on the low table.

Jasmine didn't know what had suddenly happened to Riss to make her lose control, and she offered M'chel some of her tea.

That evidently made matters worse, for M'chel

grabbed Jasmine's wrist, and let out another cry of heartbreak.

'Can't you make her stop that?' Rabert demanded.

Jasmine, intent on something else, shook her head.

'You, woman, listen to me,' Rabert went on. 'You appear to be the less out of control of the two.'

Jasmine almost giggled at that misperception, but managed to nod solemnly.

'My group grabbed the two of you because we thought you looked prosperous, and most likely have family or husbands who would pay well to have you returned.

'Undamaged, shall we say.'

A rather ghoulish smile touched Aren's lips. Rabert went on:

'Am I correct?'

To his surprise, Jasmine now started crying, with an occasional moan.

'Goddamned weak reeds,' Rabert swore. 'Would one of you answer my question — we assume you have relatives or such capable of raising a ransom, correct?'

M'chel managed a nod.

'Maybe . . . maybe Uncle . . . Uncle Baldur can raise a little money,' she faltered.

'It had better be more than a little considering how you two are dressed,' Rabert said. 'We are businessmen, you know, and have a fairly high overhead.

'Both of you will appear on a fiche, which we'll send to your uncle. Asking for, uh . . . a million—'

M'chel let out an agonized wail, and Jasmine joined her.

'Very well,' Rabert said. 'We're not unreasonable. Half a million. In Alliance credits. Or a full million in Alsaoud gelders.

'No one is to go to the police or any other armed force, or else the worst can be expected to happen to both of you.

'Your uncle will have . . . four days . . . from when we deliver the fiche to . . . ?'

'The Excelsior Hotel,' Jasmine managed. 'He's M'chel's uncle, not mine, but he can get in touch with my family and ask them to contribute.'

'Good,' Rabert approved.

'Let me make you aware of the options, if there are any problems. We can arrange to have your uncle receive certain bodily parts – a finger, an ear—'

'A nipple,' Aren put in with his horrible smile.

'Yes,' Rabert said. 'A nipple, if need be. My colleague has more violent tastes. If there are any serious problems after that, I shall turn one of you over to him – and to a couple of his assistants, and, with a recorder running, most unpleasant things can happen – and possibly there might be only one of you to ransom, or perhaps Aren would show a bit of mercy and allow the other to live, even if she would be damaged and unlikely to recover her full wits.

'*Most* unpleasant,' he repeated.

Aren licked his lips.

Both women started sobbing uncontrollably.

Rabert grimaced, got up, looked at Jasmine and M'chel disgustedly.

'Get yourselves under control,' he ordered. 'I'll have a man with the recorder come in now, and let you find your own words to ask for help. I would recommend you sound convincing. *Most* convincing, since your future, if any, depends on it.'

Jasmine bobbed her head, clearly terror-stricken and willing to do anything.

When M'chel had taken her hand, Riss's fingers had pressed out – twice, until King had suddenly gotten it – in Standard Code, the letters
B-E H-Y-S-T-E-R-I-C-A-L.

TWENTY-FOUR

'Son of a *bitch*,' Chas Goodnight said gently as he eyed the screen. 'Come to think, sons of *sixteen* bitches. How did those two manage to go and get themselves kidnapped?'

'I doubt,' von Baldur said, 'if they planned their evening around the event.'

Grok growled incoherently. 'Of course we shan't consider going to the police.'

'Not in this ballsed-up society, we won't,' Goodnight said. 'Too much chance of a leak – or that the cops are in the baddies' hip pocket. And we'll ignore the chance of a plain ol' ordinary screwup. Do we have the money to bail 'em out?'

'We do,' Grok said. 'I can renew my loan to Star Risk that you repaid recently.'

'But that is not the most important question,' von Baldur said. 'Is this ransom note to good old Uncle Baldur a setup?'

Goodnight puzzled for a moment, then got it.

'Oh. You mean, is Cerberus on to us and trying to suck us into a trap?'

'Exactly.'

'Good question,' Goodnight said. 'I don't have an answer. Not even in battle analysis mode. Grok?'

'A ploy such as this,' the giant alien said, 'is certainly within their moral parameters. But I question whether they have the plain ordinary subtlety to come up with it.'

'Questions, questions,' Goodnight said irritably. 'We could seriously handle some answers.'

He got up, eyed the ransom note on the screen for an instant.

'Naturally, if we tried to trace the note back, it'll have been routed through so many servers to be totally clean.

'Do we know where the women went?'

'They signed out for a place called Minnie's Home. From there, who knows where they might have gone,' Baldur said.

'You two hold down the fort here,' Goodnight said. 'I'm going to go out and ask a few questions.'

'I suppose,' Grok said a trifle wistfully, 'there is no way that I could accompany you. I have a concern for Jasmine . . . and M'chel as well.'

Goodnight clapped Grok on the back.

'Nope. You're still too visible. But I'll try to hold your end up. I don't particularly love snatch artists.'

His grin was distinctly unpleasant.

The two women were remembered at Minnie's Home, but no one knew where they'd gone. Goodnight did find, though, that the district was a known swarming place for Khazia's burgeoning kidnap trade.

He went into a corner with one woman who seemed a bit knowledgeable, and credits changed hands.

Goodnight bade her good evening, and went out onto the street.

It took an hour's strolling before he was targeted.

A single large lifter slammed to a landing beside

him, and three gunmen leaped out. There was a fourth, a driver, behind the lifter's controls.

'You're ours,' one of them shouted, waving his gun.

'You mean, you're mine,' Goodnight corrected, touched his cheek, and went bester.

A knuckle strike caved in the first man's wind-pipe, and he gurgled down as Goodnight spun, pulled a pistol from his belt, and blew the second man's forehead away. Another round went into the third man's chest, and Goodnight was in the lifter's cab and out of bester, as the mewling driver was trying to lift away.

'Yes,' Chas said. 'Let's take a nice ride. I'd like to find a nice quiet alley and ask you some questions about your trade and your associates, and whether you might have heard any interesting stories about people and their latest acquisitions.'

There was no sign on the café.

Not that there was anything that would attract cus-tomers to it anyway — at least, other than those of a certain type.

The building sat by itself in a grimy industrial sec-tion, with a large, open parking area.

The district was one where police had no reason to patrol after dark, even in teams, and many good reasons *not* to patrol.

It had no windows, and the interior was divided into a bar, an open central dining area, and booths where private deals could be arranged.

It was late, after midnight, but the café was crowded.

The patrons would also have discouraged trade.

Their appearance did not suggest they were the sort who traveled in honest paths, nor harbored righteous thoughts.

Goodnight slid through the door, carrying a small pack.

A burly doorman, flanked by a gunnie, stopped him.

It was that sort of joint.

'You want?'

'Nothing you have,' Goodnight assured him cheerfully. 'Looking for a pair of jokers who don't always go under the same name. One's ugly as your mother, the other's good-looking, in a dead-fish sort of way. Likes to pretend he's with some sort of uniformed mob.'

'Wouldn't tell you if they was here,' the man growled. 'Don't talk to nobody what sounds like a copper. Now, get your ass back to your precinct and tell 'em you're only alive 'cause I feel generous.'

'Tsk,' Goodnight said, and kicked him in the groin.

The man yelped, bent over, and Goodnight hammer-smashed him on the back of the neck.

As the doorman collapsed, Goodnight shot his backup between the eyes with a small pistol he didn't bother taking out of his sleeve.

The shot stilled the buzz.

'Awright,' Goodnight said, very loudly. 'Party's over.'

He scanned the room, didn't see anyone who resembled the pair he was looking for.

Guns were coming out.

Goodnight unhurriedly reached in the pack, took out a grenade, thumbed the release and pitched it into one corner of the room, then came out with a second, threw that into the other corner, and went flat as the two grenades exploded with dull thuds.

Gas billowed through the room.

There were shouts, screams.

Goodnight stayed down until the noise stopped, then picked himself up.

He'd already inserted filter plugs in his nostrils.

The room was strewn with bodies, a few moving feebly.

Goodnight went to his first target, the bartender, rolled him on his back, knelt, and touched a syrette to his arm.

The second man was a prosperous-looking sort who'd had half a dozen underlings sitting around him.

He, too, got the antidote to the gas.

The others in the room would die, without recovering consciousness, within fifteen minutes.

Goodnight lifted the man he thought to be a boss sort into a sturdy chair, and secured him at wrists and ankles with plastic restraints.

'You'll hold,' he said, as the man's eyes flickered open.

Goodnight went back to the bartender and put him in a second chair, tied him as well.

'Good evening, gentlemen,' he said, when the barkeep showed signs of alertness.

'Now, pay close attention, because I don't repeat myself.

'I'm looking for information on where a couple of your fellow kidnappers – don't bother arguing with me about what you're not – hang their hats.

'They lurk around this dive, so don't bother lying to me that you've never heard of them.

'I don't like liars.'

He noted the first man's sneer.

'Oh, you'll tell me,' he said, even though the man hadn't spoken, and set his pack on a table.

'You'll go second,' he said. 'I'll use your compatriot here as an example of my methods, not to mention listening to any skinny he might provide.

'Interesting thing,' he went on, taking some items from the pack. 'No matter how much someone doesn't want to talk, if you apply certain things to certain places — I'm talking simple things here, not drugs, which can get complicated — people become very eager to tell you what you want to know.

'Simple things,' he said. 'Such as splinters under the fingernails. Or razor blades. Or an electric generator. And I could write volumes about what can be done with two or three common needles.

'It's an interesting art, and you *will* find yourself cooperating with me.

'I say again my last, over.

'I *really* don't like snatch artists.'

TWENTY-FIVE

'It has been four days since we sent that ransom note,' Aren said. There was a slight note of pleasure in his voice. 'I'm afraid we're going to have to offer evidence of our seriousness.'

M'chel considered the situation.

There were Aren and two guards – one with a dangling pistol, the second with a blast rifle at port arms in the room she and Jasmine had been held in.

Good enough.

Aren reached in his pocket, took out an old-fashioned spring knife, snapped it open.

'I'm sorry about this,' he said, sounding very not sorry.

M'chel let out a sob, held her hands close to her face.

Aren stepped closer.

'Now,' Riss said to King in a very calm voice.

As she spoke, one hand came off her face in guard position, the other snapped forward in a palm smash against Aren's nose.

It squashed, messily.

He yelped, more in surprise than in pain.

Jasmine snap-kicked the first gunnie in the upper thigh. He grunted, spun.

Jasmine had the gun out of his hands, reversed it,

shot the other gunman in the forehead, then blew the top off the first man's head.

Riss grabbed Aren by the hair, jerked his head down as her knee jerked up, ruining the rest of his face. M'chel ran him forward, slamming his head into the very solid chest of drawers against one wall.

He collapsed, soggily.

To make sure, Riss snapped the side of her foot down against Aren's neck, and the dullish snap settled any doubts she might have had.

Riss went across the room in a rush, snagged the blast rifle from the second gunman's dead grasp, and went through the door into the apartment's main room.

The man who called himself Rabert and one other gunman were just coming to their feet, alerted by the shots.

M'chel shot the gunman in the chest, swung the rifle to Rabert.

He was lifting his hands, possibly to protest, possibly to beg for mercy.

Two guns went off almost simultaneously, almost blowing Rabert in half.

M'chel had a tight grin on her face. She was about to say something to Jasmine when they heard the roar of an engine, and a lifter floated around the corner of the building outside.

It nuzzled against the balcony, and Chas Goodnight, wearing coveralls and a combat harness, rifle in hand, leapt from its open door onto the balcony, shot the window out, and crashed through. He had a com bud in one ear, and a throat mike on.

At the controls of the lifter was Redon Spada.

In almost the same instant, the door to the apartment crashed down, taking the frame with it, and Grok rolled through, his paw dwarfing the blaster in his hand. He also wore a com.

Behind him, also gun-ready, was Friedrich von Baldur.

M'chel eyed them.

'A little late, boys.'

Von Baldur looked around at the carnage.

'So I see.'

'Come on,' Goodnight prompted. 'Less chit-chat. Let's blow this joint.'

The two women hurried across to the balcony and were almost bodily pitched into the lifter's cargo area by Goodnight. Behind them came von Baldur.

'I am getting too old for this,' he protested as he clambered aboard, carefully not looking down at the many stories of emptiness below him.

Grok took a bundle the size of his head from a small waist pack, thumbed a control, tossed it on the body of the late Rabert.

'Let us go then, you and I,' he quoted. 'Before this dive is spread out against the sky. We have thirty seconds.'

They boarded, and the lifter banked and slid away at full drive.

The side of the skyscraper blew apart, taking three stories with it.

'And so the innocent suffer with the guilty, tough titty, tough titty,' Goodnight said. 'Assuming there's any such in these parts.'

He turned to Riss.

'Now, if you two are through playing around, I think it's time to start straightening out the situation.'

TWENTY-SIX

'Premier Toorman will see you now,' the receptionist said.

Friedrich von Baldur tucked his viewer under his arm. It had a screaming banner reading PIRATE OUT-RAGES INCREASE. He smiled graciously, made sure that his old-fashioned cravat was straight, and went toward the indicated door.

The receptionist wasn't an attractive female, but a man who looked as if he'd be happier as a bar bouncer and two equally obvious goons waited at the door.

Uneasy lies the head wearing the crown, von Baldur thought, and went into the premier's office, which was only slightly larger than the average starship landing field.

The premier was a small man with a twitch. He reminded Friedrich of someone – no, some*thing*. Something he'd seen in a holo. It was an earth animal called a . . . he grasped for the word . . . a *wabbit*.

He put such frivolity out of his mind and began his sales pitch.

Von Baldur represented a firm called Research Associates, which had already done business with Alsaoud, selling them a consignment of deep-space mines, which they'd said they were quite pleased with.

Von Baldur had heard, from 'various sources,' that the system might benefit from 'more hands-on service' — specifically the direct services of Research Associates — in every area from planetary defense to high-level security.

'Particularly with the problem you seem to be having with piracy,' he added, smiling like the ever-benevolent, ever-helpful, ever-protective uncle.

Toorman managed a smile, and Freddie noted that the smile, too, was twitchy.

It should have been.

Toorman, prime minister for five years, had stood for president in the recent elections, and been resoundingly defeated by a man named Flyver, who'd spent millions ensuring his victory.

The word was that it was only a matter of time before Flyver found an excuse to impeach or otherwise remove Toorman, even to the point of using violence, and bring in a replacement who would be more than willing to jig to Flyver's hornpipe.

Von Baldur added what he thought should be the capper to his pitch: that he understood certain parties within the system — who need not be named — had dared to bring in outside agitators and organizers, which would further discombobulate Alsaoud's happy worlds.

He did not use the word discombobulate, although he wanted to.

Even as he spoke, he realized the mention of Cerberus constituted overkill.

Toorman's twitching grew more obvious, and now could be seen as something approaching terror.

'I find . . . what you've been telling me more than interesting . . . certainly worthy of my discussing the possibility of your joining us with my private advisors,' he managed. 'And you may rest assured that I will take the matter under immediate advisement, and will be responding to you within . . . well, perhaps not hours, but a few days at the outside.

'If you'll leave your card with my assistants outside, I assure you that you have my complete backing.'

Von Baldur knew that he'd just been turned down.

'Why, that chicken-hearted, yellow bastard,' Goodnight snarled. 'Doesn't he know that his ass is already in the whatchamacallit?'

'Tumbril,' King said.

'He'd goddamned better tumble damned fast out of the line of fire,' Goodnight agreed. 'His ass is buttermilk if he keeps on keeping on!'

'Regardless, Chas,' von Baldur said mildly. 'We have just been rejected from what appeared to be the easiest, most convenient way to edge our way toward the seat of power. Does anyone have any ideas on what we should do next?'

'We must do something,' Grok said. 'We cannot just stay freelance. That would only arouse Cerberus's suspicions – not to mention that we can't afford to do much of anything for very much longer, since we're woefully underfunded. I'd really rather not renew my loan to us, if there's another option.

'We need a sponsor – and I, for one, don't see one looming on the horizon.'

Riss, who'd been fiddling with Freddie's viewer, looked up.

'I have, I think,' she announced brightly, 'a rather excellent idea.'

TWENTY-SEVEN

Riss and Goodnight, bulky in space suits, hung behind the bulk of a semidisassembled light cruiser, the guts of its drive controls dangling out stern ports.

Behind them a few meters floated Redon Spada.

Around them were a dozen other ships, in various stages of combat readiness. Some sort of economy measure had driven Alsaoud to putting the harbor of what passed for its naval fleet in deep space, rather than on some nice, sensible desert somewhere.

In theory, to the ground-hugger or bureaucrat, that increased security.

In fact, all it did was create thousands and thousands of vulnerable points, in every possible direction.

And the fleet itself that Alsaoud was so proud of would have passed — to a properly martial world, system or duster — as no more than a light patrol squadron.

The three were eyeing, with greed in their souls, a small Sung-class destroyer, whose sleekness belied its twenty-year-old obsolescence.

But Spada knew a secret about the class that made it most interesting to him and to Star Risk.

M'chel was considering the single survival capsule linked to the destroyer that served as a watchman's shack. Inside, out of the 'weather,' were the three sentries assigned to this half of the unmanned fleet.

Too goddamned easy, she thought. But that was the way it was here in the outback – sloppy and casual until you started taking things for granted and got killed.

Goodnight flashed a signaling blip from his suit light, and the three went across the open space on low-power suit jets and closed on the destroyer.

M'chel wondered why, after all these years, she still couldn't be in open space without a momentary, illogical, purely mental fear of falling.

Riss took position on the capsule, and Goodnight went to the destroyer's airlock.

It had no more than a standard magnetic lock, and Chas touched a pick to the airlock's security system and turned the pick on.

He felt vibration as the pick cycled silently for a moment, then the lock clicked, and the airlock slid open.

Spada and Goodnight went inside and closed the lock behind them.

There was air in the ship, and the two flipped their faceplates open and checked the ship for occupancy.

It was empty but fully fueled, and all vital signs – air, water, etc. – were positive.

Goodnight grinned happily, and Spada slid into a control couch.

Spada had never piloted a Sung, but it took him only a few moments to figure out the operating system and activate the drive.

Goodnight went back to the lock, cycled it, and stuck his head out.

Riss floated nearby above the 'shack.' Chas flashed a signal light, and Riss replied with a double flash.

If Goodnight had been given Riss's job, he would have undoubtedly killed the three men in the capsule.

But M'chel was softer-hearted, a trait that would no doubt lead to her unwanted demise one of these years.

Instead of blasting the capsule open and letting the occupants breathe vacuum, she maneuvered to the capsule's tiny lock, unslung an emergency arc-welding kit, and, being very careful to not give any signs away, welded it shut.

Avoiding both the capsule's ports, and staying away from the flat pickup for the capsule's tiny radar, she went 'below' the capsule, found its emergency exit, and sealed that as well.

Then she used the welder as a cutting tool, and severed the two cables linking the capsule to the Sung.

The capsule should have had a com of sorts, but Riss, feeling very sentimental, attached a small suit emergency beacon to the capsule, with a timer to set it screaming into life in six hours.

Rejoicing at a job well – and sneakily – done, she entered the ship.

'Let 'er rip,' she told Spada.

Spada fired up the drive.

He punched in a course that would take the ship, on secondary drive, behind Alsaoud's nearest moon, where the Star Risk yacht waited.

'Now we've got the tools,' Goodnight said, 'we can begin our new career.'

'Aaaar,' M'chel agreed happily. 'Just call me Captain Kiddo.'

TWENTY-EIGHT

'While the children are out getting new toys,' Jasmine King told Grok, 'I think we could well be pursuing other pastimes.'

'Such as?'

'Such as the persecution and assassination of one Frabord Held, since we still don't have a clue as to why Cerberus is scheming in the Alsaoud System.'

'Umm,' Grok said thoughtfully. 'If we kill him, which sounds like an interesting pastime, will it (A) tip Cerberus that we are back in the game, and (B) worsen our situation?'

'It will certainly (C) make me feel better, at the very least,' Jasmine said, but looked at von Baldur for an opinion.

Friedrich considered, also examining his reflection in one of the Excelsior suite's mirrors and deciding he looked appropriately dignified and warlordlike.

'Killing – or, more linguistically soothing, perhaps – readjusting Mr. Held's biomass, *is* an interesting thought,' he mused.

Jasmine decided Freddie was feeling particularly pompous that day.

'The major drawback is that it could bring on a worse, that is, more skilled, antagonist,' von Baldur continued. 'From what you two have told me, Held is a worthy opponent, and not to be taken lightly. I am not assuming, though, that he is the ultimate Cerberus operator. There are, no doubt, Cerberus executives available who are more canny than he is. Our more than occasional opponent, Walter Nowotny, comes to mind.

'However, consider that any organization will develop a bit of a twitch if one of its managers is removed from the field in a sufficiently spectacular manner, which is a positive accomplishment. It might also make them, or rather their personnel, angry.

'Rage does not improve reasoning.

'So why not? Go ahead and conspire on Mr. Held, rather than just sitting here waiting for our friends to return.

'Besides, Jasmine, your mention of (C) is always important.

'Finally, idle hands can make for a devil's play-ground.'

He looked about, got the scorn he deserved, and shrugged.

'All right then,' von Baldur said, 'let us begin to scheme. First, I suppose, is figuring out what means we will use to discarnate this gentleman.'

'No,' Jasmine said. 'Both you and Grok mentioned a concern about who might be Held's successor.

'So let us start by preparing our skein. I would assume that we have some time before Riss and Company find a starship that meets their requirements.

'After Held is removed, I'd assume security around President Flyver's palace will be even more stringent, since if we lay our plot right, everyone will think he was the real target.

'We should now make our surveillance of the palace

especially – pardon the pun – bulletproof, since we will need to be on the alert for Held's replacement.

'Then we may consider the next stage.'

For the next couple of days, various elderly men in every stage of repair from impeccable to wino, and young women ranging from lovely to shuddersome lurked around the palace, unobtrusively leaving more bugs in their wakes.

Star Risk reaped an unexpected side benefit, since as King was planting one of the last of the devices, a particularly clever holo pickup that masqueraded as a statue of some sort of friendly small Alsaoudian creature, across from the main gate, she spotted Held coming out. Jasmine went to duck-and-cover mode, since she was hardly an anonymous figure, and Held knew very well what she looked like.

By great good fortune, von Baldur was providing her with a mask at the time, since the statuette was rather bulky.

He saw her slide for shelter, and, a second later, saw and recognized Held and began trailing him.

The Cerberus executive, having no particular reason to feel paranoid, was no more than reflexively careful about checking his tail.

Von Baldur followed him to what was evidently one of Cerberus's safe houses.

A stakeout of the house, a secluded villa in a wealthy residential area, over the next two days, suggested this was Cerberus's main safe house, and probably Held's own residence.

Back at the Excelsior a message from M'chel, Goodnight, and Spada waited, reporting they'd successfully acquired their ship and were proceeding to jump it out of system to have it modified – or rather, retrofitted – to Star Risk's requirements.

'Now we can proceed to debate the methods of murder,' Grok said.

'A bomb is generally the easiest,' von Baldur suggested. 'That is, assuming a certain level of expertise in its construction, which we have; a certain level of, shall we say, subterfuge in its planting; and, finally, a certain level of luck in its detonation, which we are more than due for.'

'Yes,' Jasmine said. 'A bomb. Or a long arm. With a flat-trajectoried solid slug. Or an explosive bullet. A nice quiet place for the gunner with a line of sight on the killing floor, timing, and . . .' She grinned nastily.

'There must be,' Grok said meditatively, 'fifty ways to tag your target. *That* might be worth a song.'

Von Baldur looked at him, and at King, and swore they were both licking their lips, although what surrounded the alien's mouth barely qualified as such.

TWENTY-NINE

The secret of the Sung-class destroyer about which Redon Spada had happened to learn in his travels was quite simple: The ships had been cleverly designed for a culture that was short on manpower, but long on imperial ambitions.

So the Sungs had been designed and built to be operated by a minimal crew – less than four, in an emergency – and was almost completely automated.

Why the designers hadn't gone ahead and merely built them as remote-piloted ships was a mystery to everyone but Spada, who explained, 'They'll never build unmanned spacecraft for war. Young pilots don't get to parade around wearing white scarves and waving their hands around in bars telling war stories, and generals and admirals don't get medals up the ka-giggy for flying a control panel through shot and shell half a light-year away.'

So the Sungs had gone into service – and then a wee mistake had been discovered. The ships' automation had a regrettable tendency to disregard the tiny crew's welfare, up to and including loading an unwary crewman into a missile launch tube on occasion.

Other than that, they were wonderfully lethal warcraft.

Naturally, a war had been in full swing when this was discovered by the contracting navy, and so the Sungs weren't just scrapped out, but little by little deautomated and loaded with additional crewmen.

But as every robotic assassin was discovered and rendered harmless, another appeared, so the Sungs, now no more than a particularly inefficient, if easy on the eyes, warship, were sold off to 'lesser' markets.

Which meant systems like Alsaoud.

Neither Redon Spada nor Star Risk gave much of a damn about the ships being a bit on the dodgy side — mercenaries learn, early on, they're unlikely to be given the best and the most modern in the way of tools, just as the wars they fight are seldom glamorous or 'civilized.'

Assuming there's such a thing as a civilized murder campaign . . .

Since part of the mercenary condition is fighting in a perpetually undermanned state, the Sung was perfect for Star Risk's nefarious designs.

And so, half a dozen systems from Alsaoud, in an unobtrusive shipyard, Riss, Goodnight, and Spada went to work reautomating the Sung, which they named the *McMahon*.

Spada had, to Goodnight's vast surprise, refrained from naming his wages when he'd been brought back aboard, saying only that 'When you folks are back on top, I'll rape, maim, and loot.'

'I wouldn't have been that gentlemanly,' Chas said.

'Which is why you're a sordid thug, and I'm up above the clouds,' Spada said smugly.

He called in favors and friendships from half a galaxy, and an interesting assortment of weaponry began arriving at the shipyard, all shipped URGENT and either fitted to the *McMahon* or shoved into one of its holds because 'it'll probably be of some use sooner or later.'

When the *McMahon* was air- and space-worthy again, Spada took it into space, and ran it through its paces. It performed admirably.

Riss and Goodnight went along, being most careful to stay clear of any machinery that started making Threatening Operating Noises, or just showing signs of being turned on.

The *McMahon*, other than a slight tendency to hiccup convulsively when fed navigational problems at all abstruse, worked fine.

Just what Star Risk needed to go a-pirating.

THIRTY

Spada, Riss, and Goodnight slid the *McMahon* back
behind one of Khazia's moons and took their yacht back
to the planet, exuding innocence from every pore.

They expected to be greeted with hosannas for their
bravura theft. Instead, they arrived in the middle of the
murder plot.

Goodnight listened to the details, sneered at the
other three schemers.

'Typical amateurs. Talk, talk, talk, but no frigging
bloody-handedness.'

'We were just about to pounce,' Jasmine King said
in an injured tone.

'About. Hah,' Goodnight said. 'And what method of
shuffling off this coiled mortal, or however it goes, had
you arrived at?'

'I,' Grok said, putting just a trace of emphasis on the
word so Goodnight would know who the boy genius
was, 'came up with a brilliance.'

'Oh yeah?' Goodnight said. 'Talk to me.'

Grok told him. 'And the beauty of it is, if we do it
right, it'll be seen as a common accident.'

'And if you don't do it right,' Goodnight said, 'the
bastard will be at full alert, and you'll never get a

chance that good again. Let me ask you something, O my furry friend. Who was going to bell the cat?'

'Cat? There are no felines in this project.'

'Who was gonna be the Goon in Charge?'

'I was,' Grok said. 'Since it was my idea, and I have probably the best knowledge of any of the three of us in practical physics.'

'Oh, my paws and whiskers,' Goodnight moaned. 'Have you ever killed anybody like that?'

'No,' Grok admitted. 'But it seems quite simple.'

'Hot flash,' Goodnight said. 'It ain't. There's a ton of variables – which don't have squat to do with physics, I might add.'

'I suppose you do,' Grok said in an injured tone.

'As a matter of fact, yes,' Chas Goodnight said.

'Then, of course, I would be nothing but an egotistical fool to insist on being the man with the button,' Grok said.

'Exactly,' Goodnight said, then caught Jasmine's buried grin.

'Goddamnit,' he said. 'Did I just go and trap myself into being Chas in charge?'

'Of course you did not,' von Baldur said, dripping innocence. 'But one of Star Risk's biggest virtues is its willingness to always yield to the voice of sweet reason and expertise.'

'Trapped, trapped, trapped,' Goodnight moaned.

'Don't take it so hard,' Riss said. 'I've got a good idea of what we'll be doing, in theory. I'll even volunteer to fly the cover vehicle to keep you from running into trouble – or, rather, to get you out of any trouble you do run into.'

But Goodnight was inconsolable.

Both Grok and Goodnight were correct.

The killing method he'd chosen was very simple and

old-fashioned — murder by vehicle. It had gotten a little more sophisticated than it was in the days when Indians ran cowboys down with T-model airplanes, or however it precisely began.

But not much.

The devil was, as always, in the details — making sure that the target didn't do any of several possible annoying things, such as ducking out of the way and letting the oncoming vehicle hammer itself against a lamp standard; ducking into cover, or worst of all shooting back, not to mention the evils that would result if a friendly local policeman happened on this thuggishness in midmurder.

Vehicular homicide was, indeed, one of the lethal arts Goodnight had been trained in. Trained and practiced on four different occasions, which von Baldur had recollected Goodnight mentioning one drunken night. Friedrich had suggested that the other two might find it worthwhile to put the con on Chas.

Jasmine had remembered that one of Frabord Held's more inhuman habits was to rise an hour before dawn, go for what he called 'a brisk walk,' exercise for an hour in whatever open space he reached, then proceed to his work station, and snarl at anyone who dared to come to work at a more civilized hour.

Even more stupidly, it had been his habit to indulge in this as a solitary vice, sans bodyguards or cover.

Jasmine had used a small model aircraft, fitted with a camera, to tail him from an oblique angle, and found that his habits hadn't changed.

Two days before the target date, Riss had stolen a commercial lifter. At about the same time, von Baldur, feeling this was vaguely below his dignity, had nicked a still-valid registration plate off a broken-down lifter in a slum area. That plate, which wouldn't be missed for a while, had gone onto the stolen lifter and its proper registration deposited in a nearby sewer.

The day before, Goodnight had lifted a rather expensive lifter from one part of Helleu, and another registration plate from another.

Patrolling police only see license plates and, of course, people behaving in a suspicious manner, which means being part of any scorned minority . . .

Very early the next dawn, Riss and Goodnight set out, refusing all offers of company. Both of them had heavy blasters ready at hand and were sleepy enough to want to use them. Both wore gloves, and had previously wiped all controls of their vehicles, just to make sure.

The touch went perfectly.

Goodnight was making wide orbits over Cerberus's safe house, keeping a binoc on its door. Riss was about a kilometer distant, low to the ground, watching Goodnight.

Goodnight had a momentary twitch when a police lifter swept past, but it was intent on other business or a snack break.

Held came out of the safe house and started down the street toward the park he would work out in.

Goodnight put his lifter into a shallow dive, brought it out about a meter above the ground on Held's street, keeping a couple hundred meters behind him, and holding his speed at walking pace.

Riss, in turn, was half a kilometer behind *him*, alert for any problems.

The chosen kill zone was along a walled section of the road just before the park's entrance. To make it better, the road was posted against any parking, so it was a nice, clean, barren stretch of pavement.

Goodnight put on drive as Held reached the wall, quietly so Held wouldn't notice any increase in sound.

He was doing about sixty kilometers per hour as he came up on Held.

The man turned then, saw the lifter as Goodnight kicked hard right rudder, and gaped in terror.

The lifter slid sideways, caught Held with its side cushion, and banked him hard into the wall.

Held hit the wall headfirst, and slid, bonelessly, to the pavement.

Goodnight accelerated away, and took his lifter up toward an overhead traffic lane.

Riss flew past the body, saw that it was motionless, head tweaked at an odd angle, figured there was little chance of survival, didn't figure it was worth stopping for a coup de grâce that would render all their craft pointless, and climbed after Goodnight.

He parked the lifter on a deserted street, and stepped out just as M'chel hovered up next to him.

'That's that,' he said. 'Now let's go see about some breakfast. An honest day's work makes a fellow hungry.'

THIRTY-ONE

'Let it never be said,' Friedrich von Baldur said solemnly, 'that pilots are nothing but glorified transport drivers.'

'I would *never* say anything like that,' Chas Goodnight said piously, considering the elaborate table of food surrounding him.

'Especially not within their hearing,' Riss said.

Spada sneered at them both.

Grok was paying no attention to anyone, merely hungrily considering the dinner that had been called in to their suite at the Excelsior.

'To explain the viands: I was wondering just how we might go about picking an ideal target for our first venture into piracy,' von Baldur said. 'We want an impressive taking, I would think. Something that will give us immediate stature among our desired brethren.

'I considered seizing the *Normandie* on its next trip into the system, but I did not exactly warm to the idea of having all those damned passengers to take care of. Nor did I like the basic idea of hijacking a ship under Alliance registry.'

'Not to mention,' King said, 'that when we rode it, it was escorted insystem, and had a pair of missile batteries, and there's nothing stickier than a target that dares fight back.'

'Good thinking,' Goodnight said. 'We've got enough enemies.'

'Not to mention,' Jasmine said, 'the fact that you're still on one or another of the Alliance's Most Wanted lists.'

'Not to mention,' Chas agreed.

Von Baldur tapped his champagne glass with his fork for silence, noted that it was empty, and refilled it from one of the ice buckets before continuing.

'As I was saying,' he said pointedly, 'I was looking for a target, which should not be the *Normandie* until a later date, if at all. I decided that the best ploy would be to bounce a com out-system, purporting to be a prospective importer of thingamajiggies into the Alsaoud System, and look for a nice shipping line with a nice medium-sized freighter we wouldn't have any trouble selling off.

'I then bethought myself of consulting with Mr. Spada to see if he had any idea about an easier, less traceable, way to go.

'For what the thought produced . . . well, this dinner is in his honor.'

Von Baldur drank champagne, nodded at Spada. It was his turn.

'Most of what I'm going to say goes under the heading of things I should have figured out,' the slight man said apologetically. 'Such as why this particular part of the world is so prone to piracy, privateering, and such.'

'Mean people,' Goodnight suggested.

'Or why the Alliance has sent threatening squadrons into the Alsaoud area so often, since the Alsaoud worlds aren't the worst known.

'The answer turned out to be revoltingly simple –

one of the major navpoints that everyone transitioning through this sector uses is nearby.

'Lay in wait around that area, and something worth swooping on is sure to drop by.'

Early navigators found it simple to use certain predetermined points as they lurched through hyperspace, finding out the connections and pitfalls. In theory, it was possible to go from any point A to any point B by using any sequence of 'navpoints' to step a starship on its route.

But it was easier, faster, and — strangely enough — safer, to use locales that had been previously set. There were hazards in hyperspace, many still unknown, in the same ways that 'bottomless waves' or tidal rips were unknown to early ocean navigators.

This wasn't exactly desirable as common knowledge — it was far better for the average interstellar traveler to think of his starship as jumping from place to place, under the command of steel-jawed and laser-eyed officers rather than bumbling from one place to another to a third to a fourth to eventually emerging somewhere close to where he wanted to end up.

For one thing, this produced far fewer lawsuits when the odd starship vanished inexplicably, as some still did.

'How fascinating,' Goodnight drawled. 'It's always good to know a bit about the local geography and all. But how does that justify this?'

His hand waved around the feast.

'Chas,' Grok said acerbically, 'you're a good companion, but sometimes you're slightly thicker than a stone wall.'

'Agreed,' Goodnight said, undisturbed. 'Momma didn't raise no bright ones. Proof — I went off to be a sojer boy.

'But I say again my last — navpoints don't explain real Earth pâté de foie gras.'

'Because,' Jasmine said, 'this navpoint, and the consequent traffic through the area, may explain Cerberus's presence here.'

'How so?' Goodnight asked. 'Let's get specific here. How can anybody make a buck off a navpoint? Better, how can *we* make a buck? Taking it away from Cerberus, of course.'

He looked at von Baldur.

'I don't know, yet,' he said. 'But it is significant.'

'It's significant,' Riss agreed. 'But does it mean anything? Pass the toast.'

She spread fish eggs, hard-boiled egg, and real Earth onion bits on one of the toast points.

'As long as we're talking about Cerberus . . . and over food, at that,' Jasmine said, 'have we gotten anything to suggest who the late and distinctly unlamented Mr. Held's replacement will be? I'm assuming that Cerberus isn't going to take its nefariousness elsewhere.'

There were assorted headshakes.

'Relax, Jasmine,' M'chel said. 'The evil of the day is sufficient thereof, or something like that.'

'At least,' von Baldur said, 'Mr. Spada's discovery shall make it decidedly easier to find a nice, delectable target, merely by lurking instead of having to advertise, which can always attract unwarranted attention.'

'Then Mr. Spada is more than welcome to his banquet,' Goodnight said equably, reaching for the champagne.

THIRTY-TWO

Seven of the eight board members of Cerberus Systems were gathered on Alegria IV, all but one of them present in person.

They were meeting to discuss Frabord Held's replacement.

The matter was considered that important.

'First,' one of the officers said, 'we should all be aware that Mr. Held's death was not an accident at all, contrary to what the police of Khazia claim, but a sophisticated murder.'

He looked about, as if expecting praise for his perspicacity.

Ral Tomkins thought of showing a bit of mercy, since the man was the most recently appointed member of the board, then changed his mind. Why deviate from his usual style?

'We are all aware of that,' he said coldly. 'None of us are raw recruits and I, for one, slightly resent being treated like a fool.'

The man shrank back almost imperceptibly. 'Have any of our operatives filed a report with the slightest clue of who might have done it or why?' he squeaked out.

Tomkins frowned.

'One, blathering about some group called "the People," whoever they may be with, naturally, no evidence supporting her claim. I think the most important task of the moment is to send in a properly skilled replacement, since this agent in charge is clearly not ready for executive status.

'In the course of bringing Operation Peaceful Skies to success, the perpetrator may become evident, in which case he will be dealt with. If not . . .' Tomkins shrugged.

'I'm not sure that I agree the most important matter at present is to replace Held,' Eldad Yarb'ro said from his end of the table. 'I think we should consider the validity of the entire operation.'

'Don't be absurd,' Tomkins snapped 'There are enormous benefits to be gained by its success, as I've presented over the last several months while we were debating it. With Alsaoud pacified, and piracy ended, we will have gained enormous goodwill with the Alliance, which, you will recall, is the central reason we agreed to mount it. Not to mention the enormous commercial opportunities we can exploit as this navpoint, and its security, become more and more important to projected Alliance development that we have become aware of through our friends in the government. I'll also remind you that you favored the plan at the time it was voted on.'

'I've reconsidered somewhat,' Yarb'ro said. 'Especially after going through the budget for Peaceful Skies . . .' He winced. 'Who comes up with these damned titles . . . anyway, I was once again taken aback by its cost.'

'Which is minuscule compared to its benefits,' Tomkins said firmly. 'Not only with the Alliance, but with our presence firmly established in the Alsaoud

System, there'll be great enrichment to be gained from contracts with firms whose interests develop in this area.'

'Possibly,' Yarb'ro said. 'But stick to the Alliance, since that's why you pushed for us to get involved in the first place.

'I recollect, during my own time with Alliance Intelligence, we were known to allow a government to perform a favor for us. If it required no effort or expense on our part, and they were successful, we might grant them a boon or two.

'If it didn't, that was — as the field ops say — tough titty for the kitty.

'And we laughed about those who thought they could outmaneuver us.

'I would hate to think that we here at Cerberus, thinking ourselves so clever and skilled, are setting ourselves up as nothing but Alliance patsies.'

'I think,' Tomkins said, 'that your years have sucked you into timidity. At Cerberus's present level, it is good for us to consider long-term benefits, instead of the immediate profit.'

'Quite possibly I *am* getting more careful,' Yarb'ro said, undisturbed. 'As you grow old, life becomes more precious. Obviously you are not going to listen to my cautions, so let us move on.'

'Oh, not at all,' Tomkins said, smoothly. 'I think you are wrong, but I also agree it is good to be careful.

'For this reason, I wish to suggest that Held's replacement be a man who you recently recommended to deal with that annoying competitor of ours, who seems to have done a very thorough job. My assistants report that not only was Star Risk utterly destroyed, but that its officers have been driven into oblivion.

'Their disappearance will, I'm sure, be a warning to

others, and if they ever resurface we'll continue the object lesson.

'So I think your man, Walter Nowotny, should be sent to Alsaoud with full authority and our blessing. We can then, I would think, relax in the knowledge that the next time we hear of Alsaoud and Operation Peaceful Skies, it will be a report of ultimate success.'

Tomkins smiled.

Yarb'ro smiled back, but felt like cursing.

He'd been neatly mousetrapped by his objection to the Alsaoud maneuver. If for any reason it failed, Tomkins would use the connection he'd firmly established between Nowotny and Yarb'ro to explain the failure as a plot of Yarb'ro's and claim he hadn't been involved. Yarb'ro would most certainly be destroyed.

It was a move whose Machiavellian qualities Yarb'ro sincerely admired.

THIRTY-THREE

It is not enough just to have the tools for a job.

Sometimes it's necessary to go looking for work.

Especially when it comes to a job like pirating.

Things change over the years and parsecs. Rarely, however, do the penalties for acquiring someone else's property en masse.

Punishment for being caught tends to involve tactics like humorless judges, noosed ropes, tall tree limbs, or their equivalent.

But fortune favors the bold, or so it's held among the unhanged.

Star Risk, being bold, set to work in two areas.

The first unleashed Chas Goodnight and a joyful Grok, no longer restricted to hiding in the shadows since von Baldur and all the others assumed that their murder of Frabord Held would expose their presence in the Alsaoud System.

Grok had noted that the People seemed not to discriminate against nonterrestrials. In fact, rumors that Goodnight heard suggested that if it was necessary to deal with outsiders, they preferred them to humans, the explanation being that few aliens required policemen. And so Grok began his inquiries on Khazia more or less openly, and very quickly amassed the names of certain individuals and firms among the People most interested in acquiring things without being too careful about attached certificates of ownership. He settled on the Ganmore family, who seemed to have a certain amount of probity, at least among fences.

Goodnight, on the other hand, had gone zero for zero, coming up with either lightweights or those known for double- or triple-crosses, and was starting to wonder if he was losing his fine hand for skullduggery.

M'chel and Jasmine went looking for targets, using everything from shipping holos to advertisements to word of mouth in the industrialists' hangouts on Khazia.

Redon Spada and von Baldur combed the out-system shipping news.

Riss got lucky first, hearing of a pending cargo. It was somewhat better than pure gold even though it appeared boring – a cargo of micromanipulators, inbound to Alsaoud III, the volcanic world of Tarabula.

Inbound on the starship *Fowler*.

Money changed hands, and Star Risk got the flight schedule of the ship, and took both the *McMahon* and their yacht out to lurk near the navpoint the *Fowler* would use to connect from its home world to jump into the Alsaoud System.

The *Fowler* was a well-designed and -constructed merchant ship, designed to be able to scoot in and out of almost all ports on any world, including an airless one.

It was a little short of three hundred meters long, with a surprising four thousand metric tons cargo capacity. It loaded either via a stern ramp or into either hold through side hatches, using a pair of integral hoists.

It had a crew of eight officers, twenty men, and –

here was Goodnight's near downfall – five stewards taking care of up to twelve passengers in quiet luxury.

On schedule, the *Fowler* blurped out of subspace beyond Alsaoud. The navigator keyed for precise location and began setting up for the jump closer to Tarabula.

Instead, just as its radar told it that two ships were closing, it received a 'cast on the standard emergency com:

'Ship *Fowler*, Ship *Fowler*. Hold your present orbit. Make no attempt to escape or resist.'

With the 'cast came a side benefit Jasmine was particularly proud of: layered over it was the near subliminal of a flashing human skull and crossed bones that she'd found in a library of clip-and-paste.

Also, withering static went out on all standard 'cast frequencies to jam any commed screams for help.

Finally, a very obsolete (and therefore cheap) missile was fired, just accurate enough to be certain to miss. It exploded a few dozen kilometers off the *Fowler*, Goodnight having replaced its conventional warhead with a rather stunning fireworks display.

That was more than enough.

Star Risk's yacht and the *McMahon* set orbits around the *Fowler*, and Grok, Riss, and Goodnight went out. Von Baldur stayed at the controls of the yacht; Spada in the command chair of the *McMahon*.

Riss was suppressing a desire to shout 'Aaargh,' and 'ye hearties are half-vast,' and other piratical bellows as the inner lock came open.

She didn't need to.

There was already enough chaos going on, mainly caused by the passengers, who were running up and down the main corridor in various stages of panic. There weren't more than six or eight of them, but they made up in volume what they lacked in numbers.

The loudest, M'chel estimated, was a vastly overweight young woman, perhaps nineteen, with hair frizzy enough to belong to her grandmother.

She was screaming, 'Oh, help, rape, rape, they're coming,' coupled with periodic yips.

She ran up to Riss as M'chel opened her faceplate, squealing, 'Oh, please don't ravish me, sir.'

Ravish?

Riss was puzzling over that when the young woman realized M'chel wasn't conventionally equipped for the crime, and gibbered incoherently. Then her eyes gleamed as she saw Goodnight lift his helmet off.

She ran to Chas and grabbed him about the hips.

M'chel hid laughter.

The woman squeaked, 'Oh, please, don't, don't.'

Goodnight grimaced and pushed past her toward the hold.

The woman looked disappointed.

Goodnight went into the cargo spaces, determined that the cargo they wanted was indeed there.

Grok and Riss trotted to the bridge, blasters ready.

They were met with nervous smiles and outstretched, empty hands.

'You're taken,' Grok growled.

The man at the center console nodded.

'We'll make no resistance, only, please don't hurt anyone.'

'That will depend on your performance,' Grok growled, while Riss had to turn away to hide her gun.

The *Fowler* was theirs.

It was tempting to treat the matter lightly, but there was always the possibility of a counterattack by the crew — not to mention the reminder that they were

committing a decidedly capital offense — and so Star
Risk kept their guns ready.

Grok rousted the passengers back to their compart-
ments. Most of them went, obediently.

Except of course for the young woman, who had to
be bodily lifted to her stateroom.

'Lord suffering,' Goodnight said, shaking his head.
'First thing, we get rid of *them*. Especially her.'

'In a moment,' Riss said.

She found the switch to the ship intercom, keyed it.

'All passengers. Stand by for transshipment. Have no
more than one bag per person. Be ready in ten minutes,
or face our wrath.'

She had the crew set a jump into the system, and
came out of the control room to find a small, chubby
boy with spit curls waiting in the corridor.

'Please, ma'am, my sister wants to know when you'll
be raping her.'

'In a few minutes,' Riss said. 'As soon as we take care
of a few things.' She caught sight of Goodnight. 'And
he'll be in charge of that.'

Goodnight glowered at her.

'Bitch!'

M'chel smiled back, sweetly.

'Bastard.'

The *McMahon* and the yacht kept close formation on
the *Fowler* as it came out of hyperspace off Mardite, the
fourth, sparsely settled world of Alsaoud.

The yacht cross-locked to the *Fowler*, and the passengers and crew were escorted into it.

The fat young woman caught a glimpse of
Goodnight as he ducked into the engine spaces and
gave him her most hateful stare, then was gone.

Goodnight stayed hidden until the yacht had
unlocked from the *Fowler* to dump the victims on a

deserted section of Mardite before he came out.

He went to the bridge, where Jasmine was setting a new course into the asteroids, the Maron Region.

'You know,' he told Riss, who had the watch, 'if we were *real* pirates, we would have made all of the witnesses have their keels hauled, or something fatal so we wouldn't have to worry about having them show up as witnesses.'

Riss knew very damned well that Goodnight was only partially joking, and was glad there were a few controls on the sociopath.

'Now, now, Chas,' Jasmine said. 'The course of true love never runs smooth.'

Goodnight gave her a very hard look and didn't answer for a while.

'Sometimes,' he said finally, thinking of how poorly he'd personally done of late, 'I dunno about this pirate shit.'

THIRTY-FOUR

Keeping in mind that it's not uncommon for pirates to be pirated, Star Risk entered the Maron Region cautiously. They kept the yacht well forward with its fairly advanced sensors and radar at full alert – Grok manning them, then their prize, and just 'behind' and 'above' that, the *McMahon*, while keeping another eye out for anything resembling the Alsaoud authorities, whether naval or police.

But they weren't jumped.

By anyone.

At a certain point, they took an orbit stationary to a certain asteroid, and 'cast a certain signal on a certain frequency, as Grok had been advised.

A dozen small spacecraft swarmed toward them – it seemed from nowhere – and all three ships were boarded.

When Grok had told Goodnight about the procedure he'd been advised on, Goodnight didn't like it at all.

'Suppose their ethics run out?' he objected. 'Supposing, come to think, they don't *got* none in the first place?'

'Then we're screwed,' Jasmine said.

Goodnight's mind diverted, he considered King –

what she would look like outside her space suit, being screwed – and sighed.

But nothing untoward happened.

Two dozen men and three women boarded the *McMahon*, facing them with very ready guns.

M'chel didn't know if the People's cause was righteous, but they surely packed enough artillery to make the convincing fairly easy.

Von Baldur said that he wished to conduct business with the Ganmore family.

The gunnies deferred to a middle-aged, mustached thug, who bowed and told Friedrich to suit up and come with him.

Von Baldur obeyed, and fitted himself into one of the small ships.

That ship zigged between asteroids, and 'landed' on a nearly zero-g, dumbbell-shaped world that had four rather enormous hangars anchored to it. Anchoring was accomplished by matching orbits, and one man exiting the ship and clipping a lead from its nose to a ring on the asteroid, much as if the ship were a riding animal.

Von Baldur was escorted into one of the hangars, and to a small chamber atop it, a surprisingly luxurious office.

A man about Friedrich's age, but with still-dark hair, considered him with calm eyes.

'You wish to do business with my family?'

'I do. Now, and in the future.'

'You arrived with three ships. Are any of them your proposed offer?'

'The merchantman,' von Baldur said. 'The others are necessary for continued work.'

'Do you have paperwork for the merchantman?'

Von Baldur just looked at the man, who allowed himself a brief smile.

'Do we have to deal with the crewmen, or have you already taken care of that detail?' the man asked.

'They have been dealt with.' Von Baldur didn't offer details.

'I admit to mild interest in the ship you offer, even though we have a plethora of spacecraft.'

'The ship is of secondary value,' von Baldur said. 'Its cargo is what I am primarily interested in selling.'

'Which is?'

Von Baldur told him, and admired the man as a fellow professional, since his expression didn't change.

'Ah,' he said. 'May I offer a drink?'

'You may,' Friedrich said. 'I assume you will share one with me.'

A smile came, went.

'We seek no unnecessary advantages in our business dealings,' he said. 'I shall. And, by the bye, my name is Mal, and I am, of course, a Ganmore. I have been given the title of Advisor.'

Von Baldur introduced himself, and the two shared a mildly alcohol-charged beverage that tasted slightly fruity, but of no identifiable variety.

Then the bargaining commenced.

This von Baldur thoroughly enjoyed, especially since Jasmine had earlier done one of her immaculate research jobs, so Friedrich knew exactly how much the micro-manipulators sold for on the open, legal market.

Advisor Ganmore was a remarkably honest man – for a thief. He paid sixty percent of the price. In Alliance credits.

'Might I invite you to pass some time with the People?' he offered courteously as they finished.

'Another time,' von Baldur said. 'We have to return to our other lives.'

'I understand,' Ganmore said.

'But next time, we shall — in fact, we will probably be interested in renting living and working areas here in the Region, since we shall likely be wearing out our welcome on Khazia,' Friedrich said. 'As I said, we hope to be bringing you much business in the near future.'

THIRTY-FIVE

'Not only,' von Baldur said evenly, without taking his eyes off one of the screens he was staring at, 'have I decided to become superstitious, but I shall never, ever again mention the name of someone I do not wish to crop up in the immediacy.'

'What?' Riss asked, antenna going up at his deliberate tonelessness.

Without answering, he patched the image at which he was staring to one of her computer screens.

M'chel repressed a 'yeep.'

One of the first things they'd done – after returning to Khazia and determining that no one was looking for them regarding the disappearance of a certain spaceship named *Fowler* – was to field the tapes from the various pickups they'd planted around the president's palace, to see if they could spot the late Held's replacement and how many other Cerberus operatives they might be able to pick out.

Von Baldur had found one immediately – the image he showed Riss.

'I shall be *dipped*,' she said, not needing an answer. 'That really is our boy the superagent Nowotny, isn't it?'

The other three Star Risk operatives swooped around.

Spada had preferred to stay close to their yacht, parked at the most expensive yard they could find, which had all the mod cons any zillionaire could want around his prized spacecraft.

The *McMahon* was hidden on one of the system's moonlets.

'It surely is Nowotny,' Goodnight said. 'Well, what are we going to do, kill him?'

'I'm not sure we could,' Riss said.

'Come on, M'chel,' Goodnight said. '*Anybody* can get murdered.'

'I know,' she said. 'I just think assassinating the good Walter might be a little expensive. Especially for the murderer.'

'The worst is,' Grok said, 'that I won't be able to go out at all now. He knows me well – and certainly remembers that I tried to double on him and certainly would like to pull out my dewclaws to see what I know.

'The same goes for you, Jasmine, even if you lack claws.'

'I suppose so,' King said. 'Oh well. We set out to pull the lion's tail, and we've surely succeeded.

'Not that I regret killing that horrid Held for one instant.

'But does this alter any part of the equation's progress as we'd planned it from here?'

'Maybe,' Grok said. 'I certainly think that all areas should be open to rethinking from this point forward.'

'I do think,' M'chel said, 'that it means the tightrope just got a little thinner.'

It became immediately apparent what game Cerberus was running in the Alsaoud System, although not why, nor for whom.

President Flyver – which meant Cerberus –

announced Alsaoud would no longer allow blatant law-
lessness to overwhelm his worlds – he clearly wasn't a
master orator – and would immediately form an
antipiracy task force that would both analyze the enemy
and use any and all tactics to end the 'plague of terror.'

Star Risk also decided it was time to escalate, and
determined to no longer mess around with minor
depredations.

THIRTY-SIX

One of the things that got escalated was Star Risk's expenses.

For their next strike against Cerberus, they needed some heavier guns, and they didn't have the right ones handy.

Redon Spada did. He found a pair of patrol boat owner-skippers – old acquaintances who were proud of taking any job that wasn't suicidal, charging an arm and a leg, doing the work perfectly, and not talking about it later, which was most important in the still-undeclared war against Cerberus.

It took two days for Spada to track down the p-boats, another day for them to hire a transport that would jump the short-range combat ships to the vicinity of the Alsaoud System.

Spada, with the yacht, met the two patrol ships, escorted them to the moonlet, linked them to the larger *McMahon*, and ordered them to wait.

The mercenary pilots shrugged.

They were getting paid, quite lavishly, and so they didn't mind a little leisure. As long as it didn't last too long.

It didn't.

Less than five ship-days later, Star Risk went into motion.

Target: the Alliance liner *Normandie*.

They'd debated hard whether this was either one of the more intelligent or one of the dumber changes they'd thought of, and tentatively decided it was good.

But if things went wrong, and they killed a shipload of innocents – or, worse yet from their point of view, were hit by either the *Normandie*'s own weaponry or that damned escort ship from the Alsaoud System . . .

M'chel decided she didn't want to contemplate what would happen if things went that badly wrong, which would inevitably mean the Alliance would show up to Rectify the Matter, which would mean those hanging judges and the rest.

At least the *Normandie*, being under Alliance registry, followed a fairly precise schedule, so at least their pirating could begin on some kind of a plan.

Star Risk would mount its attack inside the Alsaoud System, just where the liner would make its first jump from the common navpoint – and where the escort ship should meet it.

The escort was waiting where it was supposed to be, so von Baldur left a small spy satellite, and held his ships not far distant, on the edges of the Maron Region.

Then they waited some more.

M'chel had never been a good waiter, she realized. But there was a difference between being in a nice safe dirt bunker, or even in a nicely armored track vehicle, and sitting in a goddamned spaceship floating in the midst of nowhere.

She pushed away the memory of how she used to go mildly berserk in a troopship, waiting for a landing force to assemble, making life most difficult for her underlings.

Now, there was no one to drive mad, and so she stewed gently until the satellite beeped softly.

All ships jumped to the coordinates of their satellite.

The two p-boats, having gotten an exact description of the Alsaoud escort and having everything short of the blueprints from *Janes*, were first into action.

One small missile blew its drive mechanism apart, a second was command-steered to the ship's nose, and destroyed its C&C systems.

The escort ship whirled in emptiness, gently whining for help on the only coms left to it.

That had taken about thirty seconds, and had only cost one casualty, an electronics tech who'd been worrying over a hiccuping part of the ship's command and control network.

Star Risk then went after the *Normandie*.

They knew exactly where the twin missile launchers on the liner were, and the p-boats and the *McMahon* drifted missiles in. One blew near the stern, and the *Normandie*'s star drive went down, leaving it helpless to escape into n-space.

The yacht was broadcasting on all freqs that the *Normandie* should not, must not, fight back or call for help, or else be prepared for total destruction.

If the liner had been able to get a signal out, and there'd been any sign of a rescue force, there would actually be no alternative other than to break off the action and flee.

And if the *Normandie* opened fire from either of its two batteries, the pirates would also have to flee.

Star Risk wasn't prepared to face mass slaughter.

Half of piracy is bluff, anyway. However, being mercenaries, and having a certain reputation for lethality to hold up in their 'community,' they hadn't told the patrol boats of the reality of this secondary plan, merely saying that in the event of an emergency the p-boats were to follow Star Risk's orders exactly.

The p-boat skippers and their crews shrugged, and said they'd do as they were told.

Two missiles from the *McMahon* closed on the *Normandie*, and exploded less than three ships' length from the liner, exactly positioned off the twin missile stations, neatly scrambling the hardy state of the art command circuitry.

Then, with previously taped threats of blood, thunder, and dismemberment roaring on the com, Star Risk boarded.

Surprisingly, the passenger spaces weren't as chaotic as they'd been on the *Fowler*. Goodnight was thinking what damage one crazed fat woman could do, when he saw someone come out of a cabin, holding a small blaster.

He shouted a warning. Riss went flat as a bolt clanged off a bulkhead, and he fired back, aiming for the idiot's leg.

Goodnight missed a little, hit the bravado-crazed man messily in the intestines, and heard him scream, gurgle, and die.

'Goddamn that stupid glory-happy son of a bitch and his medal-sucking mother,' he swore to no one in particular.

But he was running toward the bridge, as were the others. Grok, as planned, took a position just between crew and passenger countries, a blast rifle cuddled in his arms.

But none of the passengers, looking at the unpleasantness that had been one of their fellows a few seconds earlier, felt inclined to fight back.

They were herded back into their cabins while Grok set a course for the Maron Region. Von Baldur called the other ships in to take a close orbit around the liner, while Goodnight and Riss found the ship's purser and had all of the safes opened and looted.

M'chel found that she couldn't stop thinking about that poor, dead, grandiose idiot.

She decided that she was getting old.

While taking the *Normandie* certainly was spectacular enough, the profit came from the looting.

Neither the Ganmore family nor any of the other middlemen in the People would offer anything for the *Normandie*, since it was entirely too much of a stand-out.

Its small cargo of luxuries, its own storerooms of delights for the passengers, and the passengers' loot made the endeavor highly profitable, though.

But the passengers were a problem.

'In the old days, we could have sold them as vassals, or slaves,' Goodnight said. But he said it quietly. He'd been a bit subdued since killing the passenger.

Not enough for anyone except Star Risk to notice, but he *was* subdued.

Advisor Ganmore sold them a small transport, and they crammed the passengers and crew of the *Normandie* aboard, sent Riss aboard the yacht and Spada to take the liner a couple of jumps back toward the Alliance, and then set it adrift with alarm bells and whistles going off for rescue.

Then they paid the two patrol boats off, who were exactly as expensive as they'd promised, and sent them on their way.

Star Risk waited until M'chel and Spada came back, then decided to linger on for a bit in the Maron Region,

waiting to see if anyone had pinned them to the crime
and planning what their next move would be.

At least out in the asteroids, among the People, they
wouldn't have to spend quite as much time watching
their backs, although Friedich maintained that having
the luxury of the Excelsior Hotel was worth the fear.

THIRTY-SEVEN

Grok got in the habit of meeting Advisor Ganmore for drinks now and again, late of an evening. Generally, Jasmine came with him.

The big alien was proud of having adopted a garb that let him fit in with the People, including a belt knife.

Of course, he was more certain he fit in than anyone else, but no one was likely to tell anyone his size that he was smoking hop.

One night, the three went to a new place, perhaps prompted by Grok saying the tavern they usually met in was entirely too quiet and stodgy, and he was interested in something more representative of what he called the People's 'cultural heritage.'

Ganmore shrugged and took them to a larger, rowdier joint.

They found a table, both Grok and Jasmine picking one that allowed them to have their backs to a wall, and ordered drinks.

Ganmore eyed half a dozen young men who were as loud as a small regiment at a nearby table, as they suddenly broke into a song that seemed to be about the right of the People to go back to their home worlds and take what had been theirs by force.

Ganmore shook his head.

'Of course, they never consider that we took it from someone else once, even if it was slugs and grubs.'

'I think someone should stand up for the slugs' and grubs' homeland,' Jasmine said.

Ganmore laughed wryly.

'Is that possible – I mean, to take back what you call your home worlds, not standing up for slugs and grubs?' Grok asked seriously.

'Of course not,' Ganmore said. 'It almost never happens that someone turns their back on the present to chase history, and succeeds.

'So those who sing – and believe – the old songs, or worse yet make pilgrimages to the old worlds, and give themselves a title for doing this, or talk about the palaces they were driven out of, are, in the long run, fools – sentimental, sometimes admirable fools, but fools nonetheless.

'The Alsaoud System, for better or worse, is ours now.'

'There appear to be those who disagree,' Grok said.

'And there are those here . . . I would imagine like those,' Ganmore nodded at the other table, 'who think we should accelerate the taking of Alsaoud. By force, if necessary.

'But that's absurd. For one thing, we're outnumbered at present.

'But we have history on our side.

'Their government is about as piskewey as it is possible to get. I doubt it can stand by itself forever.

'Not to mention the People are outbreeding them. Not this generation, nor the next, nor the one after that, but Alsaoud will be ultimately ours.'

'I notice that the People seem to welcome anyone who will favor them,' Jasmine said. 'This doesn't always win friends, if outsiders see you're welcoming criminals and pirates.'

She had the grace to blush a little.

'Like ourselves,' she admitted.

'No,' Ganmore agreed. 'It does not. But it is entirely too easy for a person, or a culture, to think that he who helps me is my friend, and to blazes with what others think. History will tend to resolve things like that . . . in favor of the survivors.'

'Even if you believe in inevitable historical processes – and I can think of a few men on ancient Earth who did as well,' Grok said, 'and were proven wrong – there could well be those on Alsaoud, today, who would be willing to put a great deal of effort and expense into maintaining the status quo.'

That was as close as Grok thought he should come to referring to Cerberus to an outsider. Besides, he was fishing to see if Ganmore knew of them.

Ganmore shrugged.

'Outsiders? Out to feather their own? I have enough faith in my people to think that we shall prevail, in spite of the dislike the Alliance and others have for the People.'

One of the young men at the other table noted Jasmine, who was a great deal prettier than any woman of the People, and made a rude gesture.

Ganmore and the others pretended not to notice.

'What we shall do is take all the support we can get – especially from nonhumans,' Ganmore said, 'who obviously have no interest in this system. In time, as we conquer, the Alliance will grudgingly accept us.

'It has not survived as long as it has for refusing to accept change or new blood.'

So, as far as Grok and Jasmine could tell, the People

had no knowledge of Cerberus, and certainly no idea of what they intended in their grand scheme.

After a final drink, Ganmore made his farewells and left.

Grok and Jasmine were about to follow when one of the young men made a rather too-loud comment about foreign whores.

Grok grunted.

'My muscles are stiff.'

He got up.

Jasmine put a hand on his arm.

'Ignore them. They've been drinking.'

'So have I.'

He went to the other table. The man who'd made the comment about Jasmine was grinning, perhaps waiting to see how foolish Grok would be to start trouble with six armed men, and what he would say.

This was a miscalculation.

Grok didn't need to swap insults before he fought.

His paw shot out in a backhanded slap against the man's chest, and the sound of the man's ribs cracking was very loud.

Instantly, the tavern was silent.

One man came to his feet as the insulter collapsed backward, burbling blood.

Others started up, and Grok kicked the heavy table into their faces.

The second man jumped clear of the tumble and drew his knife.

'Ho, ho, ho,' Grok growled as he pulled his own, oversized blade.

The second man had been in a few fights. He held his knife low, blade parallel with the ground, in his right, his left extended a bit further out as a block.

He kept moving, almost dancing, circling to Grok's right, blade weaving.

Grok held his huge knife rather carelessly in his left paw — his species was ambidextrous — and stood still, only turning to face the man.

The man was confident, seeing Grok making almost every mistake known, starting with too big a knife — a basic beginner's error.

He darted in, slashed, and learned that Grok's fur may have felt silky, but it was fairly decent armor.

The cut didn't do anything more than slice a few hairs away.

The man recovered quickly, started back to his guard stance.

But not quickly enough as Grok moved.

He not only was about twice the size of a human, but moved with a bit more than twice the speed.

Before the man could jump back, Grok's curved knife flashed out across the other's left, open hand.

It cut neatly through the palm, and fingers spun away and blood sprayed.

The man had an instant to mourn his crippling, then Grok turned his knife in midstroke, without recovering, and struck again, higher, stepping inside the man's guard.

The great knife took the man below the nose, and rather surgically severed the top half of his head.

The man was dead, and didn't know it.

He spun twice, gorily, and dropped.

The other People were up now, but frozen.

'Anyone else?' Grok asked gently.

No one answered, no one moved, noticing that Grok had drawn his heavy blaster, held it ready.

Jasmine, just now getting to her feet, had a rather slender, long-barreled blaster of her own that had come from nowhere.

The tavern held in a death-hush as the two Star Risk operatives backed out the door.

They trotted away, not waiting to see who boiled out the door after them.

'Well,' Jasmine said, 'there's another place we can't go back to.'

'Why not?' Grok asked. 'We won, didn't we?'

THIRTY-EIGHT

Star Risk crept, rather nervously, back onto Khazia. They had detected no signs that Nowotny and Cerberus and the Powers Wot Be were specifically after them, but from a distance, who knew for certain?

But their suite at the Excelsior was empty, immaculate and unmonitored, even if the hotel management was a bit nervous about getting paid, given Star Risk's long absence.

But bills were paid current, and champagne was sent up, a little guiltily, and all were happy, floating, as M'chel said, 'on a large, pink cloud.'

Next were two steps:

Finding a new target to pirate; and beginning a little counterespionaging against Cerberus.

This second job took priority, and was the hardest, since all of them were known to Nowotny. And unless the scar-faced goon was playing things a lot closer than von Baldur thought, Cerberus still didn't know that they had regrouped, let alone that they were in the Alsaoud System.

They knew they'd be discovered sooner rather than later and there'd be hell to pay, but tried very hard to keep it later rather than sooner.

They probably shouldn't have assassinated Held,

since that would be the ultimate giveaway, but what was done was done.

Goodnight summoned Jorkens, the lifter driver, and told him they had decided to put him on the payroll full-time, and asked what he made a week.

Jorkens gave Chas a figure which was, of course, inflated, which, of course, Goodnight knew.

Goodnight offered the man twice that, which made Jorkens nervous, as it was intended to do.

Nervous, but in a position where he couldn't refuse the job.

Nor would he – Goodnight hoped – kill the golden goose by selling them out.

Not that selling out would be that easy, since the only real secret Star Risk had was its identity, which was kept well concealed.

Ostentatiously scattered around the suite were various documents, cards, letterheads, false letters and so forth that Jasmine had spent time churning out. All of them were headed or addressed to that hoary phony, Research Associates, and nothing suggested Star Risk.

Goodnight wanted one simple thing from Jorkens.

'I know that President Flyver, long may he wave, needs to keep track of – hem-hem – dangerous aliens.'

Jorkens nodded, and got more nervous. Anything involving internal security normally makes most citizens of most worlds shaky, since treason is such a handy tool for politicians to use against anyone.

'I also know that one of the best ways to keep track of these dangerous sorts is to have good, reliable lift pilots who'll report any evil they see or hear,' Goodnight said smoothly.

'Not me, Mister.'

'Of course, of course,' Goodnight soothed. 'But I'm

sure you know of some that do this reporting for the odd favor or shekel.'

Jorkens tried to hold a poker face. All this was, of course, completely foreign to him.

Goodnight held up a hand.

'I don't want to know who they are, or even who you think they are. But I'd like you to make sure any of these sorts you know about hear of certain things that I'll tell you about.'

'Such as?'

'Such as the presence of some interesting people in the Alsaoud System.'

'I don't understand,' Jorkens said.

'You don't have to,' Goodnight said. 'I just want the word to get around.'

Jorkens, thinking of the money and not seeing any immediate harm, agreed. Star Risk didn't give a damn about what intelligence Flyver had or didn't have, but knew anything that looked hot would instantly go to Cerberus.

Then the team built a pirate for Nowotny's consumption, to act as a stalking horse and hopefully attract Cerberus's attention.

They named him Lapied. Von Baldur said he thought they were getting a little too cute for their own good, but Jasmine said Nowotny didn't have a great grasp of foreign languages, particularly obsolescent ones. Grok agreed, adding that Nowotny thought the world of his *own* intellect, and was fairly humorless, so their minor jape was very safe.

Lapied it was.

He was an ex-officer in the Alliance military, under his real name, never to be revealed, who'd been thrown out of the service for crimes he never committed, and had sworn an oath of eternal vengeance.

'My word,' Goodnight said. 'Aren't we getting romantic?'

'And what's the matter with that?' Riss asked.

'Nothing, I guess.'

Lapied had a sleek black ship of his own, a former Alliance cruiser, manned by Alliance and other dissolute renegades. Lapied had never been caught, because one of his practices, when he moved into a new system, was to develop a skein of informers and agents on that system's capital worlds.

Here on Alsaoud, he'd further allied himself with members of the People.

'Isn't that a bit raw?' Riss asked.

'Aren't the People actually tied in with every would-be raider that drifts into Alsaoud?' von Baldur asked. 'And would they not get in bed with our Lapied if he happened to exist?'

'Well . . . yes,' M'chel admitted.

'Then life may be a bit uncomfortable for them. Besides, if our scheme plays out the way we want it, they *will* be in cahoots with certain big-time pirates – namely, ourselves.'

Lapied's existence went out, in whispers.

Grok tried to bug Cerberus's headquarters to track events, using a model spaceship, which he crashed gently into the building's roof, very close to an airvent.

It transmitted junk sound for a few hours, then went suddenly dead.

'They have,' Grok reported, 'an active antibugging program. Cerberus usually does.'

'Or else,' Goodnight said, 'you didn't check your batteries when you stuck 'em in.'

Grok curled a lip, which he'd learned denoted human scorn. The gesture was awesome, baring one side of the alien's very large fangs, but looked as if he was about to eat the face of whoever he was showing his new expression to.

But even without a bug Star Risk was rapidly assured that Nowotny had gotten the word on Lapied:

The drivers who'd been given the phony information were rewarded, and their controls asked them for anything more they could uncover about Lapied the Dashing Freebooter; and, uglier, the holos started running negative items about what the People were, thought and did.

There were even a few incidents against them, but they didn't amount to much, since the People stayed armed and were hair-triggered.

Van Baldur made sure that Ganmore heard of these incidents; and so, in the Maron Region, word grew that it was time to make a few examples of these Alsaoud swine, and no one needed to be overly particular about guilty parties.

'I just hope,' Riss said, 'that nobody innocent happens to get killed because of our puppeteering.'

'In this world,' Goodnight said piously, 'the innocent must suffer with the guilty.'

M'chel thought of spitting in his eye, but didn't bother, since Goodnight was irrevocably Goodnight.

Then Star Risk's own agents started hearing about a particularly valuable and large shipment coming into the system:

A cargo of exotic alloys, suitable for various purposes from jewel mounting to star drive internal controls.

Just what someone who'd pirated a ship of micro-manipulators would almost certainly be interested in acquiring.

'Oh, yes, we are most *certainly* interested,' von Baldur said with a sneer.

'Just how dumb does Nowotny think we are?'

THIRTY-NINE

Cerberus laid an excellent trap.

First was the cargo ship carrying the supposed alloy riches.

It actually was a robot carrier of recent design. Instead of cargo, Nowotny put three limited-yield nuclear devices aboard.

A little investigation that any competent pirate could be counted upon to make would provide the information that the ship was to follow a widely used astrogation track, using the navpoint just outside the Alsaoud System, then would jump into the system, and make a final jump just off Khazia.

Nowotny didn't figure it would get that far, but had a bomb squad brought in from Cerberus's headquarters just in case the hijackers slipped a beat and the cargo actually reached its destination and needed a little disarming, so his petard wouldn't do any hoisting.

Two days before the cargo ship was scheduled, Nowotny had a huge hulk positioned near the out-system navpoint. Purportedly, it was a wreck that had had a drive explosion years ago, and had conveniently drifted to its present position.

Actually, the wreck was a gutted junker from an out-system boneyard.

It had been lifted into space and jumped to its position by tugs. Three patrol ships waited in the shell of the wreck.

One held the operation's commander.

Nowotny's plan was not oriented toward surrender or prisoners.

This was intended to be a nasty object lesson to Lapied and Alsaoud's pirates.

Just in case they showed up in strength, there were also two light destroyers held in n-space, linked via a subspace transceiver to the Cerberus officer in one of the p-boats.

Cerberus laid an excellent trap.

But Star Risk laid a better one.

Two weeks before the cargo ship was due, Freddie von Baldur and Ganmore went recruiting to some of the People's raiders, who politely dubbed themselves privateers, naturally claiming to attack outsiders only for the greater good of their race.

Von Baldur's pitch was simple: 'I won't pretend there's great prizes to be seized. In fact, you'll be out your operating expenses.

'But I'll give you a chance to kill some Alsaoud . . . and to hopefully shortstop any antiraider campaign before it gets any strength.'

The People were a little puzzled by such unexpected honesty, and became most agreeable. Von Baldur got four large vessels – one a light cruiser, the others small frigates – and three close-range attack ships.

He positioned them in place about a light-second from the navpoint four days before the cargo ship was due, and told them if they gave away their position with com chatter or any other unnecessary noise, he'd set Grok on them. Tales of the alien's thin-slicing of some local rowdies hadn't been lessened in the telling.

These ships were 'hidden' behind an ELINT program Grok had written.

To any sensors other than pure visual, these ships would appear as no more than a scattering of small meteors, in an orbit between stars.

Von Baldur wasn't particularly worried about encountering anyone out in nothingness with a telescope or sailing through space navigating with the Mark I Eyeball.

The day before the scheduled arrival of the 'cargo ship,' Star Risk took their yacht and the *McMahon* out.

Then there was nothing to do but wait.

On schedule, the 'cargo ship' appeared out of n-space. Before it could make its jump onto the Alsaoud System, as Cerberus had predicted, it was attacked.

But Cerberus hadn't expected anything the size of a light cruiser.

The alert went off in the ships hidden in the hulk, and they shot out to the attack.

Before they got within range, the People's cruiser very accurately blew off a missile near the cargo ship's drive mechanism, leaving it spinning in an aimless orbit.

As Cerberus's p-boats closed, the People's frigates, attack boats, and the *McMahon* jumped into normal space, and acquired the p-boats.

They disappeared in a flurry of targeting missiles and explosions.

The leader of the expedition had a moment to scream for help to Cerberus's ships waiting in hyperspace.

The scream was never answered.

The officers and crews of those two light destroyers might have worked for Cerberus, but they were mercenaries on salary. And mercenaries are traditionally loath to take on suicide missions, leaving that for the idealists and volunteers.

'And now we board,' the captain of the People's cruiser exulted.

'That's a big negative,' Goodnight drawled from the com board of the *McMahon*. 'First we look up the lady's skirt.'

That was Grok and King's department, aboard the yacht. Half a dozen modified missiles went out, and closed with the 'cargo ship.' Very high speed cameras and other sensors went into action.

Grok sent a remote piloted vehicle piggybacking on a missile to the 'cargo ship,' brought it down on the ship's skin, and trundled it across to an airlock.

The RPV extended a claw, and began fiddling with the airlock control the lock iris opens.

The RPV entered – and two of the three nukes that Nowotny's technicians had installed went off.

The various missiles continued recording as the robot ship blew itself to flinders.

'As we thought,' Goodnight 'cast with satisfaction. 'It was a trap all the way around. All units – mission complete, all commanders take command and return your ships to their bases. We owe you one.'

Grok and Jasmine paid little attention, busy analyzing what their surveillance missiles had gotten.

When Star Risk rendezvoused aboard the *McMahon*, Grok reported.

'As far as any sensor told us, the boobytraps aboard the false cargo ship weren't triggered by any specific command, but almost certainly set off by the attempt to enter.'

'They wrote off their crew?' Goodnight asked in some amazement. 'Cold-blooded bassids. Might as well be working for the Alliance.'

'Odd that you should mention that,' King said, and told Chas that the ship was a robot.

'Well, aren't we taking no chances,' Riss said.

'That isn't the most interesting thing,' Jasmine said. 'Unlike most of the other hardware we get out here in nowhere, *Janes* lists the robot as a relatively new design, currently in production for the Alliance battle fleet.'

'Oh, dear,' M'chel said. 'Cerberus has some interesting contacts.'

'Or worse,' von Baldur said.

None of them wanted to discuss one of the probabilities that occurred.

Walter Nowotny was livid – and scared.

His trap had not only snapped shut emptily, but expensively.

Ral Tomkins would not be pleased.

And Nowotny knew Tomkins tended to strike fast and viciously when he was displeased.

Nowotny determined to strike back before Tomkins had a chance to consider and prepare disciplinary measures.

He was a well-trained Cerberus executive, which meant, among other things, that he had the company's reflexes ingrained at cellular level.

One of them was to respond to any challenge or any threat instantly, with the heaviest tools available.

This meant, after the failure of his trap, that he had to take care of the Maron Region and any notion these refugee People had of independence.

One of the many advantages Cerberus had was keeping a small cruiser squadron on near-instant response.

Nowotny knew of this squadron, and had the rank to summon it.

The squadron arrived off the Alsaoud System within ten days, and Nowotny met and briefed it.

The orders were simple:

A small, inviting merchant ship was to precede the five cruisers into the Maron Region.

Any hostile attempts on the merchantman was to be met with heavy response, first on any attacking ship, then with a raid on whatever asteroid the attempt came from.

No surrender would be accepted.

The squadron commander was told that Nowotny wanted the utmost severity applied in this 'object lesson.'

That officer knew well what that meant, and verbal orders were given to all hands to give no quarter.

There were only two things wrong with Nowotny's response: first, that any automatic response to a challenge should be considered of questionable value; and second, that Nowotny didn't know Star Risk was on the other side of the equation.

Jasmine and Grok had told von Baldur what Nowotny's response would be, and so the Maron Region was ready.

Von Baldur had noted Nowotny's love affair with decoys, and thought he might repeat himself.

He had raiding captains among the People who thought he was a tactical genius after he'd magically scented Nowotny's first attempt against them, and had been most interested when he 'just happened' to discuss his plans for great plunder, raiding into the Alsaoud System once they'd been humiliated a bit.

So when he asked for a dozen or so smaller vessels for standby, they'd been eager to provide them. He got twenty-five.

When one of them reported a fat, happy merchant ship wiggling its sexy bottom through their asteroids, there was no hesitation to send a couple of these light raiders against it, and have the others ready.

But not to take on the merchant ship.

They were to go after whatever came behind it.

Nowotny's five cruisers popped out of n-space, summoned by the merchantman's screams for help.

And they were swarmed before they knew what was happening.

One cruiser for each five voracious raiders . . .

Two were destroyed, two surrendered to the glee of the raiders, and one managed to make its escape.

Von Baldur encouraged that – he wanted at least one survivor to, as Goodnight said, 'let our Wally know what it's like to get a tit in the wringer.'

Nowotny knew he was in deep trouble.

Star Risk was planning the next step in the slow humiliation of Cerberus Systems.

Neither of them had allowed for other agendas.

They should have.

FORTY

The Right Reverend Rob Patson had some very negative qualities: he was short, overweight, had archaic dandruff decorating his thinning hair, fairly advanced halitosis, and, like most religious zealots, was heavily opinionated and poorly educated.

But he could hate.

And he could rouse the rabble.

He'd reached middle age before he discovered his two talents.

He'd never amounted to much before, not having a cause, and had had little more than seven children, a defeated wife, a dozen or so disciples and a storefront 'church' in the city of Helleu.

But when the People started trickling down onto Khazia, he had his cause.

The People not only spoke a strange tongue, but dressed weirdly, were violence-prone, and almost certainly used drugs.

They also bred too fast, and, within a few generations — Patson knew anyone listening to him didn't have the ability to figure out how many — would breed the 'rightful' citizens of the Alsaoud System into minority and then nothingness.

The existence and continued success of the pirates

was grist for his mill, proof that the People had a Plot In Development, and he railed against it.

Pretty soon he had to give up his storefront for a much bigger auditorium.

He attracted half a dozen wealthy contributors who either bought into his nonsense or wanted followers on the bottom rung of society.

No mob can exist with just preaching, and so Patson used to take his rabble down to the People's quarter to jeer and pray loudly for their conversion to something acceptable.

Shouts are also weak tea, and so the odd idiot took to picking up a bit of paving or a bottle and hurling it at anything resembling an emanation of the People, from a business with an indecipherable or foreign-sounding name, to anyone 'dressed funny,' to whoever the idiot thought wasn't one of them.

A woman with two children got caught out, and stoned, fortunately not fatally.

That, of course, sent Patson's horde into high glee, even though the good reverend deplored, *deplored*, such violence.

The rowdies among the People now had their feet held to the fire, and their boasting of manli- or womanliness called to account.

Rowdy they may have been, stupid they weren't.

The next time the noise of Patson's goons assembling filtered into the People's district, the young women and men were waiting, after they'd thrown up barricades that appeared flimsy and badly planned at first, but when the rabble filtered down them, they were proven to be most effective channels that put the mob at the end of a one-way alley.

And waiting in the buildings on either side were the rowdies. With guns.

Elders pulled them off after a dozen goons had been shot down. The mob fled in panic back the way they'd come. Bricks, bottles, clubs littered the alley, alongside the bodies.

'Tsk,' one woman mourned, replacing the half-empty magazine in her black-marketed blaster. 'Isn't it just like an Alsaoud to bring a club to a gunfight.'

Alsaoud holos screamed, generally taking the line that 'no one approves of Patson's murderous rabble, but someone must prevent further violence, and disarm the gunmen of the People. Violence of this sort settles nothing.'

Actually, it settled the mob back on its heels for a week.

Scouts for the rabble reported that these hooligan youths had set up patrols around their district, and anyone who had business outside was escorted by armed guards. Police, ordered to stop such outrages, looked at the determination in the eyes of these escorts and — being the cowards police normally are, unless they outnumber their opponents by the dozens — left well enough alone.

During this week, there was time enough for the elders in the Maron Region to meet.

And time enough for Star Risk to consider what they might do.

'We sit back and watch the bodies bounce,' Goodnight opined. 'And see if it gives us a chance to further outrage Cerberus.'

'Wrong,' M'chel said flatly. 'We're at least partially responsible for these mobs — if we hadn't stirred things up by using the People against Cerberus, none of this might have happened.'

'I question your logic,' Grok said. 'The People were a-pirating before we arrived in the Alsaoud region.'

'I'm a sentimental saphead,' Jasmine King said. 'I vote with M'chel.'

'Who's advocating what?' Grok asked.

'Maybe,' Riss said, clearly thinking aloud, 'making sure the People down on Khazia have even odds.'

'Which means what?' von Baldur asked suspiciously. 'Running guns to them?'

'That's not a bad start,' M'chel said.

'That's ridiculous,' Goodnight said. 'All that'll do is stir up – oh. I get it. More trouble for Cerberus, probably.'

'That wasn't why I suggested it,' M'chel said. 'But it'll do for a reason. I vote yes on my own measure.'

'I think I shall, too,' Grok said.

Von Baldur considered. 'It certainly won't make life any easier for Nowotny and company. Make it four.'

'Hell's tinkling little bells,' Goodnight said in disgust. 'I'll vote with the sappy sentimentalists. Make it unanimous.'

'Things like this,' M'chel said, 'warm the cockles of my little heart and make me proud of all of you.

'Of course, we're not going to *give* any guns away.'

While Jasmine and Grok plotted on the theoretical aspects of street mobbing – that is, what kind of weapons one should give others to lug to a brawl – von Baldur consulted with Ganmore on just how they were going to get their varied bangsticks to the injured parties on Khazia.

'I am not sure,' Ganmore said, 'that I ever should have told you my title of Advisor,' he said. 'For now you are truly requiring me to play out my role, when it is supposed to be honorary.'

'Star Risk,' von Baldur said smoothly, 'expects only that from its friends that which they have shown themselves very capable at.'

Ganmore squinted warily at von Baldur. 'I somehow feel I shall be paying for that compliment the next time you bring me a cargo for valuation. Nevertheless . . .'

There was an excellent conduit:

The People, having more than a passing familiarity with extraborder dealings in their wanderings across the galaxy, knew well the ways of customs officials.

When they moved onto Khazia, they realized they might need to provide certain items for their people from time to time, such as foodstuffs that were outside that planet's health laws, or people themselves who didn't wish, for whatever reasons, to appear on anyone's immigration rolls.

So, even though there was no maritime tradition among them, a dozen men and women suddenly took up the trade of ocean fisherman.

A commercial boat, beyond sight of land and the reach of radar, is an entity unto itself, and is seldom, without a tip, regarded as interesting to any regulatory agencies beyond a game department.

Von Baldur reported this to the others.

'Those poor wights,' Grok said. 'One of these centuries they will have their own planet and government again, and all of their citizens will be master scofflaws.'

The first rule of running a successful uprising, whether a full-scale revolution or just minor banditry, is to use the same weaponry as your enemy. It makes resupply a lot easier, and helps add confusion to the issue when trying to determine where a bullet came from and who was responsible.

No one in Star Risk had paid much attention to what the local cops carried, and as the small Alsaoud land army was kept mainly out of sight, they didn't have much of an idea on what sort of gunnery to provide.

Since everybody was trying to keep hidden to conceal their presence from Nowotny and Cerberus as long as possible, Redon Spada had to do the eyeballing.

His casual investigation produced another interesting discovery – both police and military were armed with current-issue Alliance blasters and blast rifles.

'Interesting,' Grok mused. 'Between spaceships and pistols, they do seem to have an inside to the Alliance, don't they? I sense Cerberus's fine hand at work here.'

Interesting – but the idea didn't seem to be immediately relevant, and did give Star Risk the way to go.

Using current weapons, though, was going to be a trifle expensive, and they weren't trying to bankrupt the People – at least, not until Cerberus was properly dealt with.

Goodnight and his compatriots had to go out and hijack a couple of small freighters for the front capital.

Then von Baldur went to Hal Maffer, who was surprised to hear from him.

'I thought you people folded your tents and started living the clean life. Glad to see you're still around,' he said cordially. 'I hope you settled that nasty business with Cerberus.'

'No problem with that,' von Baldur lied. He didn't trust Maffer – or anyone else any more than he distrusted him – or anyone else. 'We're doing an excellent business a long, long ways from any of their interests. And we're paying for these hem, tools, up front.'

'That's good,' Maffer said. 'I always like dealing with you people. Keep me in mind if you need any other devices as the situation develops. So what do you need now – and do I deliver?'

'No,' von Baldur said. 'We'll pick up.'

He gave Maffer the shopping list.

Grok and Jasmine had come up with a rather draconian inventory. Since they weren't combat veterans, they'd consulted with M'chel, who certainly was, to see if their logic and theories were too rigid.

She shook her head.

'No. You two are as hard-hearted as a pair of supply sergeants – but you're right. Or, at least, you're not very wrong.'

They'd chosen blast rifles and blasters, ten with clip-on shoulder stocks, for each rifle. Of course a rifle is always more useful than a handgun, but a little hard to conceal, sometimes. At least with the rinky-dink add-on stocks, which have never increased a pistol's usefulness much, these guns would be a bit more lethal.

But not by much. A good rule of thumb with a pistol is to never deploy one unless you can also throw it at your enemy and do damage.

They'd allowed a dozen crew-served weapons, no more. These could be used for ambushes, but there deliberately weren't enough of them to encourage any development of positional warfare.

There was quite a lot of plastic-type malleable explosive, and various sorts of detonators, for ambushes and booby traps.

Finally, there were grenades.

Grenades come in two general types: offensive and defensive. An offensive one can be thrown at the charge, with a small enough exploding radius so the thrower shouldn't have to worry too much about getting caught in his own explosion.

Detonating grenades can be pegged from a nice, safe hole or wall to duck behind.

Again, because they didn't want to encourage their rebels down on Khazia to start thinking they had fortresses, there weren't any defensive bombs provided.

Spada and Goodnight picked up the cargo in the *McMahon* and brought it back to the Maron Regions. Commo went back and forth, code words were arranged, and then the ship took them down to Khazia, rendezvousing with the fishing boats at sea, in the dark of the moons.

All the weapons were safely hidden in the People's district before the sun came up.

A few days later Patson's rabble got themselves stirred up with rhetoric and other, more concrete stimulants, and determined to make a stand for their own beloved streets, by burning down the People's quarter. But this time they'd give the scum a surprise, and since Khazia had fairly strict civilian gun laws, brought a scattering of sporting arms, various stolen weapons, and an assortment of antiques.

The People's district was well barricaded.

The mob, shouting brave slogans of Khazia for the Alsaoud and such, closed on it.

A few bravos with guns thought they saw targets and chanced a round or two.

There was no response until they got within ten meters of the barricades, and then blaster bolts cracked out in volleys. Even given the untrained and excitable aim of the People, thirteen Alsaoud sprawled on the pavement.

The mob fled at lightspeed, trampling another five of their brothers as they went.

Were the People 'normal' rowdies, the next stage would have been police riot squads, the People's retreat back into pretended innocence, and everyone fuming and fretting for the next escalation. Or, conceivably, that might have ended things for a few years.

That was what Star Risk had been depending on. Given that the People were sometimes, as had been noted, 'a bit excitable,' that was not what happened.

The People held firm behind their barricade, even after the mob had fled.

Police riot squads did show up, and advanced rather timidly.

Their armored lifters were charged.

The police opened fire.

The People didn't break and run.

Instead, they opened fire with all weapons, and, screaming their rage, ran on.

The police lifters wheeled and fled as the People were on them.

They hid back at their stations and barracks, claiming to be regrouping.

The People rioted happily that night, burning and destroying anything that looked profitable or inimical. Among the losses were both the reverend Patson's storefront and auditorium. Unfortunately, the reverend was not in them when they burnt.

He, his wife, and brood were able to flee to Tarabula, the system's third world, and vanished from history.

The next day, four of the People's most respected Advisors called on the presidential palace, to discuss and end the troubles.

Walter Nowotny considered the situation absurd. How could a minority, less than a fifth of the population of the city of Helleu, be able to cause such chaos? Utterly preposterous.

He had other problems, such as the pirates or the looming confrontation he would have with Ral Tomkins of Cerberus — and, most likely, his 'mentor' Yarb'ro, to which he was hardly looking forward.

He 'requested' that the Advisors be turned away.

They were — most rudely, with nightsticks — and the People ruled the streets of Helleu for a second night.

Star Risk was almost as upset as Nowotny, impor- tuning Advisor Ganmore to end this madness before the situation got out of hand, and whatever gains they might have gained were lost. Now was the time for negotiation and ultimatums, not more rioting. In the necessary conferring, Star Risk hoped to see another opening in Nowotny's armor, and strike for that.

But the cheery anarchists in the streets weren't lis- tening to their own Advisors, let alone Ganmore in the far-distant Maron Region.

Even out there, a good half of the People thought it was the time to strike against the Alsaoud, and gain what was their due.

Former pirates were now loudly declaring their patriotism, and a vision of having their own worlds again.

Starships were arming, massing, and discussing what had to be done.

The People also had their own sudden visionaries to contend with, that this was the Day of Redemption.

'We have created a hell of a mess,' von Baldur said haplessly to M'chel Riss. 'Do you have any suggestions as to how we can improve things?'

She shook her head, completely blank.

She was a soldier, not a revolutionary.

'We could just bail, and leave Nowotny up to his belly button in shit,' Goodnight said. 'But the bastard might wade out. We'd better tough it out and see what develops.'

It was announced that President Flyver would talk to the people of his system and implore them to calm themselves and be reasonable, and that the Proper Authorities would bring order back, with justice for all.

Being a bit of a grandstander, he said he would make his address from the balcony of the presidential palace, and his most trusted advisors would be with him, System-wide holos would be 'casted.

'You think,' Goodnight said, 'Nowotny'll be dumb enough to show up for that? And maybe we could slip a missile in their laps?'

'I'm truly appalled,' Jasmine King said. 'Do you know how many innocents would die just to take out one man?'

'And besides,' M'chel added, 'there's not a chance Nowotny'll be watching the show from anywhere but a holo screen. He's not a complete dunce.'

Grok just shook his head.

Goodnight even went into bester, and while in battle-analysis mode had von Baldur ask him about the likelihood of Nowotny being there and being vulnerable. He had to listen to his own superbrain tell him he was a romantic dreamer.

But they all decided to watch the show.

It was quite a show, indeed.

The great square in front of the palace was packed. Even a hundred or so People had dared attend, well bodyguarded by young women and men with Star Risk's weaponry.

President Flyver had the most dynamic, inspiring speech of his entire career written.

'We are all common people, of a common blood, and must learn to seek peace for all, and listen to our most secret, most loving hearts. Only then can we—'

He looked away from the screen he was reading from, out over the crowd, annoyed by a sudden, approaching whine that definitely should not have been there.

Five thousand meters overhead, three military starships patrolled, alert for any intrusion from space.

Three hundred meters above the palace, police lifters

loaded with alert marksmen and the best operatives Cerberus had swung back and forth, watching overhead for forbidden aircraft.

A young woman of the People had found her calling.

She had been taking light flying lessons, intending on making a career with her own transcity delivery service. She was considered quite a skilled flier, soloing in a dozen hours.

But now there was something more important than her career.

Something more important than life itself.

She was airborne an hour before the speech was scheduled, orbiting out of Helleu over the ocean, keeping low under any radar screens, eyes flickering from her controls to the holo screen showing the palace.

When Flyver's introduction began, she swung her lifter back toward land, and went to full speed.

She came in over Helleu only fifty meters above the rooftops.

The palace loomed large in front of her.

Flyver looked away from his screen, saw the bulbous nose of the onrushing aircraft, had time to notice a scratch on the nose paint, opened his mouth to scream.

The woman's lifter never wavered, her grip on the controls never shifted, as she sent her aircraft smashing into the center of the presidential balcony.

FORTY-ONE

M'chel never thought the word frozen applied to anything but ice cubes or certain, irregular, states of matter.

She was wrong.

The five members of Star Risk stood motionless, watching the smoke boil out of the president's palace.

The crowd around it was also frozen.

'Let's roll,' Goodnight said suddenly.

'Where?' Grok said, seeming a bit amused by the humans' astonishment.

'Whatever is going to happen will begin in that proximity,' von Baldur said, jerking a thumb at the screen. 'I think better when I am on – or at least close to – the scene.'

'When,' Grok said, definitely amused, 'you bother to think at all.'

But he reached for a com, and called for Redon Spada to stand by the yacht.

The crowd outside the palace recovered slowly, and when they did, they wanted scapegoats.

They found some close at hand – the small contingent of the People. Even better, they were mostly women and children.

With, fortunately, a thin screen of armed men and women.

The guns came out, and the crowd stopped cold.

The People retreated, back through the streets toward their own district.

The Alsaoud started after them.

At that point, the military inadvertently saved the day, swooping down, very late, to see what they could do to save their rather incinerated president.

The crowd didn't know who owned the spaceships that were screaming down on them, and assumed that more diabolical attackers were at work.

They scattered.

The People would have done the same, but there was nowhere to go.

One Alsaoud patrol boat captain, angrier than the others and slightly more collected, snapped a screen into a tight shot of the street, recognized the People by their costumes, assumed they had something to do with the assassination of the freshly elected Flyver, and launched a missile.

It missed by blocks, and destroyed a government office handling consumer affairs.

Then the ship's executive officer jerked his superior out of the launch station, and took over the controls of the p-boat.

For this act of mercy, he was later courtmartialed and reduced two grades.

Across Alsaoud, alarms were gonging the military to full alert.

Someone had killed their leader, and they were going to seek revenge.

As of yet, they didn't know on whom, but it had to be somebody.

*

Someone came on the official government com frequency and announced that Prime Minister Toorman would be taking over the government until the 'situation clarified and elections can be held.'

Star Risk had reached their yacht, and Spada had trapped the 'cast.

Goodnight started laughing.

'Ho-ho, with Toorman in charge, that'll mean Nowotny is eating several meters of boiled shit.'

Of them all, he and Grok were the least disturbed.

In Grok, that was easy to understand.

But M'chel puzzled over Goodnight, unable to decide whether he was simply used to dealing with the unsettling because of his background in special operations.

She preferred that thought to its alternative – that Chas Goodnight was just an utterly cold-blooded son of a one.

There was a real, armed enemy – even if they weren't shooting yet.

The freebooters of the People entered the Alsaoud System at battle stations.

Even though the People weren't in any sort of battle formation, the Alsaoud ships met them.

Someone – no one ever knew who or on which side – touched off a missile, and fire was returned.

Ships swirled through space around Khazia, firing on anyone they thought was unfriendly. Frequently these were on their own side, warships that either didn't respond as expected or were just late on the password.

It was nonsensical, but it was bloody.

Walter Nowotny hoped his flopsweat wasn't showing on his face as he bowed deeply to Premier Toorman.

'Of course, Cerberus Systems extends the same contract to you as to the late President.

'We merely struck our deal with President Flyver because he was the head of the government and of the same party as his predecessor, with whom the original contract was drawn up, and it will be our privilege to give you the same kind of aid as before.'

Nowotny couldn't have known, but Toorman's twitch had worsened since he took over the government.

'That . . . that is good,' Toorman said. 'I haven't had time to review your contract, but I must assume that everything is in order and we shall have an excellent working relationship.'

'I'm sure we shall,' Nowotny said, thinking if we don't, we will with the new man.

He was still waiting for a reaction, some kind of reaction, from Ral Tomkins.

FORTY-TWO

But whatever arrangements Cerberus had made with Flyver, either they hadn't carried down to the Alsaoud fleet yet, or else in the general excitement, their Fleet Admiral, an intensely political sort named Poel, had forgotten them.

It was an interesting sort of mess.

Since Poel hadn't survived the event, he'd evidently decided that the motlies of the People could be easily wiped out, or shoveled out of the system, and so hadn't had much of a coherent strategy going in.

His crumbling excuse for a strategy wasn't helped by the problem the Alsaoud had with the fleet itself.

Huge, sprawling battleships go in and out of style, depending on how removed from reality the admirals are, and how easily overawed the fools who pay for the defense budget are.

Friedrich von Baldur was one of the few experienced combat leaders who loved battlewagons.

Of course, his adoration had less to do with their combat handiness — which was marginal at the best of times — or their efficiency, which had always been non-existent.

He loved them for their size, for the enormity of their admirals' quarters, the number of cooks that the officers' mess would accommodate, and other non-battle perks.

Why the Alsaoud loved them was never known, but their fleet consisted of some twenty superheavies, bought from various mothball yards for their size and beauty.

No one worried about how reliable these vessels were, so long as they were sleek and striking.

After all, Alsaoud hadn't fought any sort of fleet battle for two hundred years.

Their navy was not only rank-heavy and -happy, but the enlisted man's condition was accurately, if vulgarly, described by Goodnight as 'sucking hind tit.'

Their quarters were cramped, their food was marginal, their discipline was draconian – but by the gods, their uniforms were gorgeous.

Needless to say, there weren't long lines in front of the recruiting booths, and so the Alsaoud had instituted conscription, which didn't make service in the military any more popular.

Yet another problem was that these battleships, frequently maintenance queens, kept the Alsaoud from being able to afford the proper number of escorts for a rational fleet.

So the fleet, instead of being somewhat pyramidal in construct – one battleship, two cruisers, ten destroyers, twenty patrol boats, thirty logistical ships, as it might have been – was, roughly, one dreadnought to three or four destroyers and an equivalent number of supply ships.

This was not good.

But it didn't stop Admiral Poel from charging into the heart of the Maron Region and its myriad asteroids.

The marauders from the Maron Regions, many of whom weren't People, but out-system bandit sorts, may have nobly flashed into the Alsaoud System looking to save any beleaguered People, not to mention any loot left lying about. But they were hardly fools, being very aware that a good big man beats hell out of a good little man a hundred times out of a hundred.

And the Alsaoud dreadnoughts appeared to be good *huge* men.

So the intruders decided the hell with the ground-pounding People, they could fend for themselves. And they went, precipitately, back the way they'd come.

One raider, which had been rather hastily set up for space-worthiness, wasn't, and one drive chamber, already pitted, blew out through the side of the ship, fortunately taking only one wiper and one assistant engineer with it.

But it left the ship pinwheeling in an obnoxious and helpless orbit, and under observation by the officers of one battleship. Its officers grinned tightly, and bore in for the kill.

The pirate's commanders may have been a bit less than competent at combat-worthiness, but were evidently excellent at making friends and alliances.

Two destroyer-sized pirates, who'd operated with that raider before, heard its bleats for help, and, amazingly for warriors for profit, came back to assist.

The Alsaoud battleship was as intent on its prey as any spider closing on a small fly, and didn't 'see' the other two ships from the Maron Region until they were within a light-year and had launched four missiles each.

The battleship's countermeasure officer yammered orders, arms windmilling, to launch AA missiles. Three were spat out in time, but without much guidance, and all eight incoming missiles blew the battleship into three separate pieces, all of which began screaming for rescue.

Other raiders and ships of the People heard the

screeches, observed the situation thoughtfully, and wondered if maybe the Alsaoud fleet wasn't a bit long on bluster and short on bombardment.

A scattering of them turned back just as the Alsaoud fleet entered the Maron Region, and within minutes met incoming missiles.

The 'battle,' which hadn't been much so far, had lasted two E-days since Poel had gone to war.

Space was alive with the slash of missiles and wounded or dying ships.

The Alsaoud lost eight more ships, two destroyed, three crippled, all battleships, before they set emergency orbits back toward home.

The People and the pirates boarded the crippled vessels, looking for anything from spendable loot to lootable weapons to surviving officers whose relatives might pay a ransom.

It was, by pirate standards at least, a famous victory, and the Alsaoud System went into shock as reports trickled into the media, in spite of Cerberus and Toorman's best censorship, and they realized how badly they'd been hammered by nothing better than thieves and thugs.

Worse, there didn't appear to be anything much between the Maron Region's monsters, and invasion, murder, rape, and looting.

Even Star Risk, from a vantage point 'below' the Alsaoud System's ecliptic, were shocked.

Von Baldur's most astute comment was an incoherent 'well, well, well,' to M'chel's question about what they should do next.

She growled, and told Goodnight to put himself into bester and give her an analysis.

The best that Chas's unconscious could provide was 'Insufficient data for an accurate prognosis.'

'Awright,' Riss growled. 'So we can't do much of anything until Cerberus shows us how it's gonna step on its dick and we can take advantage.

'So let's us go recruit us some goons to do a proper job of it.'

FORTY-THREE

Ral Tomkins had finally gotten the word — or, more likely, had figured out he'd best respond to it.

The manner of his response froze the air of the conference room on Alegria 87's capital world.

'We cannot allow these marauders to get away with their depredations,' Tomkins said, his voice leaking cold power.

'Why not?' Yarb'ro asked mildly. 'It's only a defeat if we acknowledge it to be.'

'What are we supposed to do,' Tomkins growled. 'Shrug and move on?'

'Why not?'

'Because we will have been embarrassed in the eyes of the Alliance!'

'So?' Yarb'ro asked. 'It wouldn't be the first time.'

'Maybe in your day things like this disaster were meaningless. But not now. Not in the world we live in these days.'

'Pfoh!' Yarb'ro said. 'Things that are not immediately in front of us can safely be ignored. Or, if you're particularly concerned, we can have some word-pusher make up some kind of story that we've suddenly discovered everyone in the Alsaoud System has pellagra, and we're doing the Alliance a favor by pulling out.'

'No,' Tomkins said firmly. 'It's no longer that simple. And you *would* make a suggestion like that, considering it's your protégé who's responsible.'

'I suggested Nowotny because he's done a superior job in other assignments, no more. I'm hardly sleeping with him,' Yarb'ro said. 'If it makes you happy, replace him. I have no particular concern one way or the other.'

'With whom?' one of the other board members asked wryly. He nodded at one of the wall screens, with Nowotny's report on it. 'You'll hardly get one of our best and brightest to volunteer to oversee this disaster.'

There were mutters of agreement, a wry smile here and there.

'True,' Yarb'ro said. 'But perhaps, Mr. Tomkins, you have a replacement in mind?'

Tomkins glowered at Yarb'ro, then reluctantly shook his head.

'So, setting aside all of the screaming and yelling you'd planned,' Yarb'ro went on, 'taking the tantrum as a given, if it pleases you, what, specifically, are we going to do next, assuming you discard my suggestion of abandoning the project, and finding another way to ennoble ourselves in the eyes of the Alliance.'

'We *must* win in the Alsaoud System,' Tomkins declared, as if it were a given.

'Very well,' Yarb'ro said equably. 'How?'

'Very simply,' Tomkins said. 'We must intensify our efforts against these bandits until they're either wiped out, or flee to other systems.'

Yarb'ro didn't respond, but sat, clearly awaiting the new grand strategy.

'I shall order Nowotny to recruit new, outside strength,' Tomkins said. 'The billing will be sent to the Alsaoud System. We won't need to endanger more of our own resources. With more forces in place, victory shall be close at hand.'

Tomkins looked around at the various screens and the four directors actually present.

There were no heretics present. He got nods of assent, a few mutters of agreement.

'And what do you find so funny?' he demanded of Yarb'ro.

The slight smile didn't vanish from Yarb'ro's face.

'Nothing,' he said. 'Nothing at all. You are the chairman – and you clearly have the votes.

'Make your charge.'

Tomkins stared at Yarb'ro, who refused to drop his gaze. Tomkins was the first to look away.

FORTY-FOUR

Friedrich von Baldur considered the image of Walter Nowotny as he strolled, unaware of being recorded, through the palace gardens. He turned to the other Star Risk members.

'You know,' Goodnight said, 'if we weren't still playing invisible, it might be interesting to do a nice solo run into Khazia and relocate Mynheer Nowotny to a different level of existence.'

Von Baldur ignored the suggestion.

'What am I supposed to deduce, class, from seeing our Walter still perambulating about town?'

Jasmine and Grok looked at each other.

'Obviously,' she said, 'the bastard is still on the job. Damn it.'

'Obviously,' von Baldur agreed. 'What else?'

'Possibly,' Grok said, 'that the Cerberus strategy, such as it is, continues the same, which means he won't be replaced. They're going to hammer on, regardless.'

Von Baldur lifted an eyebrow, turned to Goodnight.

'I don't need to go into battle-analysis mode,' Chas said, 'to figure that conclusion isn't necessarily justified by the facts we have.'

'No,' Riss said. 'But to keep on keeping on is pretty much the way Cerberus thinks.'

'Not thinks,' Grok corrected. 'Reacts. Thinking has little to do with it. That was one reason I left their employ.'

'If they continue their present course,' von Baldur said, 'that would mean they'll be bringing in more and better troops, since we have beaten their flunkies and pet stooges hollow.'

'Which means hiring, since they aren't real fond of bleeding their own blood if they don't have to,' Goodnight said. 'So we'd better do the same.'

'We lack only one thing,' M'chel said. 'The geetus.'

Von Baldur sighed.

'We *are* a little short in the cash department at present. That last cargo has been just about spent.'

'So let's go back and do the same again,' Goodnight said. 'Why fiddle with success?'

'Will anyone be thick enough to run more ships through this sector,' von Baldur wondered aloud, 'especially since we beat them last time around?'

'Now, none of us know the answer to that,' Riss said. 'You might want to light your little torch, Diogenes, and go looking for some truth.'

'I might at that,' von Baldur said. 'I shall report back.'

He called Star Risk together a day later, quite happy.

'Yes indeed, they are trying again. This time on the convoy plan. Which I happen to have acquired the details on from – hem, hem – *friends*, at a fairly reasonable price. They are dispatching seven ships, with five escorts. This will likely mean emergency, which means exceptionally valuable cargoes.'

He ignored M'chel's inadvertent 'Yum.'

'I have already secured ten of our allies to go ahunting with us,' von Baldur continued.

'And to take a seventy-five-twenty-five split in the matter.'

'You silver-tongued devil,' Goodnight said with admiration.

'I am, am I not?'

It was an interesting action. The convoy's five escorts were all hired guns, which meant they had a very fine regard for casualties, especially their own.

Star Risk, having the advantage of von Baldur's intelligence, knew to the moment when the convoy was scheduled to leave n-space and set up for its next jump beyond the Alsaoud System.

So they were waiting.

It was almost as if the raiders had managed to find and attack in hyperspace, a near impossibility.

Nevertheless, the convoy escorts swore that was exactly what happened. Their sensors reported launches from everywhere, and ten ships appeared onscreen.

The first escort to blip into reality was met with a pair of missiles, completely destroying the ship.

The second had its stern blown off, and it went spinning off into inconsequentia. Its crew later claimed they'd fought off two raiders with close-range missiles and chain guns, which no one believed, since there's never been a pirate so mad that he lusts after warships instead of fat merchantmen.

One other escort was hit in the midsection, and, leaking air and courage, went back into n-space, bleating for help.

The merchant captains, not particularly foolish, immediately began flashing the interstellar code for 'Need Assistance,' which in this case meant surrender.

The raiders took no casualties, which, together with

the rich cargoes brought back to the Maron Regions, produced still greater status for Star Risk.

'Now,' von Baldur said, looking at the screen that showed the transfer of gelders from Advisor Ganmore, '*now* we can go hiring ourselves some allies.'

He started to lick his lips, saw M'chel watching him, and stopped himself in time.

FORTY-FIVE

And so Star Risk went back to Boyington, the haven and employment hall for mercenary pilots, ship crew and starship maintenance experts.

Since Star Risk was still an anonymous enemy to Cerberus, at least as far as they knew, Redon Spada went as the front man with M'chel Riss as invisible backup, at least until they saw how things floated.

They slid onto the planet quietly and booked into the Bishop Inn, where the pilots hung their helmets.

Just as quietly, they found themselves sharing a bed again, but both of them systematically denied to themselves that it was anything more than a way of keeping the four a.m. mournfuls away.

Boyington itself was fairly quiet when they arrived — a decent-sized war between a couple of clusters had siphoned off a lot of the availables.

'There's another reason to get pissed at Cerberus,' Riss said. 'If it hadn't of been for them, we might be able to get involved in that fracas and make some serious money.'

'I've heard it's getting nasty over there,' Spada pointed out. 'You could also get yourself dead.'

'Not me,' M'chel said. 'I'm immortal.'

'Of course,' Spada agreed. 'How *could* I have forgotten.'

Riss threw a pillow at him.

Things got a bit unquiet as ships and men suddenly streamed onto Boyington from nowhere.

They wore a common uniform, in a motley of repairs, and most of their ships had the same insignia. A few had hastily spot-anodized the markings over.

Spada inquired.

It was a mournful story.

They represented the last trickle of a defeated fleet, and a vanquished planetary system.

'Typical,' Spada reported to M'chel. 'Exploited, without rights or representation, valiant rebellion against all odds, the brave little guys with truth and justice on their sides—'

'And they got their butts beat,' Riss interrupted.

Spada nodded.

'As I said, typical. But with a bit of a difference,' Redon continued. 'After the surrender, their fleet was ordered to report to a certain world, and their crews scheduled for, quote, *retraining*, end quote.

'The admirals, being the subservient types who always get promoted and the bridge of battleships, obeyed. Their ships got sold as scrap and they're planting p'raties in some paddy somewhere.

'These that we've got here on Boyington said screw that for a lark, and took off. Now they're looking for someone to pay their rent, and mourning about never being able to go home.'

'Exiles make crappy fighters for anybody except The Cause,' M'chel said cynically. 'But have a gander at them.'

Spada reported back in a couple of days.

Riss had occupied herself with reading an abandoned

and very thick treatise on mathematics as a sixth-dimension construct, and trying to teach herself how to do light-sensitive nails.

By the time Spada came back, she'd failed at one, and discarded the book as simplistic.

'You were right,' he said. 'They're still too busy feeling sorry for themselves to be battle-worthy. But I gave them my card. In a year or so, we'll see.'

'Oh, well,' M'chel said. 'There's others.'

There were, and these looked very unprepossessing.

But Spada — and Star Risk — knew what they were looking for.

These were the singletons, uniforms of whatever army they'd originally belonged to abandoned long since, as well as six or seven others for whom they'd fought after going freelance.

Riss felt braver now, and chanced going out interviewing with Redon. They did this carefully, looking for things most recruiters didn't: what shape their possible hires' ships were in; how well-kept their maintenance records were; the state of their electronics, particularly fire control systems; the quality of their messes.

And, most importantly, the 'feel' of a ship or team — how well the men responded; how many of them looked happy; how many officers knew the names of the women or men in their sections.

Democracy, even though this was fairly common among mercenaries, wasn't important — there were troops who seemed perfectly content under a jackboot.

Star Risk signed up a dozen ships, and then some two hundred-odd maintenance specialists.

Riss still had pots of money left over. Or so she thought for the moment.

Enough so that Spada chanced talking to some people he'd admired from afar.

They called themselves Rasmussen's Raiders. Their CO wasn't Rasmussen, but his former XO, a lean, hatchet-faced man named Caldwell.

Rasmussen had gotten himself dead a half dozen wars ago.

For some obscure reason having to do with unit morale and a sense of history, Riss thought more of them for not having renamed themselves Caldwell's Crew or Cacophony or anything like that.

And they were sharp.

They called themselves a wing, but were slightly overstrength for an equivalent Alliance unit. Their ships were just off state-of-the-art for the Alliance, which of course never sold off their best and most current. Their heavies were a pair of cruisers, another heavier cruiser that had been stripped of some of its armament and converted into a Command & Control ship, a dozen heavy destroyers, some eighteen patrol ships and a dozen logistical craft, plus a pair of very large hangar ships.

All were fully manned, and the women and men of the Raiders wore snappy uniforms of tan and deep blue and were sharp, sharp, sharp.

'I don't know,' Riss said when Spada proposed the Raiders to her. 'We need sneaky slobs, not parade sorts.'

Spada handed her a fiche, and she ran it through a viewer.

She came away somewhat impressed. They'd been on the winning side in four of their last five contracts, which was very rare for mercenaries, who were far more used to fighting for the losing underdog.

'They don't seem to have got in any knock-down drag-outs lately,' she said. 'Not, anyway, since the one that got Rasmussen killed.'

Spada just looked at her.

'Awright,' she surrendered. 'We're not supposed to be wading through blood up to our belly buttons if we can find a way around it.

'Let's go talk to them.'

Riss was impressed that Caldwell, who gave himself the fairly unegotistical title of Commander, had heard of Alsaoud, and had a vague idea of what the problem was.

She was also impressed with the grand tour he gave her and Spada. Caldwell seemed to have no secrets to hide.

Everything was fine, until after a fine meal aboard the C&C ship, they sat down to negotiate.

Riss had refused the wine with the meal, as had Caldwell and his executive officer. Spada allowed himself a single glass.

'What, exactly, would our duties be?' Caldwell inquired.

'Perimeter support around the asteroids our clients control. Raiding into the Alsaoud System. Seizing merchant ships on occasion — nothing in violation of Standard Wartime Practices,' Riss said. 'Support in isolating and controlling the system's home worlds.

'We do not anticipate needing your unit in a physical invasion of any world. We hope to be able to settle the matter without getting into a brawl,' she said.

'That's a relief,' Caldwell said. 'Invasions get expensive, in every sense of the word.'

'One problem I see,' the XO said, 'is making implacable foes of Cerberus Systems. They're very big — and frequently are tied in with even bigger sorts. Not good enemies to casually collect.'

'We don't anticipate matters getting nasty enough for Cerberus to be making a list of everyone with us, and the People,' Riss said. 'Once they've taken a few more defeats, they should get out.'

She didn't mention the state of utter hatred between Star Risk and Cerberus – as she'd said, she didn't think matters would get that brutal. She also hadn't used the name Star Risk at any time.

'The prospect is interesting,' Caldwell said. 'Especially, given your victory, that interesting reparations could be demanded.'

Riss didn't say anything. One of Star Risk's policies was never to grind victory in – although on Cerberus, if not Alsaoud, they were willing to make an exception. But talk of things like that lay well in the future.

Caldwell considered, scribbled a figure on a bit of paper, showed it to his executive, who nodded.

He named the price.

Riss was glad she didn't have a mouthful of anything, as she might have choked.

'You *are* expensive,' Spada said, in a completely neutral voice.

'But well worth it,' the executive officer said. 'And we don't waste your time or ours by haggling.'

That definitely settled that – the named price was about double Riss's remaining resources.

She made polite noises about having to consult with her principals, thanking them for the dinner and the dog and pony show, and she and Spada left, somewhat shaken.

Caldwell waited until the pair had cleared the flagship, then touched an unobtrusive stud.

'Yes, sir?'

'Did you have any problems?'

'Negative, sir. All images turned out perfectly.'

FORTY-SIX

Walter Nowotny, even though he was an experienced gambler with a good poker face, blinked at the size of the figure that Commander Caldwell had mentioned.

'Your services are quite steep,' he said.

'True,' Caldwell agreed. 'But well worth the price. I will also mention that Rasmussen's Raiders will provide an additional most valuable service, gratis.

'If a deal is struck.'

A smile twisted Nowotny's scarred face.

'Cerberus is not accustomed to making any arrangements on the if-come system,' he said in his eerie near-whisper.

'We don't expect you to,' Caldwell said. 'In fact, we'll offer a proposition: We shall present our service right now. And if Cerberus still declines our offer – well, then, so be it.'

Since Nowotny was sitting in a conference room aboard Rasmussen's C&C ship, he assumed, correctly, that everything was being recorded.

Caldwell didn't need to add that if Cerberus reneged on the deal after making it, they would have a certain amount of trouble in the future making arrangements with other firms, even in the most amoral world of the mercenaries.

'I know,' Caldwell said, sweetening the deal, 'that Cerberus is, shall we say, swinging gently in the wind here in the Alsaoud System.

'My information will significantly load the odds in your favor.'

Nowotny was intensely curious. Not to mention that he knew very well that Ral Tomkins, his boss, was sharpening a dagger that even Yarb'ro couldn't keep out of Nowotny's back forever.

He needed any help he could get to get back in Tomkins's graces, and quickly figured that, even if this information was fairly specious, he could still use Caldwell's unit in the worsening situation. Not to mention that if Caldwell was playing games, there would be a terrible revenge taken at the first convenient opportunity.

'Very well,' Nowotny said. 'We have a tentative arrangement. Now, can we go into the details of this ever-so-valuable intelligence?'

'There is nothing to discuss,' Caldwell said. 'I'll give it to you right now.'

He reached in a drawer of the cabinet behind him, took out a burnvelope, put his finger on the pore-pattern tab, and the envelope opened.

He took out a hologram, gave it to Nowotny.

This time the Cerberus executive actually hissed an intake of breath.

The holo, of course, showed M'chel Riss and Redon Spada sitting where Nowotny currently was.

'Since Cerberus clearly has had no idea who its main opponents here happen to be, I thought this might be of interest, considering Cerberus's known dislike of the firm formerly known as Star Risk,' Caldwell said. 'The holo was taken within the week, when these two attempted to hire Rasmussen's Raiders.'

Nowotny was staring at the holo.

A thin smile came, stayed on his face.

'Yes indeed,' he said softly. 'Your information will be most useful indeed.'

'It seems to be posted across half the galaxy,' Jasmine said. 'On every channel that might conceivably have an interest in us, including Alliance open intelligence postings.'

Star Risk collectively stared at the printout:

Reward

There were six thumbnail pictures below the screamer, of the members of Star Risk plus Spada. Below them, the legend:

Dangerous armed dissidents, not to be approached without caution. Wanted for various crimes against the public interest.

'Cheap bastards,' Goodnight said. 'They don't even name the size of the reward. Hard to brag on having a price on your head when you can't put a figure to it.

'And I've taken a much sexier shot before.'

'Where did they get the information about us?' von Baldur wondered. 'We knew it was going to get out sooner or later, but . . .'

'It must've come from either a snitch here in the system,' M'chel said. 'Or, since Redon's on the poster, maybe when we were on Boyington?'

She examined the poster more closely.

'Boyington,' she said. 'That was the tunic I was wearing.'

'Let me simplify your reasoning, O Sherlock,' Grok

said. 'Cerberus has just hired an organization named Rasmussen's Raiders.

'Which report said you two had interviewed.'

'Those bastards!' Riss said. 'I'll have their guts for a winding sheet. Whatever a goddamned winding sheet is.'

'Ah,' Friedrich mourned. 'This is truly an age of immorality and distrust.'

Two days later, Jasmine brought Riss another poster. This read:

WANTED
$1,000,000
Alliance Credits
or equivalent
No questions asked

Below that was a picture of Walter Nowotny.
Below that:

For war crimes, including murder,
attempted genocide, bribery and
coercion of public officials, and being
ugly in a public place

'The image is one we took with one of our cameras inside the palace,' Jasmine explained. 'We dodged the background out since we think Nowotny doesn't need to know about them at the moment.'

'Wish they were bombs,' Riss muttered. 'I notice we put a price tag on Walter's head. If somebody wants to collect, where'll we get the credits?'

'We shall worry about that when it happens,' King said, a bit loftily.

'Also, there's that bit about being ugly in a public place,' M'chel said. 'I assume Chas came up with the copy?'

She was fairly sure Jasmine hadn't, since she wasn't particularly impressed with the depth of her sense of humor.

'Actually, no,' King said. 'It was Grok.'

'Grok?' M'chel asked in an incredulous tone.

'Grok,' Jasmine said. 'He has depths.'

'He does indeed,' Riss said. 'Now, we'll see if this shakes Walter's little equanimity enough to make him do something stupid.'

'We can hope,' King agreed. 'But if nothing else, it makes me feel better for the moment.'

FORTY-SEVEN

'I am most pleased,' Ral Tomkins announced. He'd assembled Cerberus's entire board in person for this announcement. Or almost all of them. Yarb'ro was conspicuous by his presence only on a com.

'We now have terror by the throat.'

On cue, the reward poster for Star Risk flashed on a wall-sized screen behind him.

'Thanks to some selfless citizens of the Alliance, we now know who these thugs and pirates are who've been striking terror into the hearts of the innocents of the Alsaoud System – none other than the goons who dubbed themselves Star Risk. Now that they have been identified, their eradication is a certainty, and without them masterminding the terror campaign of these self-styled People, victory will be immediately at hand.'

He waited for applause, frowned slightly when none showed itself, and continued:

'To make our task easier, not only have I increased the size of our forces assigned to the Alsaoud System and the space surrounding it, but this day I was also successful in having assigned to us the 441st Signal Intelligence Detachment of the Alliance Navy, to enable us to narrow Star Risk's location, and then to deal with them as harshly as they deserve.'

This time, after Tomkins's frown-around, there was a spatter of 'here, heres,' tapping of knuckles against real wood, and a few gentle claps.

Tomkins smiled.

'The thing that amazes me,' Yarb'ro's dry voice came, 'is that I think you've been reading your own press releases long enough to believe the crap you're spouting.'

Tomkins reddened, started to reply. But Yarb'ro continued.

'There is nothing wrong with such drivel for the masses who generally believe it,' Yarb'ro continued. 'But not to us, and most of all not to yourself.

'Realize something, Tomkins. There is no difference, save in size, between Cerberus and Star Risk, nor in our evident intentions: to bring Alsaoud under our hegemony, and thereby increase our profits.

'So please don't bore us with any of this terror by the throat shit that you've been burbling.'

Yarb'ro realized he was burning every conceivable bridge that might end the feud between him and Tomkins, but he no longer cared. An hour earlier, a com from Nowotny had made it very clear that his former pupil had now firmly cast his lot with Tomkins. Yarb'ro was feeling very alone.

'As I've said before,' he went on, 'I think Cerberus is getting overly involved in the Alsaoud worlds, and now we've hung our intentions out to dry, to mix a metaphor, with the Alliance, and by borrowing this SigInt unit.

'For what end? So a government, which we must realize loves only itself, will think well of us, when we operate by the same self-interest? How absurd.

'I think this is foolishness, and dangerous as well. And I now introduce a measure of censure against our chairman, Ral Tomkins, and further direct him to end all involvements in the Alsaoud worlds, and to cancel this request to the Alliance.'

He waited.

There was utter silence.

No second for his motion, not even a request for debate.

Cerberus's board thoroughly approved of the course chosen.

Yarb'ro slumped in defeat, and his screen blanked.

Ral Tomkins smiled, tightly.

FORTY-EIGHT

The explosion came exactly sixty seconds after Yarb'ro turned on the burners of his old-fashioned natural-gas-powered stove.

The man fancied himself a gourmet cook, and had studied the cuisine of half a hundred worlds in his assignments, first for Alliance Intelligence and then Cerberus.

He was a real rarity – a man who was just as happy cooking for just himself as for a party of twenty.

Yarb'ro was studying the dish he was making for the first time, Sung-tzu-chi-ssu. He had toasted his pine nuts with a bit of salt and thyme, and was getting ready to brown the chicken with the habanero peppers, sitting in its marinade.

There was a very slight click.

Yarb'ro's stove did not normally click.

He dove behind a butcher block table as the stove blew up.

The fire flashed over him, but he was barely burned The blast did most of the damage, shattering his left leg and arm.

The fire department rescued him and put out the flames before his mansion could ignite, but his kitchen was gutted, and his huge collection of cookbooks, fiches, and files was a dead loss.

Official investigation blamed the explosion on an 'industrial accident.'

Yarb'ro, painfully recuperating, knew better.

FORTY-NINE

The 441st Signal Intelligence outfit arrived in the Alsaoud System fairly unobtrusively, at least for an Alliance unit.

Fortunately for them, they were organized as an independent, space-based detachment, with a dumbbell-shaped artificial satellite and a pair of obsolescent destroyers to guard against interlopers.

That kept them a ways away from the roiling chaos of Khazia.

Being professionals, they went immediately to work.

They'd handled harder jobs.

The main code the People used had begun life as a commercial cipher. One of the People's computer sorts had put a scramble on that cipher, then a further scramble.

The end result was more than enough to keep Alsaoud in the dark.

But not enough for the Alliance.

While their computers were ticketing away at the task, their signal analysis specialists were working away.

The main com bands used by the People's ships were quickly found, and even though they couldn't be read yet, their transmissions were logged.

A third and fourth destroyer hung above the Maron

Region and monitored outgoing coms that were evident responses to the People's ship transmissions.

That gave them a possible location for the People's headquarters.

That information went to Walter Nowotny.

His second in command wanted to launch on the data they had.

'No,' Nowotny said. 'Not 'til we're sure. We'll most likely have just the one chance.'

Walter Nowotny was a careful man.

Three local days later, the 441st broke the People's code and confirmed that the signals going into the Maron Region included requests for instructions.

The transmissions out were orders.

That gave Nowotny confirmation for the probable location for the People's high command, which must include Star Risk.

In the interim, Star Risk itself had a break – or, more correctly, a solid analysis of data.

The People's agents on Khazia had reported an increase in supplies being sent offworld.

The supplies were interesting – support items for various electronics, plus food and other items not commonly used by Alsaoud natives.

Star Risk found this interesting, and drew the obvious conclusion – that there was a new player in the game.

Grok began breadboarding circuitry, and installing what he'd rigged in Star Risk's yacht, much to von Baldur's displeasure as he saw rich real wood paneling and carpets being ripped out to be replaced by utilitarian plas and little wireless transmission points.

Nowotny decided he had enough for a strike.

A pair of Rasmussen's best patrol boats were slaved to a light transport, and the ensuing lump sent on a jump out of the system, then a second blind jump to make sure they weren't tracked, then a return to the navpoint just outside the Alsaoud System, close to the Maron Regions.

The transport that had carried the patrol boat crew members in relative comfort within range of the target was parked in an orbit well out of anyone's way, after the crews were transferred back to their ships.

The patrol boats went in, jumping into the Maron Regions, then taking a high, looping orbit to where those commands had originated, which could only be the People's High Command.

The ships were detected, and destroyers were launched against them, too late.

Each patrol boat launched a pair of heavy missiles, set to home on the command source.

Then they fled back to where the transport waited.

One of them made it; the other was tracked and destroyed by one of the People's strike craft.

Radar picked up the incoming missiles, and launched countermissiles against them.

Only one was destroyed.

All three of the others impacted and blew up within half a kilometer of those outgoing transmissions.

The com channels blurped static, then went ominously silent.

Walter Nowotny was monitoring the mission, and for a brief moment, rejoiced that he – Cerberus – had finally rid themselves of that damned Star Risk.

But within hours, the command transmissions began once more, from another, unlocated spot within the Maron Regions.

Star Risk had tried to get the People to change – and keep on changing – their code and the com channels, but without success.

But at least they'd been able to convince the People's leaders (such as they were in that fairly anarchic society) that all transmissions should be remoted.

So Rasmussen's Raiders only blew up a quadrangle of 'cast towers, and they were the last set of three.

Star Risk was also careful.

It would be their turn to strike next.

FIFTY

'What we have is an intelligence triumph,' Grok announced.

'Yeah?' M'chel asked, a bit suspiciously.

The team was gathered around the remains of a late meal.

'We have located the unit that was responsible for sending that missile after us,' he said.

'Very good,' Friedrich said. He poured wine for all of them.

'Not only do we know where it is — sitting out in deep space, just waiting for a hit,' Grok went on, 'but we have a positive ID. It is the 441st Signal Intelligence Detachment.'

'Out-flipping-standing,' Goodnight said. 'I call that good snooping.'

'Actually,' Jasmine said, a bit sheepishly, 'once we found out where it was, it was simple to backtrack to the Alsaoud military post office handling its mail. And then to have one of the People's agents down on Khazia bribe a clerk to give us a couple of pieces of their mail and descramble the cover on the address.'

Grok ducked his head, which the others decided meant he was sorry he'd been so boastful. Maybe.

'Still,' Riss said. 'Very damned good.'

'So now it's payback time,' Chas said, not quite licking his lips.

'Maybe,' Friedrich said, his voice suddenly gloomy. 'And maybe not. The 441st. From where? Or, rather, belonging to whom?'

'The Alliance, of course,' Grok said. 'Cerberus, as we've already concluded, has some friends in very high places.'

'Oh, hells,' von Baldur said.

'Why the piss-off?' Goodnight wondered.

'We aren't going to hit any mainline Alliance unit,' M'chel said. 'We've got enough troubles right now.'

'Why the hell not?' Goodnight asked.

'Because, my simpleminded friend,' Riss said, 'if we go blow up these electric spooks, we're on the Alliance's shit list. And it won't matter if we use cutouts for the operation – frigging Cerberus will make sure the tail is pinned to the donkey, whatever the hell a donkey is.'

'They *will* hunt us after that,' von Baldur agreed.

'So?' Goodnight wondered. 'I've been on the Alliance's hot list for a while now, and I'm still footloose and fancy free.'

'You're one man, with only what, a lousy murder rap on you?' Riss said patiently. 'There's five of us – and putting a whole unit blippo will make us a lot hotter than you've ever thought of being.'

Goodnight glowered around at the other four.

Grok also didn't seem worried by the prospect of Alliance revenge. He bared his fangs at the others and emitted what he thought was a disgusted growl. It merely sounded homicidal.

'So now we've got this hot skinny – and there's zip-burp we can do with it?' Goodnight said. 'We're just gonna duck and cover?'

'Not forever,' von Baldur said. 'But we are certainly

not going to do a death ride of the battle cruisers against this 441st until we can clarify matters somewhat. And a little generic hammering might be in order.'

Goodnight worked his lips and suddenly stood.

'This is about a royal piss-off,' he announced. 'Just beating up the nearest bad guy around isn't going to relieve my high blood pressure. If there's nothing *we're* going to do but sit and wait for Cerberus to try again, *I'm* going to do something.'

'Such as?' M'chel asked.

'I'm going to kill me a Walter Nowotny.'

FIFTY-ONE

So, while Chas Goodnight vanished into obscurity for a time, or so he hoped, together with a goodly assortment of tools of mayhem, the rest of Star Risk went looking for some blood and thunder.

It didn't take long to find it.

The People's always-anarchic High Command, for want of a weaker word, decided it was time to take the war home to the Alsaoud.

After a great deal of back-and-forthing, the People decided to level the planet of Mardite, the fourth world of the system, from the air. All spaceships and aircraft would be blown out of the skies or destroyed at their fields, and all known government institutions would be obliterated. The People intended no particular harm to the civilians of Alsaoud, but if they happened to get in the way . . . life was tough.

Naturally, the People's plans had to be discussed at great length by everyone from squadron commanders to ship commanders to engine room wipers, a fair percentage of them freelancers.

Equally naturally, the existence of these plans leaked like a sieve.

Even more naturally, Star Risk — or rather, Grok and Jasmine — learned that Alsaoud, which meant

Cerberus, was most familiar with the People's schemes.

Suggestions that their beautifully laid, if a little roundheeled, strategy should be aborted were sneered at by the People.

'Oh well. That at least should give us an opportunity to wreak a little havoc,' von Baldur said. 'And perhaps suggest to our friends that sometimes papa knows best.'

'I assume you have some sort of scheme afoot,' Redon Spada said. 'How will we keep Cerberus from learning about that, too, when the People blab it all over hell's landscape?'

'Very simple,' M'chel said, smugly, having figured out von Baldur's intent. 'We just won't tell them.'

And so it was.

Spada put the mercenaries Star Risk had hired on Boyington on alert. He'd asked Jasmine if she felt competent to pilot her own ship on the raid, but she hid a shudder, remembering the not very distant past and politely told him 'Not yet.' She'd rather ride along as Grok's copilot.

Spada also arranged for missile packets to be prepared for each of their ships. These were five heavy shipkillers linked to a sixth, which had its warhead stripped away for a slave repeater controlled by Star Risk.

Star Risk and company then went out, well before the People were mobilized, and parked themselves in a high ecliptic above the target world of Mardite.

Waiting, for M'chel, wasn't quite as bad as usual. The patrol ship Spada had given her was smaller than the normal transport, but the skeleton crew kept away from the bridge, after having been growled at a few times.

She tried to keep her mind occupied with the new

edition of *Trans-Reimann Equations*, but her eyes kept drifting to the radar repeater that showed nothing unusual. Half a dozen times she wanted to summon her electronics tech and make sure the radar wasn't broken, but she managed to restrain herself.

But at last the time came, and a motley of the People's warships blipped into existence off Mardite.

With a sigh of relief, she brought her crew to General Quarters – not much more than a formality – and notified Spada's ship. Von Baldur had thought he should lead the company, but restrained his ego, knowing Spada was infinitely more experienced in space, particularly when it came to small unit actions.

The People formed themselves into waves and closed on Mardite, clearly paying no attention to anything other than their fellows and the planet they were going to hammer.

It was long seconds before any of the People saw the nearly two dozen warships, Rasmussen's Raiders, as they came out of hyperspace and went instantly on the attack.

Then the com was a yammer of alarm, and space became a swirl of fighting ships.

'Tallyho, and all that rot,' came Spada's calm voice, and Star Risk dropped down, Riss thought, not remembering where the hell the phrase came from, like the Assyrian on the fold.

Rasmussen's crewmen weren't much more alert to nonessentials than the People, and so Star Risk, holding a very loose formation, was almost within launch range before the alarm was given.

It was a multilayer sandwich: First Mardite, then, just out-atmosphere, the People, then beyond them Rasmussen's Raiders, then as a thin top crust, Star Risk, its bundled missiles hounding along obediently.

Riss remembered to keep auxiliary screens on, and a spare eye on them, so she suddenly didn't become another layer in the sandwich if some other enemies materialized.

'All units,' Spada ordered. 'Missile homing units on. Launch in fifteen seconds . . . five, four, three, two, turn 'em loose.'

On command, the missile bundles unbundled, and each missile acquired and locked on a target.

Techs had installed safety circuitry, so the missiles ignored any ship 'casting on the People's standard Identification Friend or Foe circuitry, scattered and went for Rasmussen's ships.

What had been a melee became a blanket of explosions, hits and near misses.

Rasmussen's unit was doubly decimated.

M'chel looked at the momentary balls of flame and smoke on a real-time screen. She should have rejoiced at a remarkable slaughter, but was thinking what a particularly nasty death breathing space was if it didn't come quickly.

'Let us go on home, troops,' von Baldur 'cast, 'and prepare snooks to be cast at our allies.'

Riss obeyed the command.

She felt no particular sense of wild victory. She decided that automated battle wasn't her style — and, anyway, generic hammering wasn't very satisfactory.

FIFTY-TWO

Chas Goodnight was not a man who believed in over-work, particularly when it came to dirty deeds.

Assassinating almost anyone isn't a terribly difficult job, even the most carefully guarded. The problem comes if the assassinator has the slightest interest in living in freedom after his or her gun goes bang.

Goodnight wasn't a strong believer in one-way trips, and had decided long before that he made a rotten fanatic.

He had himself inserted onto Khazia by a fairly reliable agent, broke contact with the agent's network, and went to ground. He stayed in the People's ghetto even though people might talk, since he figured that was somewhat safer than trying to innocently swim among the Alsaoud as one of them.

He had a full evaluation of the palace, which now included Nowotny's quarters. His first plan was the easy one, just using a large bang. But a variant of that had been done before, and if it failed Cerberus would certainly know a plot was in the works.

Besides, Goodnight valued a bit of subtlety when he got bloody-handed.

The palace was, of course, constantly hiring people in various categories.

The best, for his purposes, would be in the security division.

Goodnight slightly darkened his skin, enough that he could pass for an Alsaoud, and applied for a job.

But Cerberus had that rather well covered – a new hire would spend some time in outlying areas before being trusted in the heart of the great mansion.

Also, at least initially, he would be paired with a more experienced guard.

Chas didn't have time to spare, so he looked at other openings.

He found one as a kitchen scullery type, figuring that no one would be interested in a pot-walloper.

He was right – no one was, particularly since the shift supervisor made sure none of the scut-workers got out of the kitchen, even on a break.

Three shifts of being the low man in the kitchen, and becoming most familiar with arcane kitchen tasks like cleaning the grease trap and polishing steam tables, and he moved on. If he'd wanted a career like that, he could have stayed with the Alliance.

Goodnight thought of another method that he'd used with great success on other worlds – to leave the Alsaoud System, apply for work as a mercenary, reenter the system, and then start being nefarious.

He used the rather exotic com he'd brought with him, which bounced both outgoing and incoming signals through several relay points, to have Jasmine check on the possibilities of that plan.

There really weren't any – Cerberus was tightly screening applicants for any job that sounded like it would get near the palace, and Goodnight wasn't about to join Rasmussen's now somewhat humbled Raiders and bash a square.

Very well, he decided. If I can't do it up close, I'll do

it from a distance. Even though he wasn't a huge fan of long-range touches, he didn't consider himself too proud for that option.

The problem there was that Walter Nowotny damned near didn't go out of the palace. When he did, it was to duck into a heavily guarded craft and vanish into the stratosphere, together with a *lot* of escort ships.

Chas Goodnight was starting to get irked, and understand why the whispery-voiced bastard had lived so long.

He decided, most reluctantly, to go for the obvious, and so he set up a missile and a control station a kilometer away.

Goodnight had a sort of itinerary of Nowotny's, gotten from the still-undiscovered cameras studded around the palace, and knew that Nowotny left his bombproof quarters for his equally bombproof command center just about noon each day, returning at dawn.

That gave Goodnight a route where the man wouldn't be in the open, but would be moving along an evidently unshielded hallway, then through a garden.

It was the best option that he could find.

Grok set up a blurp signal that would alert Goodnight when someone was moving in the garden, which should, at that time of day, only be Nowotny and his immediate bodyguards.

Goodnight let two days pass, making dry runs, thought he had a pretty good chance of success, and determined to go for it.

On the third day, his receiver blurped at the correct time, and Goodnight launched the slender missile. It was no bigger than a man, and the size of a double fist in diameter.

Its launch point was about half a kilometer from the

palace – Goodnight couldn't figure a closer secure point.

The missile did just what it was supposed to do, homing precisely on those steps that led out into the garden. It would detonate with a blast that should shred the area, and that would be that.

That was very definitely not that – sensors picked up the missile as it reached the palace walls, predicted its impact point, and, as alarms screamed, a skein of slender magnetic wires shot up from hidden automated launchers around the garden.

The missile touched a wire, was told it had reached that impact point, and exploded.

The blast over the palace walls was fairly spectacular, and gave Nowotny a start.

But no more.

And now the man knew he was a target.

'I'm getting old,' Chas Goodnight gloomed as he touched self-destruct buttons and slid out of his launch center.

'Either that, or murder isn't as easy as it used to be.'

FIFTY-THREE

Even over a com, with a synthed, neutralized voice, Goodnight sounded most piteous.

M'chel thought about the problem, then a flash of sorts came. It had a slightly malevolent quality for all hands that she sort of liked.

She commed Goodnight back at once.

'Now, Chas,' she said, grateful for the luxury of being able to grind it in through a lengthy transmission, since the com was being bounced between a dozen relays, 'don't give up. You merely need some guidance. We learned in the marines how to give that kind of help to lesser soldiery.'

The synthesizer couldn't handle his rather outraged splutter. M'chel ignored the burst of static.

'And we're more than willing to help out our fellows when their strategic planning falls short.'

'You realize,' Goodnight came back, 'that one of these years I'll get you for this, Riss.'

'I never worry beyond the next chow call,' M'chel said. 'Now, stand by, and I should be back to you within the day with an idea or so.'

She signed off, actually having had the thrust of an idea, coming from the memory of Grok playing monster on another world for another contract.

M'chel talked to him about it.

'I love this,' he rumbled. 'I was starting to think I was no more than another damned technician. Nobody seems to be aware I have certain . . . needs of my own.'

Jasmine patted his hand, and Grok bared fangs in what he imagined to be a friendly manner.

The plan, designed to lure Walter Nowotny into the open, went into effect that day.

It took about a week to implement, during which time Chas stewed and watched holos of Walter Nowotny playing Imperator Rex, which hardly improved his mood.

The plan, M'chel admired, was most sneaky and left-handed, if she did say so herself.

She admitted that possibly she could admire generic mayhem if she were the puppetmaster.

Especially when, amazingly, things went perfectly, as they did in this case.

The plot began by picking a target.

That was fairly simple.

'Everyone' knew that, sooner or later, the Alsaoud would be forced to invade Ras and Locand — the fifth and sixth worlds in the system, held by the People — plus, of course, their 'homeland' — the asteroids of the Maron Region.

The invasion force was already being created.

The first wave of whichever world Premier Toorman decided to invade, at the behest of Cerberus, would necessarily be an elite formation.

The cheapest way to make heroes, someone discovered a very long time ago, on Earth, was to hand out bits of metal and ribbon called medals. It wasn't necessary to create knights or lords, or grant land. People would cheerfully immolate themselves for one of these chest-hangings.

An even cheaper way to create an elite formation,

without going to all the bother and expense of intensive training, selective recruiting or providing the best leaders merely required giving any formation an appropriately special title.

The sad thing, which spoke volumes about the inherent stupidity of mankind, was that sometimes it worked.

Of course, said flashily named formation might realize the fraud, but it wouldn't do them much good, since most of them would shortly become cannon fodder, and their morale, or lack of same, could be tsked over by unreadably dull military historians in the dim future.

Hence the Alsaoud Second Infantry Division, newly dubbed the Second 'Guards' Division.

They were headquartered on Khazia itself, in a great, sprawling camp a couple of hours' flight time from the capital of Helleu.

There were two other units that had been named Guards, but the People just happened to have subverted five troops inside the Second, corrupted by that most trustworthy and dependable of causes – money.

That made them the pin-tailed donkey.

The Second was no better or worse than any other Alsaoud battle group, with its own transport, assault, and support units.

Intensive training was begun, and the troops knew they were doomed. It was only a matter of time before someone waved a saber and ordered them into the attack on some airless armpit of a world occupied by hateful people.

Suspicions were confirmed when they began training in space suits.

Some of the brighter members of the Second started reading up on the Maron Region.

Next step for M'chel was developing the problem.

Jasmine, working through the People's agents, had the subverted men and women within the Second start building a rumor.

They weren't to hang themselves out by actual defeatism, but, rather more subtly, to state firmly and patriotically that their designation as a Guards unit proved that the old story about the Second being a jinxed, doomed unit, wasn't true.

Of course, denial spreads the word faster than formal confirmation, and everybody wanted to know what this was about a jinx.

M'chel let those denials percolate for three or four days, while Spada and Grok prepared the next step.

This was the acquisition of a perfectly normal lifter cab.

It was packed with explosive, and had a simple autopilot installed.

At just midday meal the next day, the taxi went screaming over the Second's outer posts, and slammed into an enlisted mess hall just as it began serving.

Riss had coldly picked the lower ranks dining area, because they were the most innocent, and therefore the most likely to feel incredibly wronged and complain loudly.

The disaster killed eighty-three, wounded ninety. The disparity from the usual killed-wounded ratio was due to the sudden flash fire that shot through the debris after the explosion.

Now the rumors of the Second's hard luck spread more rapidly, particularly when one of their field grade officers had the insensitivity to shrug the deaths off as having affected 'only nonvital personnel.'

Grok was turned loose next.

Spada inserted him behind a hill about three kilometers beyond the main gate to the Second's base.

He didn't bother bamboozling the primitive security on the perimeter fences, but slipped through the gate itself, deep in the night, as the gate guards were blinded by an entering convoy of lifters.

It was very foolish, frequently lethal, to judge Grok's stealthiness by his bulk.

He knew, from studied aerial holos pirated from Khazia libraries, just where to go – the division commander's quarters.

There were two sentries in front.

They died, very quickly and silently, but messily.

Grok went through the front door, not bothering to unlock it, although that would have been simple. He thought it would be more impressive if the heavy, solid door was merely smashed in half.

He left as quickly as he'd entered.

Behind him, the division commander's body sprawled outside his bedroom, his head still rolling two meters away. In the bedroom, a distinctly underage officer cadet squalled loudly.

Now the rumors of jinx spread more rapidly.

A pair of outside agents of the People, with access to the holos, made sure reports were carefully written and given prominent play, denying the existence of the Second's bad luck.

The new division commander snorted about the jinx nonsense, and was quite busy preparing the unit for a major war game, although no one could figure why such a game, which posited the invasion of Khazia by two divisions of the People, would have anything to do with the planned invasion of the People's worlds.

Nevertheless, the Second moved into the field, lock, stock and lister bag.

Division Commander II prided himself on being 'one of the troops,' and so had a small bubble shelter instead of the usual prefab palace most generals favored when they actually had to go into the boondocks and associate with their smelly underlings.

He also traveled by standard small lifter, with only a pair of aides and a single bodyguard/driver.

One of the People's agents put a beeper on that lifter so, on the second day of the problem, as confusion was beginning to settle toward normalcy, it was easy to track DCII as he hastened to solve the latest catastrophe which one of his previous brilliances had most likely caused.

His lifter was just outside a unit's position when it inexplicably grounded.

His driver had landed at the general's order when the commander saw what appeared to be a strange animal in the brush.

Grok had deliberately allowed himself to be seen by the man, just as he allowed himself to be seen by the line soldiers as he roared out from cover, slaughtering the driver and one aide in his onrush, and smashing the second aide as he tried to protect his leader.

Grok ripped the blaster out of the hands of the general, lifted him high, then, while the man was screaming, tore his throat out with his fangs.

Then he vanished back into the woods, spitting to get rid of the unpleasant taste.

The troops went looking for an animal, not someone who hurried to a hidden lifter and was kilometers away before the first searcher reached the brush line.

Two generals murdered in four days – the Second Division was in a bit of shock. Or, at least, its officers were.

The shock was worsened the next day.

The assistant division commander was ordered to take charge of the formation while a suitable official leader with the appropriate number of stars was found, and cozened into accepting appointment to command of the Second.

The troops were told to hold in their encampments and send out patrols looking for the monster. When the new general had assumed command with the appropriate amount of ceremony, the war games could rebegin.

That day, just after the noon meal, an aircraft swooped across the division camps.

It looked like a standard Alsaoud military medium lifter, but for some reason its markings had been hurriedly obscured with what looked like mud.

The lifter sprayed a thin mist as it overflew the camps, then disappeared.

No one had an explanation for who the lifter belonged to.

Redon Spada had found the near-duplicate of the military model in a seedy back-alley lot, bought it with high-quality counterfeit credits, and had it hurriedly painted like it was service issue, then muddy paint sprayed over the paint. He wasn't about to offer explanations, nor say just what slough he'd sunk the craft into after its single mission.

Soldiers started getting sick with a rather disgusting virus that caused a high fever, spots and diarrhea. Almost no one died, but everyone who caught the bug wished they would.

The only fatality was Division Commander III, who supposedly died of the virus, although rumors insisted that his body was found in his rather comfortable field quarters in several parts.

Morale in the Second Division was at rock bottom.

It was bad enough not only for other units to hear of the Second's jinx, but wonder if bad luck was contagious.

The Alsaoud Command and Cerberus realized that the Second was up there with leprosy when it came to morale-building, to the point that the glooms were communicable.

Walter Nowotny was getting angrier and angrier, trying to figure out what the hell was going on, particularly the repeated stories about some strange goddamned monster stalking the Second.

He even thought for an instant that this nonsense might somehow be the doing of that damnable Star Risk. They did have a resident alien, one who'd worked briefly for Cerberus. But the records showed he'd been no more than an electronics technician, hardly the mobile slaughterhouse the Second was terrified of. Besides, the descriptions of the monster were of a creature far larger than this Amanandrala Grokkonomonslf. Nowotny looked elsewhere, found nothing, and assumed it was a mass delusion.

But *something* had to be done.

The first step that Fearless Leaders normally take to make the troopies happy is to provide alcohol or drugs in staggering amounts for free.

It may appear cynical, but it seems to work a lot of the time.

It didn't, in this case. Big bubble shelters were flown in, barrels of beer rolled up, and the troops were given a stand-down to celebrate a freshly made up holiday honoring something the Second did before living memory.

It didn't work very well.

First, Grok made a couple of flashing appearances, was seen by panicking troops, then vanished before anyone could even fire a shot in his general direction.

The beer had been adulterated by agents with a variety of interesting, tasteless liquids. Some made the drinker evacuate his bowels, others caused parabolic vomiting, still another simply turned the teeth bright magenta.

The soldiers started grumbling, then someone took a swing at someone else.

Several satisfactorily bloody riots ensued, and the military police came in with truncheons.

Someone didn't like it, and had a few live rounds and a weapon to voice his discontent.

The MPs retaliated, and some thirty-four soldiers were wounded, only one fatally.

M'chel now held her breath, waiting to see if the Alsaoud Command responded as she hoped they would. She was assuming they were no brighter than the average set of generals and admirals.

They did just what she'd hoped.

For some reason, soldiers above a certain rank really believe that everyone loves a parade.

Maybe spectators do, but the poor bastards who've got to spitshine their very souls and march up and down and back and forth in endless rehearsal getting screamed at, do not.

It's worse when it's a pass in review, with full equipment, since that means not only do the crunchies have to be polished and buffed, but so does their gear and vehicles.

And so the Second washed, brightened, and burnished in a state of numb rage. A handful of sensible soldiers, given a bit of luck and an opportunity, went over the fence until the goddamned mess was over.

The others massed, sullenly, on a great plain with their lifters and ships and such.

It would be a famous show.

And to especially honor the Second Guards Division, Premier Toorman and a very high-ranking advisor from

the Alliance itself would attend, plus full media attention.

After the pass in review, there'd be a serious crowd-
pleaser – a live-fire demonstration of the Second's, and
its supporting arms', awesome capabilities.

M'chel heard this gleefully, and seriously considered
renewing her faith in a handful of gods she'd abandoned
over the years.

Chas Goodnight needed no more of a kick-start.

The day before the review, he entered one of the
ancillary fields where an aerial support battalion was
based.

He was quite familiar with the small, in-atmosphere
tactical support craft there, derived from Alliance ships
he'd trained on years ago.

He slid to the flight line, where rows of attack ships
waited. Since there weren't enough barracks to go
around, the pilots and crews of the ships had been
ordered to sleep aboard, and mess from iron rations,
which also didn't help morale, already lowered by the
seemingly endless preparations for this goddamned
parade.

Sentries were posted on the flight lines, but as a formality – for who, a dozen kilometers from the field,
would bother with anyone in this unit?

Goodnight would and did, not even needing to go
bester to slip past the guards to the small, four-man
ship he'd chosen at random.

He triggered bester as he went through the ship's
lock.

In a blur, he killed the two crewmen who were
awake, then the two sleeping men.

Goodnight had tried to deal with them as neatly as
possible, since he'd be in the company of corpses for a
while.

He dragged the bodies into a cargo room, closed it off, then sat down to consider the ship's command computer.

The parade instructions for the parade were not only at hand, but neatly printed off.

He studied the orders, then the ship controls.

Everything was most straightforward and well-remembered.

There was only one glitch, early the next morning, when the ship's section leader wanted to come aboard.

Goodnight let him in, broke his neck, and put him with the other bodies, hoping no one would come looking. Or, that if they did, they would look somewhere else.

Commands began chattering an hour later, and Chas obeyed them, starting his ship's engines, setting a course, and taking off.

He wasn't very pleased with his flying abilities, but he wasn't the sloppiest pilot that day.

The Alsaoud didn't have much of a parade ground tradition.

The squadrons swept out over the sea for one hundred kilometers, then formed up in very sexy combat vees to sweep over the great parade ground, then reform once more a kilometer distant, for the live fire part of the parade.

Goodnight didn't plan on taking part in that.

He had not only the required links to his commanders on, but a pair of coms on commercial channels. These showed the lines of troops, the lifters, and the reviewing stand.

Not that Chas needed them – other screens showed the bands, fireworks and panoply around them.

But one channel did show Toorman . . . and beside him, finally winkled out of his goddamned palace,

Walter Nowotny, looking a bit uncomfortable in the poorly fitting uniform of an Alsaoud general.

Chas Goodnight, busy as he was at the controls, found a moment to blow him a kiss.

'All Voortis elements,' one com sent. 'We are approaching the stand . . . hold your formation precisely . . . this is our chance to shine.'

'Yeah, right,' Goodnight said, flipping on autopilot for an instant while he slipped over to the late weapons officer's console, and armed up the ship.

Then he had the stand on a target screen, just as one of the commercial channels cut away to a long shot of the V formations approaching in a nice, slow, stately manner.

'Have fun, boys and girls,' Goodnight muttered, and hit full power, and sent his ship screaming in a dive toward the stand.

Every frequency he had on was screaming, either at him or for somebody somewhere to do something.

He paid no mind, but put a sight pipper on the center of the stands, and fired every missile he had.

As he closed on the boil of hell the stand had become, he locked a chaingun trigger back, and emptied its magazine over the chaos.

Goodnight's ship flashed low, less than a hundred meters, over where the stands had been.

Below him was a charnel house.

'Awright, Nowotny, you bassid,' Goodnight muttered. 'If you lived through that, you're an angel. Or a demon, anyway.'

Then he went for the hills, where Redon Spada waited with the yacht.

Walter Nowotny's body was never recovered.

But Star Risk had a bit of trouble believing that their longtime nemesis was really gone.

There were at least six hundred admitted dead.

'A little in the way of overkill?' Friedrich inquired mildly of M'chel.

She shrugged.

'He didn't give us a chance to be surgical.'

'No,' von Baldur agreed. 'He did not. Now, let us see how many more bodies we have to bounce before Cerberus decides it wants to go home to mommy.'

FIFTY-FOUR

'This day, we have lost one of our best,' Ral Tomkins intoned. He let his face show sorrow for a brief moment, then fierce determination and anger.

He was particularly proud of his speech – he'd even written parts of it.

'But Cerberus Systems, terrible as an army with invisible banners, will continue on, relentlessly helping bring freedom and justice to our client worlds.'

He nodded, thinking how well his message would be playing to the thousands of coms on as many worlds, to the scattered operatives of Cerberus.

'And as I know Walter Nowotny would have said, were he still among us, now is not the time to mourn, but to strike back!

'To this end, I am personally going to go to the Alsaoud System, and take charge of the mopping-up operations there.

'Our foes will rue the day they stood against us, for we shall show no mercy.

'And our merciless hammer will be aided by the strong, secret anvil against which we shall be striking.

'I cannot tell you what this secret is, although you shall know it soon enough, as shall our enemies.

'Their doom is nigh . . . and our final victory is imminent!'

FIFTY-FIVE

'Ah-hah, yee-hah, so vee haffa haffa haffa da secrety weapon against da infeedel, eh?' Goodnight chortled from where he lay, drink in hand, sprawled on a sofa in Star Risk's quarters in the Maron Regions. 'Soon dee foe shall fribble and frabble, and da secrety weapon shall no more be named, eh?'

Riss laughed, was about to gently chide Goodnight for being overly euphoric, even though he was entitled after all the time he'd spent dragging around the bushes waiting for Nowotny to target himself. Spada was curled at one end of her couch, sipping some sort of nonalcoholic tea.

Jasmine King lay on another sofa, a blissful smile on her face. She had a half-empty bottle of some high-alcoholic swill clutched in one hand, and wasn't bothering with a glass any more.

Friedrich appeared sober, watching his partners celebrate, tasting a large snifter of brandy from time to time.

'We now,' he said, 'with any luck, can help hammer the Alsaoud back into next week, and allow the People to reward us richly. I hope.'

Grok sat at a com, its volume muted.

Suddenly he spun the set toward them.

'There *is* a secret weapon,' he announced, and patched into a channel whose picture was streaky and frequently blurred.

Goodnight started to laugh, saw Grok's seriousness, and focused on the screen.

'This is somewhere on Khazia,' Grok announced. 'The transmission is from one of the People's agents.'

The picture spun, swung, and steadied on a large landing field.

Settling down on it were ranks of starships.

Riss blinked.

'Those are *Alliance*-type ships!'

'*Farragut*-class destroyers, at least two *Quon*-type cruisers, three mother ships with a dozen or so patrol ships,' Spada agreed. 'This is not good. We surely aren't suicidal enough to go to war against the Empire.'

The agent found the zoom button on his camera, and the view closed on the nose of one ship.

Blazoned across it was, indeed, the starry black sash of the Alliance.

There was complete silence for a very long moment in the Star Risk room.

'We,' Goodnight said with finality, 'are truly and completely screwed.'

FIFTY-SIX

'Aw, crap,' Riss said in considerable disgust. 'Why does God *always* have to be on the side of the big battalions?'

She'd just returned from a futile attempt to convince the mercenaries she and Spada had hired to keep their words. None of them had done other than sneer and leave the Alsaoud System as quickly as they could.

'I want to know how the hell that frigging Tomkins managed to convince the Alliance to come in backing Cerberus,' Goodnight said in an injured tone. 'Just what we didn't need.'

'The man definitely must have a silver tongue,' Friedrich said. 'But that isn't the biggest problem.

'The People have just won themselves a notable victory,' he continued. 'Or, at least, that is what they think, Rasmussen's cohorts being the strongest forces they have gone up against lately.

'Given the fact that the People tend to be, shall we say, excitable sorts, do you think we are going to be able to convince them to fold their tents until another time, and going up against the Alliance, even if it works one time, is going to be nothing but suicide in the long run? Not that long, either.'

'No,' Grok said. 'Even trying to think like you humans, I can't convince myself of that.'

'And,' Riss said, 'since Tomkins thinks we're the root of all evil, if the People harm one lousy hair in one lousy Alliance troopie's nose, isn't he going to be telling his new buddies in the Alliance that we're behind it, and deserve to have our little peepees whacked?'

'Probably,' Jasmine King said. 'But we have to try, don't we?'

'I shall set an appointment with Advisor Ganmore,' Grok said. 'Friedrich, you might be polishing your language skills.'

It didn't work, especially when the People's agents got word that an especially juicy convoy was being set up, quite openly, to run into the Alsaoud System from half a dozen worlds, since the Alliance presence was supposed to guarantee the system's safety.

'Doesn't the word "trap" occur to them?' Riss snarled.

'I mentioned it,' von Baldur said. 'But Ganmore said that he felt the Alliance units are still unfamiliar with the People's tactics, and will not expect them to be attacking in strength on a flash in-and-out attack.

'Especially when Ganmore has put out a disinformation program that says the People are in a state of panic, and bickering among themselves, and afraid to attack. A trap's jaws, he said, can spring both ways.'

'Maybe the Alliance will buy that,' Jasmine said. 'But it sounds way, way too obvious to fool anyone from Cerberus.'

'Jasmine is right,' Grok agreed. 'So what are we going to do about it?'

'I don't know,' Friedrich said. 'Every avenue I can think of is mined.'

'I think,' Goodnight said, 'that at least we ought to saddle up and go out and meter-meter the matter.

Maybe something will occur to pull our ass out of the crack.

'Or maybe not.

'Anyway, it's got to be better to be doing something instead of picking our noses and waiting for the Alliance to show up here on our doorstep with bells and bombs.'

FIFTY-SEVEN

As the *McMahon* ungrapneled from the asteroid to which it'd been linked, and Spada prepared to jump close to that navpoint that had caused so much bloodshed, Friedrich was fixed on a commercial broadcast, showing the arrival of Ral Tomkins of Cerberus, called by the commentator 'a high-ranking commercial attaché.'

He was aboard a large and particularly sleek armed merchant cruiser, with a pair of equally glossy destroyer escorts from the Alliance contingent, and the field was surrounded with bands and dignitaries.

'Bastard,' Friedrich muttered. 'Not only does he appear to be winning, but he has all of the perks as well.'

Riss took a moment to admire von Baldur for never losing his affectation of precise speech, even at the worst of moments.

'Now, Freddie,' she said. 'Talk like that is bad for the morale of us common crunchies.'

Von Baldur came back to present.

'You are right. It is bad for mine as well.'

Spada studded the space around the navpoint with enough sensors to have filmed an epic, and found a drifting piece of moonlet to hide on. Star Risk waited for catastrophe to develop.

A day later, Grok pointed out a rather odd incongruity, a distortion on one of their radar screens.

'Interesting,' he said.

'I call it fascinating,' Goodnight said. '*Damned* fascinating.'

'Don't be sarcastic, Chas,' Jasmine said.

'I'm not,' Goodnight said. 'I'm brooding because something that I saw is tickling at me and I don't have the slightest goddamned idea what it is. So what's so wonderful, Grok, about one of our radar sets being screwed up?'

'There's nothing wrong with the set,' Grok said. 'Nor is there, as you might describe it, a wiggle in space. That distortion is an electronic creation. Behind it we shall no doubt find the Alliance ships, waiting for the convoy and a chance to trample the People.'

'Wonderfuller and wonderfuller,' Chas said. Then a glazed look crossed his face.

'Uh, Jasmine, are we keeping recordings?'

'Of course.'

'Can you bring me up a copy of that foohformatiddle of Tomkins showing up to bless the fish and fleet that Freddie was watching?'

'Of course.'

'Why,' von Baldur asked, 'do you want to look at that, when battle is about to be joined?'

'Because I might be guilty of that old ah-hah phenom,' Goodnight said. 'Or I might not.'

Jasmine found the file and patched it to a viewer in Goodnight's cabin, and he disappeared.

The others were intent on the developing battle.

It developed slowly, over a course of hours, and moved in a stately manner toward catastrophe.

Not a major catastrophe, but a catastrophe nonetheless.

The convoy, almost fifty ships with their escorts, came out of the navpoint as predicted.

From everywhere and nowhere came the People — not a fleet so much as a swarm.

They might have scorned the idea of having a coherent strategy, but in an odd way, they did.

First was to rat-pack the convoy's escorts, taking care to avoid taking casualties. This meant the People weren't as interested in destroying the destroyers and frigates with the convoy as smashing them into impotency or, better still, making them flee back into hyperspace.

Some did, and some of the transports tried to do the same.

Most of them were closely tracked, and attacked in n-space.

The merchantmen, not particularly wanting to die, especially in that fuzzy imaginary universe, came out into normal space quite rapidly, bleating surrender on all frequencies.

At that point, the incongruity vanished, and was revealed as were the Alliance ships, augmented with Rasmussen's Raiders.

'Interesting,' Spada said. 'Notice how Rasmussen's Rumpkins take a spread envelopment formation, and the Alliance holds to a nice, safe, secure, old-fashioned bloc. Maybe our boyos have a chance.'

'Maybe,' Riss allowed, but said no more.

One of their coms, on a scan of frequencies, picked up a 'cast in midperoration, of someone saying, 'time now to take a stand.'

'That is Ganmore,' Grok identified.

Some of the People's ships obeyed, and drove in for a

counterattack. Others, most likely the freelances who'd gathered around the People, scorned foolish bravery and tried to flee.

But their attackers were too close, and, as with the merchantmen, ships jumped in and out of hyperspace, spitting missiles, fighting, and, all too often, dying.

It was not going well for the People.

'A goddamned disaster, even if the People are doing better than I would have thought,' von Baldur said softly. 'And it shall all be all our fault.'

'Not necessarily,' a suddenly cheerful Goodnight said as he reappeared. 'Jasmine, could you patch what I've been looking at up here?'

'Can't it wait?' von Baldur asked.

'Nope,' Goodnight said. 'Because there's light on yon horizon.'

Jasmine looked at him curiously and touched sensors.

The battle disappeared, and the image of Tomkins's ship was onscreen.

'If you'll be so kind as to push the pickup on the nose of either of those destroyers,' Goodnight requested. 'Ah. There you are.'

Star Risk stared blankly at the repeated image.

'You will notice the Alliance banner on those DDs,' Goodnight said. 'And you will also notice the smallish sort of device below it?'

Jasmine reflexively pushed into a tight shot.

'What is that emblem?' Goodnight asked.

'Umm . . . Capella IV?' she identified tentatively.

'Thank you. I didn't know who, but I knew goddamned well it wasn't a mainline Alliance banner.'

'So?' Spada asked. 'Alliance is Alliance.'

'No, it isn't,' Riss said, getting it. 'A main force unit is sacrosanct . . . if that's the right word.'

'As good as any,' Grok said.

'Cerberus . . . Tomkins . . . wasn't able to ring in that big a favor,' she said. 'All he got was the reserves.'

The image of Tomkins vanished, and the battle reappeared.

'Which means what?' Spada said.

'It means,' Grok said, 'that whatever happens today is whatever happens today. I imagine there will not be any major repercussions if the People happen to win, other than a certain amount of whining within the Alliance.'

'Egg-zackle,' Goodnight said. 'No paybacks, in other words. Which translates as nobody hunting us into perdition.'

Von Baldur was nodding in agreement, staring at a screen, just as the day's one piece of luck happened.

For a change, it was on the side of the People.

A missile had been launched at an Alliance ship, and missed. It drove on for awhile, then should have self-destructed. However, whoever had owned and fired it was a thrifty sort who had disconnected the suicide switch, and so the missile sulked in space, not blowing up, without a target.

Then it found one. A large one, one of the *Quon*-class cruisers, within a parsec.

The missile came alive as the cruiser flashed past, and went in pursuit, homing on the cruiser's drive.

The missile showed up on one of the cruiser's escort's screens, and it yapped a warning.

A bit too late, as the missile smashed into the cruiser's storage areas.

That cruiser was the Alliance flagship.

Its sailors may have been very spit and polish, but as combat novices they weren't as careful as they should have been about ship integrity.

A ball of flame rolled down the ship's main corridor, feeding and growing as it went.

It reached the ship's midpoint and exploded.

The cruiser simply vanished in a ball of dirty flame.

'Well, dip me,' Goodnight said, as a screen on the *McMahon* IDed the casualty.

Within minutes the command loss showed, as the Alliance ships' tactics became as incoherent as those of the People. Rasmussen's Raiders changed their fight to a defensive one.

'Wonderful,' Friedrich said softly. 'Sometimes, M'chel, God is not always on the side of the biggest bullies.

'Redon, my lad, could you happen to do a search around where that cruiser was, with your parameters that lovely armed cruiser our friend Ral Tomkins arrived aboard?'

Spada's fingers flashed across sensors.

'There it is,' he said.

'Standing out like a maiden aunt at an orgy,' Goodnight said.

'I wonder if Mister Tomkins is a brave man, leading from the front and all, and decided to attend the final destruction of Star Risk?' Friedrich murmured.

'Yes, indeed,' von Baldur said, answering his own question as the ship onscreen flashed into motion. 'Things are suddenly not going well for the Alliance, and so our friend settles on the better part of valor.

'With no one noticing.

'No one but myself, that is. Mr. Spada, could you pursue that ship?'

'No problem,' Spada said. 'We've got legs and legs on it.'

The *McMahon* was in pursuit.

Star Risk was watching the forward screens, paying

only slight attention to the battle still raging on, its outcome no longer clear.

No one said anything as the armed merchantman grew larger.

There was a single destroyer with it.

'Unless he turns to fight,' von Baldur said, 'ignore that escort.'

Spada didn't bother replying.

'Closing . . . closing . . .' he reported, checking a proximity screen.

'Would you care to do the honors?' he asked von Baldur, indicating the weapons console.

Von Baldur didn't answer, but sat down at the weapons station and hit sensors, a rather holy look on his face.

'Closing,' Spada said. 'Four seconds to launch range. In range. Fire when ready.'

But von Baldur waited.

'I will make sure,' he said firmly.

'Well, don't wait until we're up his arse,' Goodnight said.

'And this is now that,' von Baldur said, and hit a launch key.

A missile spat out of the *McMahon*'s tubes.

Friedrich took it under manual guidance, and looped it over the fleeing Cerberus ship, then smashed it down, just behind the command area.

Flame flashed and went out.

There was a sudden shout on a com.

Riss guessed it was from the stricken ship.

Its escort paid no mind, but held at flank speed.

'Uh, Freddie,' Riss said. 'I think we've got a lifeboat launch.'

'So we do,' von Baldur said. 'I cannot see the justification for *that*.'

A second missile shot out, homed on the tiny craft holding no one knew whom.

The missile exploded, and there was nothing but empty space when the roiling gasses cleared.

'Well, well,' von Baldur said, turning from the weapons panel. 'The quality of mercy is, indeed, somewhat strained.

'You know, this did not turn out to be such a bad day after all.'

FIFTY-EIGHT

Eldad Yarb'ro tried to ignore the throb in his arm, as well as the worry about whether they might have to amputate and graft.

A word had come to him:

Baraka.

It came, he remembered, from an extinct Earth culture, and he didn't know where he'd come across it.

It meant luck, but more than luck.

The gods would be on your side if you had baraka.

Star Risk had baraka.

Yarb'ro could have been angry.

He wasn't.

The disaster to Cerberus was so total he almost wanted to laugh.

Especially since his personal nemesis Ral Tomkins was most surprisingly quite dead, and vanished somewhere as he fled the battle in the Alsaoud System.

The Alliance forces that Tomkins had been so proud of had turned out to be nothing but some third-ranked reservists, who had been quickly withdrawn by their home system when the casualty rate of that disastrous battle was reported.

And so Star Risk had won.

More than won, Yarb'ro thought.

After the battle had subsided, without a clear victory on either side, they had the temerity to orbit over the capital, whatever the hell it was, and threaten the Alsaoud government with bombardment if a ransom was not paid.

It was paid, and then the government had hastily resigned, in favor of whoever those goddamned immigrants were who'd started this nonsense.

Yarb'ro sighed.

With Tomkins dead and his satraps in disfavor, Cerberus had turned back to Yarb'ro to take charge again and bring about some kind of order, and try to reestablish their rather injured reputation with the Alliance.

That, Yarb'ro knew, wasn't quite the task others in Cerberus thought it would be.

Time would pass, memories would fade, and others would make bigger errors.

Of course, Cerberus was out of the Alsaoud worlds for all time.

And equally of course, there were those who wanted Star Risk to be hunted down and obliterated.

Yarb'ro smiled wryly.

Maybe they should be.

But they had baraka.

And, at least for the time being, they were to be feared and shunned.

The Galaxy was a very large place, with room for everyone.

FIFTY-NINE

M'chel Riss sat against a tree and listened to the sounds of her island being rebuilt.

It was a beautiful day.

She had credits in the bank. A new bank. Although Alliance Credit had whined their apologies, that wasn't good enough.

Maybe not as many credits as she would like, but enough to reconstruct her home so that it was even better than before.

Next, she would have to start looking for work.

Not, she thought smugly, as a solo act, but once again as a member of Star Risk, Ltd.

The others were scattered, intent on their various forms of rest and recovery.

Except for Freddy, who was bustling about supervising the finishing, custom touches on the completed building they'd bought on Trimalchio.

Work.

Yes.

In a while.

There would be the perfect assignment, somewhere out there, she knew.

M'chel Riss felt very lucky.

FIFTY-NINE